**PRA**  **ID RUIN**

*"Enth                                          vivid, invigoratingly weird, ...  ....   ...tion offers an enviably varied feast to nourish the imagination."*

**—Ramsey Campbell,
author of *The Incubations*
and *Ancient Images***

*"An accomplished debut collection by a young author who has already found his voice."*

**—Dean M. Drinkel,
author and filmmaker**

*"The remarkably chilling tales collected in Unsworth's* Into Wrack and Ruin *feel like some sort of literary ritual to conjure the spirits of long since departed masters of the uncanny. Told with lurid, confident prose, these grim and inventive stories are distressing, strange, and very surprising."*

**—Eric LaRocca,
author of *Things Have Gotten
Worse Since We Last Spoke***

*"If you like your blood fresh, your horror raw, and your humour dark, look no further than* Into Wrack and Ruin *by new kid on the block Benjamin Kurt Unsworth. The author's love of genre literature and film shines through as he crafts novel abominations to astound and disturb."*

**—Anna Taborska,
co-author and co-editor of
*Discontinue If Death Ensues:
Tales From The Tipping Point***

# INTO WRACK AND RUIN

## BENJAMIN KURT UNSWORTH

*Into Wrack and Ruin* copyright © Benjamin Kurt Unsworth and Phantasmagoria Books 2025

'Paradigm of Pains' originally published under the same name in *Criminal Pursuits 2: This is Me* (Telos Publishing, 2025, ed. Samantha Lee Howe)

'A Final Repose' originally published under the same name in *Beautiful Darkness 3* (Dragon Soul Press, 2024, ed. J.E. Feldman)

Cover artwork and frontispiece copyright © Randy Broecker 2025

No part of this publication may be reproduced, stored in a retrieval system, stored in a database and/or published in any form or by any means, electronic, mechanical, photocopying, recording or otherwise, without the prior written permission of the publisher.

Published in September 2025 by Phantasmagoria Books through KDP/Amazon by arrangement with the authors and artists. All rights reserved by the author. The rights of the author to be identified as Author of this Work has been asserted in accordance with the Copyright, Designs and Patents Act 1988.

This book is a work of fiction. Names, characters, places and incidents are either products of the author's and artists' imaginations or are used fictitiously. Any resemblance to actual events or locales or persons, living or dead, is entirely coincidental.

Cover design and layout by Adrian Baldwin
Interior design and layout by Trevor Kennedy

# CONTENTS

Page 7: **Foreword by Lawrence C. Connolly**

Page 15: **A Lenity for Ghosts**

Page 35: **The Tale of God-Fang**

Page 63: **Crucial Decisions**

Page 75: **Hollow Eyes**

Page 99: **A Loathing for Ghosts**

Page 115: **Counting to Oblivion**

Page 155: **In the Forest of Bones and Shadows**

Page 177: **The All-Embracing Nature of a Plastic Bag**

Page 181: **Paradigm of Pains**

Page 205: **Mother Dearest**

Page 219: **A Final Repose**

Page 235: **The Fifth Demographic**

Page 253: **Epilogue: O Little Town**

Page 257: **Author Notes and Acknowledgements**

# FOREWORD

## Lawrence C. Connolly

I FIRST BECAME aware of Benjamin Kurt Unsworth in 2008. It was at the World Fantasy Convention in Calgary, and I was there to take part in the launch of *Shades of Darkness*, a new anthology of supernatural and macabre stories from the Canadian publisher Ash-Tree Press.

The book event took place on the first day of the con, and it was there that I met Ben's father, fellow anthology contributor Simon Kurt Unsworth.

At the time, Simon had been writing professionally for barely a year. Indeed, his story in the Ash-Tree anthology was only his second sale. His first, the remarkably chilling 'Church on the Island', was a finalist for that year's World Fantasy Award.

No doubt about it. Simon was a writer to watch.

Over dinner that evening, he spoke about his hometown (Manchester), his approach to writing (he did much of it while travelling on trains), and his young son (Ben, then age three). His trip to Calgary was his first time so far away from the boy, and it was clear, despite the excitement of being a WFC finalist, that he missed his son terribly.

The following morning, at a reading featuring the World Fantasy Award finalists, Simon read 'An Afternoon with Danny'. Inspired by a time he took young Ben to play at a local park, the story is a what-if exploration of every parent's worst fears, a frightening account of a playtime outing gone wrong.

I continued following Simon's career in the years that followed, and since several of his stories ('The Derwentwater Shark' and 'A Different Morecambe' come most readily to mind) were also inspired by outings with his son, I got to know Benjamin Kurt Unsworth shortly before he embarked on a literary career of his own.

I say *shortly* because Ben got off to a remarkably early start.

As Simon tells it, "My son began to write. I mean, not just write, but *write*, seemingly every waking moment he was with me. I'd wonder where my aged, battered Mac was and invariably find it with him, perched on his knee as he hammered out stories."

Soon enough, some of the stories were ready to share, and in late 2019, Simon messaged me about the pending release of *Uneasy Beginnings* (Black Shuck Shadows Book 21), a slim collection edited by Simon and containing stories by both father and son.

The book was set to debut at StokerCon in Scarborough, UK, in April 2020, and I was determined to be there and finally meet Ben in person. But fate had other plans. COVID struck. The con was cancelled. And so, instead of visiting the UK to join the celebration, I sheltered in place with a copy of *Uneasy Beginnings*. It was a fast read. Seven stories: four early tales by Simon, three new ones by Ben – all presented without attribution. As Simon explains in the book's introduction, "I'm not telling which is which. Want to know who wrote what? Read them and then, if you can, guess."

It was a clever way to present the stories. Simon had by then produced a trifecta of fine collections (*Lost Places*, *Strange Gateways*, and *Quiet Houses*) and two very impressive novels (the highly recommended *Devil's Detective* and *Devil's Evidence*). By contrast, Ben was still in his mid-teens. Nevertheless, each of the stories in *Uneasy Beginnings* is the work of a fledgling writer, and the fact that those writers happen to be father and son results in a kind of close harmony that makes the collection a unique experience. Reading those stories during lockdown, I was able – for a short time – to forget the real horror stories raging in the world at large.

It was also around this time that Simon reached out to me again, this time with Ben's email and the suggestion that I get in touch with him. Thus, I soon found myself corresponding with an engaging young writer whom I had previously known only through those unattributed tales in *Uneasy Beginnings* and some stories told and written by his father.

In the ensuing years, Ben has continued writing, turning out reviews on topics ranging from cinematic horrors to *Doctor Who*. He has also produced a steady stream of published stories. How he manages it all while still finding time to pursue his studies in Latin, Ancient Greek, and Ancient Classical History at Newcastle University is a mystery to me. But manage he has, and the result is this book that you are about to read.

It's always a kick experiencing the work of a promising young writer. But for me, this book is doubly rewarding by providing an opportunity to read the work of a fellow pilgrim whom I came to know first through conversations with his father, then through his father's fiction, and ultimately through writings of his own.

I feel fortunate to have been granted such a glimpse into the early career of this up-and-coming author, and I remain in great anticipation of what is to come.

*Sic parvis magna!*

**—Lawrence C. Connolly,
August 12, 2025**

*To Aidan. You are, in a word, brilliant. And that you've stayed one of my closest friends even after all my nerdy monologues and inane witterings over the last three years means you deserve a medal.*

*"Every village has its idiosyncrasy, its constitution, often its own code of morality."*
**—Thomas Hardy,**
***Tess of the D'Urbervilles***

# A LENITY FOR GHOSTS

*"We are the dead. Our only true life is in the future. We shall take part in it as handfuls of dust and splinters of bone. But how far away that future may be, there is no knowing."*
**—George Orwell,**
***Nineteen Eighty-Four***

THERE WAS NOTHING like the smell of fresh ghost in the morning. Rathbone and Asquith both thought so as their boots sank further and further into the grassy brown and green sludge beneath their feet. Even with their toughest of boots, as they broke the ground's frosty, hardened surface, it made noises like slugs locked in battle and each step seemed to take just a little too long.

Amongst the sludge, the shovels, plows, scythes, and anything else the locals had used to extract life from the ground littered the section of the field they'd started to voyage across: like the carrot and twig remnants of snowmen after an early January thawing. If the current chill in the weather were any judgement, the snowmen this year might be the valleys' best yet. It was a farmer's graveyard of sorts. Navigating the discarded equipment and kicking them aside like disgusting rags, Asquith brought up the rear of the procession. They were a short, silent, and steady snake over the land. The wildlife, had they nearly all not sought shelter or hibernation by now, would've seen similar processions before, but at least then there was nearly always a wooden box on their morose shoulders.

With the way Spires tackled the frozen and blasted gorse, he seemed more immune to the landscape that was at war with their feet; he was maintaining quite a pace as he bounded over disrupted earth. It was tough work to navigate, but a route across this field was now their best option for reaching the Castle Tree, and promptly set about leading them across it. Rathbone saw in the man a steely coolness which he recognised in himself. Or at the very least, he recognised the impression which he himself aimed to give out.

The world of The White Feather, from inside the swirls of mist stretching out from the forest, seemed like distant memories to Rathbone and Asquith – united in marriage and in their joint treks across England's cultural cesspits. The redness in their cheeks that that public house's hearth had brought remained now as mere pinpricks. Both enjoyed the warm tingles firing away under their skin for as long as possible, rigid iciness fighting to slow their blood and make every breath visible – punishingly visible. Since the letter to their London address, the God-fearing pair had been thrust into shivers and a town entrenched a decade or more in the past. While both had matured incredibly quickly and neither had ever felt at home in the late nineteenth century, Little Hodbury, with carriages and winding tracks and simple townsfolk honing their trade in stitchery or field labour, was an isolated, distinct world of its own. It lived outside condemnation or praise.

Both Rathbone and Asquith, far more accustomed to the life of train tracks, knew the calling would bring them where they needed to be, not where they'd rather be. That was the joy of mentally living in the future, foreseeing a better time: they felt the light of equality before its dawning. Feeling that plight for every man and woman's truth was hardly an easy one, they understood the risks of most of their clientele being "Howlers", Howlers who appeared to take some pleasure in grounding themselves to Earth and causing havoc for one and all.

So, a request, not from the mortal plane but from one beyond, wasn't just rare, it was unheard of. Ever since the letter from Spires had arrived, Rathbone had felt a sharp warmth in his chest, a wary mass against his heart; he hadn't been without *it* since his father's unanticipated death. Carrying the crucifix was the constant which instilled hope in him when his work persuaded him it was wholly in vain; it was what now gave him the patience to withstand Spires' phlegmy snorts currently piercing his eardrums. Naturally never a sure-fire indicator, nonetheless he couldn't not see that Spires possessed no religious accessory of any kind. That made a change from those mingling in the village, who seemed to cover themselves in churchly iconography – Rathbone wondered if simply outdoing one another's religious appearance was a religion in its own right here, in this cold and blasted world. About Spires though, he doubted the Lord's prayer had ever separated his stern, crusting lips. If he said it in the man's presence, he imagined the man's skin would crack like fine porcelain and find nothing except a hollow heart.

Pushing aside wispy strands of freezing mist, the shotgun barrel exploded not with just a bang, with an explosion of gunpowder and encroaching wars. Rathbone and Asquith alike ground to a stop. In the distance, amassing into a giant darkened cloud above them, the murder took to the sky. Not a single crow cared for the ornithophobic Asquith, who fought between pushing her hair from her face in the icy wind and trying to find the nearest patch of ground free of mud soup where she could hastily divebomb. Stepping back and ducking away from one bird flying far lower than the other, the sole of her boot caught the protruding edge of a scythe half-merged with upset ice. The mass of crows soon flocked every inch of her space, and her world quickly flipped to a view of the sky. Her mouth had begun to taste the dirt, a tingle of which infuriated some of her hair too, when the hand hauled her back to her feet. Apologising for his rough manhandling, Spires made sure she was steady before releasing his grip, maybe a moment or two later than was acceptable of a man with a woman he barely knew.

"If you're quite finished making a fool of our business," Rathbone barked, an impatience with all the gentleness of gravel invading his voice, "I suggest we go on." He was already clearing the few feet ahead of them with his boots, upturning a few of the other discarded scythes poking from the dirt.

Asquith was finishing tucking her hair back into a less dishevelled state. As for Spires – the only description was that he was agitating. Though he wasn't still, as if brimming with energy, he was also refusing to let even breath visibly pass his lips – it came across more like that of a ventriloquist's doll than of a warm-blooded mammal. A manic current of *something* was passing through him, entombed under hardened surfaces of unsmiling and fixedness.

"This ain't my business anymore. Go your own way."

"Excuse me?" replied Rathbone, jaw clenched and arms by his side, and his eyes flicked to look at Asquith. Spires' feet remained firmly planted. He stood like a statue observing the silent message which passed between his two accompaniments. Curiosity had never afflicted him too badly – he was a farmer of singular purpose – and the man didn't care what the silent message was, he'd walk no further.

"You heard me. It was that tree you wanted, and that tree you've got. I even cleared it of the devil birds for you. Rest's up to you." Not before exchanging another glance at Asquith, whose jaw was also now clenched in an awkward lock, Rathbone allowed a little froth to form in the corners of his mouth: "Mr. Spires. You called us in. It was *you* who precipitated this little interference, pardon me if the expectation is that you see it through with us." Stood there amongst palpable testosterone, prone like a schoolchild being admonished, Asquith watched every crease on Rathbone's face replicate itself on Spires', and felt a tenser version form upon her own. Like the religious pair's unspoken bond, she sensed a stoic, begrudging one building like an iron grip between the men. Lesser men than Spires would've used that iron grip by smashing it into Rathbone's face – that was her reckoning over how he'd got a broken nose that hadn't ever quite reset itself properly.

"Listen," Spires' retort of venom began, "you haven't seen this thing. You just haven't. You've never had a spirit demand your attention like that thing has. Ask you to pass on a message, a summoning. I've got a flock that want me, and you've got that." Neither bothered to correct the farmer, nor tell him again, as they had done a few hours ago, of one particular banishment they'd had to perform. Suffice to say, on that occasion the result was a localised outbreak of zombified citizens, heartbroken widows, and smouldering houses – they *had* seen things like this before.

Spires turned on his heels, upturning a spray of mud into Rathbone's socks, and began his pilgrimage back to a small stone cottage in the distance, clearly in the process of renovation. She sighed. Just dawning on her was the fact that, tonight, she'd likely have to sleep in that unfinished place, with an explosive farmer, a mulish associate, and a shrill cockerel's wake-up call.

"Right, let's get going. A Howler won't sort itself out, will it." Rathbone spoke into the chill. Now, it was Asquith's turn to adopt the gravelly, harsh bark, and her partner's honed glare of steel.

"He's gone now, George. No need for that tone now." Whenever they were alone, it was always George – one day, he would have liked to reciprocate, call her personally, if only she'd tell him her true name. Rather, she would only be known as "Asquith". Her husband, however loving they were, never quite felt as though he could understand her. Not to say their marriage wasn't brimming with love, it was. However, Asquith had some doors she never let her or anyone else open, and that included nearly everything personal about her. Rathbone imagined he couldn't pick out her family photo with any conviction even if he was only given one photo to choose from.

Asquith and Rathbone's insight, their living in the future, only ever went so far when the material world around them didn't accept that a woman might have a greater pedigree than a man. The pair had struck up an agreement: Rathbone would exude authoritative grumpiness in the presence of others. She never totally relinquished the handle on any situation they faced though, even if it was obtuse farmer folk ringing them up and saying that a malevolent spirit had requested the pair *by name.* Their current life was simply a costume which society gave them no choice except to wear.

"Handkerchief," she barked into the mist, before mellowing her face and looking at the returned, downtrodden gaze from her partner, "if you would." Her fight for equality rivalled her plight for avenging Howlers, sometimes even overtook it. For her, the inevitable was that that meant occasionally handing over the dominant role. It was always with a harrumph though.

Fishing in his pocket, he produced a handkerchief, one embroidered with a pattern of gloriosa lilies and snowdrops intertwined, asking "What's the matter?"

"Must've been when I fell back. Got some gooey stuff all over my glove," she responded, "Damn it, I hate that damsel routine. All that whining and pretend screaming at birds." Bringing the patterned cotton away from her glove, she found it coated in some oily substance, bluish and clumping rapidly before both their eyes. In a way, the fact that it appeared to smell of *absence* was somehow worse than if it had smelled of some noxious, supernatural chemical.

"What do you reckon it is?" asked Rathbone, removing another handkerchief, patterned similarly, to wrap the first one in. He followed this up by getting out a third and final one, patterned plainly with just blue dots, to wrap the bundle in.

It wasn't so much his hands he cared about protecting, it was the lining of his coat pockets which he'd recently had patched up. Taking it back again to Madame Fleur in Soho, within a couple of weeks, she'd most probably kick him out onto the cobbles, accompanied by a chorus of vexed sobbing.

"Not sure," she responded, "Any other time, I'd assume it was ectoplasm, but it seems a bit too . . . sophisticated."

"Spires may know?" he proffered.

Gone.

Asquith turned around, only to find his hurdling of the stone walls and churned farmland must have carried him home already, and she wasn't going to deny that that gave her more bitterness than the thought of exorcising a tree. After the handkerchief had pulled away – with most of the slime slithered onto the cotton – a few scentless globules were still managing to creep their way into the glove's seams. With a clumsy moment of decision, she scrabbled at her hands, cast the glove into the frosty grass, and, determining only one glove was inane, dispensed with the second as well.

Handkerchief within handkerchief within handkerchief within breast pocket, the pair recommenced the arduous walk. The remaining trudge was a mute affair. All that chanced breaking it was the unusual, jagged plop of the rimy mud, lasting all the way to the Castle Tree. If the name somehow had significance, they couldn't see it. Its gangly roots and branches extended far around the tree, even to the forest's edge. Not that either of them had expected beauty or a welcome, it seemed to them both like some unnatural guardian, and Asquith feared that if she took one of the matches in her pocket to the thing, it'd burst into an orange-red funnel, then filter smoke over the land.

Years ago, not long after the two had married (which itself felt like an arduous trek into the past), they'd tackled an unsavoury, riverside brothel in East London, called Castle Den. That had been a place worthy of that title without a shadow of a doubt: high, blackened stone, barred windows, doors that sounded as though you'd released the Devil himself whenever they thumped their mighty wooden panels open, and tall in the same way the seedy street was lengthy. Inside, the Howler had matched that seediness and monolithic influence. The beastly thing had wasted no time in smashing stone against stone or attempting to obliterate the brains of visiting clients. Once or twice, the malevolence had even sent vaulted panels shooting from the roof, aimed precisely for passers-by who weren't allowed the chance to comprehend the sanguine splatter which instantly pooled in the cobbles. During the onslaught, Asquith had added concussion to her quiver of ailments suffered in the line of duty, and Rathbone had almost lost one of his legs, not to mention his life when they attempted to perform the original exorcism. If she hadn't thrown herself at her new husband, the blazing candles wouldn't have only been sent spiralling into the holy scriptures they had brought with them, but also George Rathbone himself. She didn't care which laws of nature that broke, Asquith appreciated the power at work that day, and she now expected to see it again here. Yet it seemed the purgers now faced a tree. Wood and a system of roots beside ample forest and wrinkled leaves.

A tree.

Around the roots' edges, warmth seemed to be spreading, stopping any of the frost encroaching back. Perched on every other tree except this one, there wasn't a single crow who dared fly over it, never mind rest upon it. Humans may be warm-blooded creatures of intellect, reason, the ability to fight the demons, but their conscious mind was slow to decipher the dread – the wildlife knew far quicker. As they watched, one crow did actually try to perch on the tree's branches; that was as far as the natural order of things would allow. Upon reaching the perimeter, rather than finding a nice place to sit and keep watch over the misty fields, it swerved aside in a conniption fit of some kind. Almost immediately, its eyes rolled back in its little skull, its wings flapped fast enough to create a localised storm, before finally it struck one of the trees on the forest's edge and dropped to earth like a stone.

"George, thoughts?" she asked him, after they'd stopped gazing open-mouthed at the bird's death.

An absence of method defined their work, in a way. No two Howlers were the same, and neither too were the exorcisms, even if they found that word loaded with connotations. An exorcism implied they were evicting some demonic spirit out of this world. Instead, they always perceived it simply the good had managed to leave this plane, and the malice simply needed an extra push. That was where they stepped in, Bible in hand, and obliged. If anything, they were administering a kindness.

"Nothing too sinister, I can see. The tree's been singled out for some reason, that much is obvious."

"Any obvious damage to the tree?"

"Nothing visible," he mused, circling the tree. He was keeping his feet resolute, refusing to step across the threshold of root and bark. The circle which the spread of roots was creating extended a good twelve feet around the spindly structure. "Certainly, no evidence of catastrophe. No scorch marks, all the branches are still there, and no dead animals in the branches."

Now, it was his turn to enact the damsel routine.

When it happened, Asquith's view was blocked by the tall, brittle tower; its roots were so contorted and craggy that even if she chose to abandon her senses and dash over the wooden mass, she'd have likely fallen flat on her face before she could interfere. At least he didn't scream, or yelp, or tumble too loudly. This didn't stop his crash into the ground being met with the splat of the thin surface of drying mire breaking though. When she'd traversed the edges of the root system, she found her husband lying flat on the ground. His dignity was probably injured more than his bones. To her, nothing was instantly amiss.

"What happened, George?" she asked, letting one or two more breaths of nerve than she'd usually allow into her voice. In most situations, it'd be about this time that the ground would explode with flames, or some ectoplasmic entity would float out of the forest, headless and riding on a wild boar. To her annoyance, he didn't reply straightaway. "Are you hurt?"

"I'm not actually sure. I didn't see anything."

"Let's get you to your feet," Asquith replied, each word crispier than the frost. Having grasped his wrists, she gave a small tug. He almost made it upright as well, the world was once again vertical, but as soon as he thought his boots had found purchase in the soil, the soil decided it wanted him back. And, worse, this time it wanted Asquith with him. "What happened that time?" she spat, tumbling onto the patch of ground beside her husband.

The blast of creaking and snapping came from somewhere to their left, along the forest's boundary. Parting the cold cloud surrounding them, neither of them felt anything, but they both flung themselves downwards, not that either of them had far to go.

"The blue blazes! What in God's name's that?" Rathbone hollered into the air, as his back took the brunt of being recoiled back to the floor. The reprimand for using his Lord's name in vain could come later, over a warm drink and roaring fire. Only now did it dawn on the man why he couldn't escape; around his ankle, a manacled lesion of wood and squirming bark was developing. The circlet of tree roots must have formed round his left foot and then seized the chance to keep him there, no matter how much he contorted and thrashed with flexibility which might have put some of the world's greatest circus performers to shame.

Picking up a sizeable stone near her foot, she knelt in the mud – partly out of strategy, partly because muddy grass and her boots rejected any co-operation – and then brought it down on the timber. The first strike struck only bark, massing like a shield over the restriction. The second landed a blow against the wooden base, and the third splintered it further. Two more sufferable batterings later, and a chunk of wood fell to pieces. This didn't stop it continuing to congeal on the floor, spasming to itself. It was still attempting to engulf his foot, Asquith realised as she watched Rathbone tug his ankle free of the fragments of wood.

Beneath them, they could feel a fluctuating hum like horses bounding over distant streets, or like the burrowing of an unseen mammal. A second later, they were on their feet.

Even that was too late. Rustling, the ground was starting to seethe and give way to tendril-like branches sprouting seed-pod-like from the soil – the movements were jerky, clearly just extensions of the root structure. It was the way more and more emerged, crunching over one another, that made their eyes widen. In that moment, the full mass looked fluid. And if it had a face, it would have salivated.

It was hungry.

They ran. The direction didn't matter – wherever way danger wasn't. Their faces widened, aghast, when they discovered that that wasn't so easy a feat.

With the splintering and creaking aggressor rearing up for attack, Asquith and Rathbone picked haste and blind doggedness to be the best course of action. True, an oleaginous mass of wood and bark, like an erratic spill of oil through the misty miasma and over the grass, was spurting ever closer, and that didn't exactly coax rational thought. However, they had no time to be baffled. The invading mist was only getting thicker, as was the writhing splinters behind them.

They dashed aside. Jumping a particularly vicious root system that had sprung from the soil, gnarling into a small and malformed fence, the line of trees seemed the most agreeable retreat. No tree was more than about ten feet from another, and they were praying that it'd lend them some advantage; surely the trees would hamper the creaking growth pululating from the Castle Tree? Their panting terse, the pair tore through the forest. Asquith had only just enough breath to croak to her husband, "This is . . . mad!". She found herself wondering when the pink elephants would appear.

Skidding over the withered remains of leaves, propelled at this point more by the forest floor's incline than the need to get away, the woman grabbed her husband's coat sleeve. Allowing momentum and gravity to relinquish control, she tugged him towards her, and the two spun into a small, curved ditch, seemingly carved into the landscape. Her slide to a halt was more graceful, using the root system of a tree that wasn't out to kill them to slow herself; on the other hand, Rathbone stumbled into a spiralling drop, in the same way a boulder may roll down a slope. His feet connected only with leaves, and he flopped forward at Asquith's feet.

"You fine down there, George? We'll need to get you a new coat at this rate," she said to him, stifling the smallest of laughs, and subsequently fathoming that it might've been her first in months. That was what terror did to you when it stalked you like a shadow. His reply had the same hint of humour they each were allowing themselves: "Oh, capital. I'm capital." Her husband couldn't consume her attention for long though – if the shoe were on the other foot, no man of nineteenth century England would extend any such courtesy for her.

Protruding her head from around the curved land, she parted the strands of a bush, devoid of life or leaves, and peered out. Stretching out before them, the landscape between them and any chance of a rational explanation was pure oppugnance. To her surprise, Asquith discovered it wasn't just the bush that was devoid of life, but the inclined forest. Shouldering herself against the ashy tree roots, nothing crossed her line of sight. She didn't resort to pinching herself or getting Rathbone to slap her, although a quick check that her eyelids were open wasn't ridiculous. In their little cave of dead forest and disturbed foliage, she didn't flinch. A wolfen howl would have completed the scene – none obliged. Somehow, she felt safer than before – though that was still a mammoth distance from safe. Expecting something to part the mist and begin its assault again, Asquith settled into place. Rathbone did likewise.

Each snap of twigs.

Each shift in weight.

Each crunch of the dirt.

Trapped within the woodland's heart, nothing had the nerve to move.

The first snap, one of true concern, they were to find shooting out from *behind* them. The pair spun around.

"Can I help you?" the encroacher called up the incline to them. Not Spires and his coarse physique, a man clad in overalls, an aged sack coat, and wide brimmed felt hat stood there. Rathbone, before he could think, manifested as a string of words unrepeatable in even the most disreputable of social settings. How the approaching man didn't hear him and afterwards take immediate offence confounded her. She, or God, would chastise him later.

"You need to get out of here!" Rathbone shouted. The farmer returned a confused expression, even from that distance, hurling back, "That doesn't explain what you're doing here! Private property, fella!" Asquith wished her husband hadn't made the situation so obvious, but she couldn't help except agree with him. Why wouldn't this man go away and fast? Or, instead, what kind of explanation might he consider soothing?

"No, no. We were shown here by someone called Spires! You need to go, we're . . . from the local council! This forest is closed . . . due to a dangerous breed of bull roaming free!" splurted back Asquith. By the end of that last sentence, she didn't even know how the first started. She hoped it was adequate.

"Spires? There's nobody around here called Spires!"

"He lives at the cottage being renovated up there."

"Renovated? That cottage isn't even complete yet. I daren't imagine it'll be finished before the summer."

The ground exploded. Where once the farmer stood, there was a shower of erupting soil and writhing wood.

Asquith flung herself sideways. Patches of the wood had reared up to splinter and writhe over her; but they had stopped. She understood how it must be to look a bloodhound in the eye. Its movements were less jerky now, more one combined entity than individual wooden snakes. It was only these few movements, readjusting and settling before splintering and trying again, where it looked like tree branches. Yet, a mere two steps later, they were pitching after the woman.

Looking between his wife and the snapping, creaking mass, two tendrils of which were misshaping themselves in his direction, Rathbone barrelled himself out of his hiding place too. And stopped a moment later – an intense burning had struck his chest. A second later, it was a twisting force. Then a brutal wrenching. His feet disappeared beneath him, and the muddy ground consumed his vision.

It was an odd sight, thought Asquith, when she turned around to see her husband being dragged up the forested incline, led no less than by his breast pocket. And he'd gained quite some velocity, rebounding between tree and pile of withered leaves.

A burning sensation of her own cut off any chance she had of observing the mad sight further.

Spreading from her forearm, the source was the bluish, glistening blob – more had originally seeped through her glove than she'd imagined. Its hardened crust was now cemented onto her skin. Grimacing, she realised it likely was ectoplasm, but there was something more to it.

Of course, she realised, it was a flag.

A flag for what, in that moment, shot from one the ground's muddy orifices. Where once was a pile of leaves, spasmodic wooden tendrils shot up and then adjusted, ready to dive at her.

She was about to croak some prayer when the searing heat of the ectoplasm took hold of her again. Where the outline of the encrusted substance was, tiny hooks had spawned beneath her skin in the same way the wooden pursuer was doing beneath the ground. She didn't have time to consider scraping open her skin and gouging out the terrifying mass – but the thought wasn't as distant as she'd have liked. Caught off guard, the time it took for her to fall to the floor was all the wooden lashings needed to loop around her ankles.

A moment later, she too was making a reluctant voyage up the hill, dragged by her forearm as the ectoplasm guided the wooden mass's flight. Her kicking and hollering, for all the energy she was putting into it, went unheard.

Mostly.

One man stood at the edge of the forest. His spectral form was melting away quickly, its use no longer required, but it didn't stop him taking up the job of smiling as he watched. A second later, it didn't matter anyway – what had once been Spires was now just a bluish sludge on the ground. As for Asquith, she was now in the tree's jaws. She never saw the waving, melting form of Spires. The taste in her mouth was all she could battle now, and that battle was lost before it commenced. Ectoplasm mulched together with splinters of wood and with lumps of mud and with disturbed leaf had reached her lungs.

The only consolation she could find in the unfolding mania was, for the first time since arriving in Little Hodbury, that there would be no more ice and mud beneath her.

At least she could die knowing what had happened to her ever-faithful, her George Rathbone. The tree and he were one. Her last sight, the man managing two small nods of the head before he was cut short by splintering tentacles inveigling themselves up through his shirt. A scream would've been a luxury at this stage; the offshoots exploded outwards only to curve inward and pollute his mouth. In a way, it was a surprisingly gentle way to go; no blood was spilled. Squirming chains of bark forming around her were the last things she could remember feeling.

Puckered and rippling like the skin of spoiled milk, the tree gulped in the last bit of Asquith to see daylight, her boot.

Under the wooden prison. No senses working. Splinters ebbing and flowing over their skin. The tree was delighting in its meal.

Resigned, each of the duo held solitary images in their minds as the creaking twistings of the wood engulfed them, soul, mind, and body: for Asquith, it was that distant dream of hers, that dream where her intellect might possess greater value than her subservient function, or where sin was so abhorred it simply shrank and accepted death. Whereas for Rathbone, it was only two words, two he'd yearned to say for longer than he might've admitted – "Hello, Da."

# THE TALE OF GOD-FANG

*"One does not hunt in order to kill; on the contrary, one kills in order to have hunted . . . If one were to present the sportsman with the death of the animal as a gift he would refuse it. What he is after is having to win it, to conquer the surly brute through his own effort and skill with all the extras that this carries with it: the immersion in the countryside, the healthfulness of the exercise, the distraction from his job."*
—**José Ortega y Gasset,**
***Meditations on Hunting***


"EVERY CONTINENT HAS forged terrible and curious myths, each able to wrench a gut or bring up tears of fear, often quite literally. But none has done this in such a weirder way than God-Fang. Said to pluck teeth from those who meet their demise at its hand, this insatiable animal, jaw slavering over the blood of its vanquished foes, will not rest until it has killed a person of every walk of life, be it one of savagery or one of tranquillity, or maybe even one with seldom an interesting thing to be said or do. And only then will it be able to either descend to be with its brother, Cerberus – the Guardian of the Underworld – or ascend to be with its other brother, T'ien Kou – the Dog of Heaven.

"Among its many powers imbued by the Greek Goddess Artemis, this creature was not restricted to only walking on a full moon like the werewolf, nor deterred by religion like the vampire. It is said to breathe poison onto the plant life and disintegrate it beneath its great paws and it is claimed that its howl can deafen all who hear it; and it is thought that to stare into its eyes is to begin a contract with Hades himself.

"Hellacious, the beast stalks the moors of Cumbria, although the idyll of Little Hodbury is the only place multiple witnesses have ever spotted it. A long-lost diary, found in the grasp of one of its hapless, indolent victims, is said to tell of this dog's only weakness: stakes rubbed with both wolfsbane and hemlock. When it morphs from beast to man, for shapeshifting is yet another power it derives from Artemis herself, this is the only moment it is susceptible to lethal harm.

"Its final fearsome trick is the creature's ability to summon the screams of previous victims and weaponise it against—"

"Honestly, where do you find all this nonsense?" Tim interjected into James' recital, closing the age-old volume's dusty cover for his brother in the hope that *he'd just stop*. And – as ever – his brother's counter to his scepticism was always utter scorn. From dawn until dusk, and probably in his sleep too, James' hackles were up and his face was paralysed with irritation.

Tim was prone to wondering if it was hereditary. Their parents, Madge and Eustace, were the stuffy type who had had kids very late in life; on the sporadic occasions when they'd been ordered to holiday, they had found the crumbiest end of Brighton, wrapped up in two blankets per pensioner, eaten corned beef sandwiches, and bet between them on who would be the next hapless tourist to have their fish and chips scattered into a culinary whirlwind by a seagull. Especially since

Madge and Eustace's death (nasty accident with a train and faulty traffic lights), James' face seemed to wear their acidity as some kind of commemorative badge.

"You realise T'ien Kou and Cerberus are different religions?" he barked back at his brother, wincing at his own words only once it was too late to apologise for them. "You've admitted yourself that this book is the only reference you've ever found to 'God-Fang'. Despite what it might claim."

"Listen, Tim."

"No, you listen for once," he retorted. "Stop dreaming up wild goose chases. They're just hogwash. Understand?" He hated talking to his younger brother this way. From time to time though, Tim felt he had to. Otherwise, it'd be only a day before a new nonsense swallowed James up rather than the week's respite his brother's sulkiest moods afforded him.

Then Tim heard the book's pages turning again and he twirled around. As he lodged his hand against the battered book's spine, the brothers locked eyes. It was fortunate that James had never been good at staring competitions; he tossed the wad of mythology onto his cluttered desk a few seconds into the stalemate and sank back in his chair.

Anything to hinder the endless trawls through Reddit, Facebook, and some of the seediest websites on Earth. Anything to hinder the cycle of James letting his job fall by the wayside, being fired, discovering his newest craze was all a hoax, and then plummeting into abject despondency. Such a cycle was why the pair lived together. Tim took his younger brother in before he went bankrupt, having abandoned his last job in favour of a frightfully cold jaunt into the Himalayas in search of nobody's favourite cuddly monster. He'd never found the right time to request James pay proper rent rather than the miserly sums he contributed at present.

Tim left him be. A university essay due in five days somehow felt more enticing than watching this lump of sadness stew himself into a bigger grump. Although not much of it was left to do, he found deadlines were like trains: one moment so far away, the next moment speeding past you and you're wondering if it will ever stop.

Given this, he didn't know where his next words came from, "We could go there, if you want. To the Lake District, I mean. This Little Hodbury place." Had he said it out of pity? Or just to be the saintly big brother? He hoped not – he reckoned maybe some time away would do them both good – however he had to admit he was glad to see the thankful burst of energy spreading into James' face as he jolted upright, snapping to attention with the speed and accuracy of a radar dish. His face reminded Tim of their grandpa's dog, even down to the curious whine.

"To look for God-Fang? You mean it?"

"For one night only!" he quickly said, a hug threatening to break a rib or two as he further added that they could leave early the following morning.

It'd be tight, but Tim knew he'd still be home in time to finish his essay.

For every pothole it ducked into, the car sprang twice as high and twice as erratically back onto the main road. Little Hodbury was scarcely more than a mile away at this point and scarcely four miles from the motorway, yet the brothers felt as though they'd be zooming along the meandering lanes for many bumpy years. Winding their way through the pastures of green, the twisting roads wouldn't cease.

James, ensconced by bags of camping equipment containing everything from tents to mess cans, had spent most of the car trip with his head in a sick bag. He always made a point of grabbing a few whenever he went in an aeroplane; over the last decade, he'd created a vast accumulation of them, at least two from every airline he'd travelled on. Sadly, most went into use straight away and had to be disposed of hastily. Tim had felt somewhat green around the gills himself before he'd opened the windows and allowed the mephitic fumes of his brother's regurgitated chicken curry and burnt toast to escape.

With a considerable breeze swooshing into the car and the contents of James' stomach only vaguely starting to settle, the village shot into view through the tangle of dense weeds and shrubbery. Little Hodbury resided deep in the nearest valley, the hills surrounding it almost vertical drops in places. As the crow flies, it couldn't have been more than three or four minutes away, but the twisting and unnatural angles of the landscape around it meant they'd have to drive about for almost half an hour in order to reach it. There's always a disparity between reality and Google images, and it was clear the village in full view was more tightly packed than either of them thought possible. What had seemed in the photos to be a grand place, idyllic and full of the sentiments of a simpler time, houses and shops intertwined beautifully, was actually a town arranged like a bicycle wheel. All the streets led out from a tiny town square and even the passageways appeared to be pressed together. The construction of tall and monolithic flats broke the quaintness which the furthermost areas of the village might have had. Once built, they would covet almost half the edges like the moat of a castle. The forest – Farrowpine Forest, James' quick search on his phone told him – was in sight on the other side of that same edge of the village, yet even it appeared to be an antibody keeping anything from entering the body of whichever outside world lay beyond.

They had no intention of needing to go to the village as they'd stocked up on petrol and supplies before coming; there was something about which seemed to suggest it wasn't comfortable in the landscape. As if its various facets had plummeted into existence, like teeth wrenched from their moorings and spat onto the floor – blood and all.

"Pass us the map," Tim asked while he pulled the car into a lay-by. "I don't want to spend tonight sleeping in here again."

"Totally. How did we not kill each other during that trip to Grimsby last year?" his brother replied. Afraid any movement might upset his stomach even further, he looked about in the footwell and tentatively reached out to grab it. James hadn't anticipated the last shudder of the car's engine. His head thrust forward in unison with it and a last torrent of visceral noises filled the car. Tim winced before making a quick apology. At least James had managed to land it in the sick bag again – or at least most of it.

While James continued retching, Tim forced his attention to wander to the nearby valleys. One side was unfalteringly green: unkempt foliage covered the hills and a layer of leaves tumbleweeded across the roads, the surrounding trees creating monolithic shadows. Everything on the other side appeared more alien. The sunlight trying to dapple the streams and hills couldn't fragment the Martian look it possessed; the bracken and stinging nettles swallowed it up before it struck the ground and warren openings peppered the minimal patches of open grass remaining. Tim reckoned he wouldn't have been able to do even half a mile of cross-country running over it without turning his legs to tatters or giving his ankles a funeral.

After James finished his latest bout of vomiting, the map landed on his lap. Tim grabbed it and turned to the dog-eared page, checking the route they'd drawn to the unofficial campsite. It wasn't actually labelled among the various icons, however James' trawls of the internet assured him it was there. While his guess was that the campsite couldn't be much further, everything seemed trapped within a kind of dolly zoom of false perspectives. A step in one direction and you're immediately in one place, ten steps in another and you're both elsewhere and in the exact same spot.

Tim began manoeuvring the car further down the road. He was taking it extra slowly so James' stomach wouldn't do cartwheels again, but as the tarmac turned into mud tracks his control over the vehicle lessened. He cursed at himself for not taking out the additional insurance at the rental company. The autumnal sunlight didn't take any prisoners either, every angle he shifted his head somehow was as useless at avoiding its bright rays as the last. He was concentrating on the gear stick too much to chastise James as he discarded one of the full sick bags out of the car window and as he descended further along the road the gusts creeping up beside the car were getting stronger. Mouldering wildlife was the nearest he had for signposts, in spite of his brother's unhelpful attempts at directions behind him – of course the one time he decided not to throw up he elected to be a backseat driver.

Neither brother knew how long the car had skidded and bumped and spluttered and disagreed and fought back by the time the campsite became visible. Not that it deserved to be called a campsite; in reality, it was a grove of trees vanguarded by a couple of streams. There was only indication anyone had used the site in recent months – a line of lankier trees, chainsawed down, vanguarded the area's eastern edge. Unlike the valleys above, the greenery hadn't filtered down here and it gave the impression this grove actually understood what autumn was – wilting orange and yellow leaves carpeted the dirt floor. In the dark, they'd be lucky to walk a few feet without losing balance and cantering into one of the trees.

James didn't need to see his older brother to know the uneasy look he was giving him.

As the car came to a halt, Tim thought about giving James a piece of his mind, but decided against it. It was early evening already and they weren't going to go home now; he might as well wait until the morning and clip him round the ear then.

The brothers got out of the car. Even with the windows open, Tim was glad of a break from the stenches collected within the steel box. James was of a different mind, releasing his body like a coiled spring and at once dashing out of the car and over to one of the streams, traversing it for a brief while and then darting over to the felled trees.

It was the same fervour James had used to

blaze through holidays with Gramps. Holidays with any of their relatives, particularly on their dad's side of the family, had been rarities; if anyone took them somewhere though, it was always Gramps. He had twice taken them to a small town outside of Falmouth, where James had spent his entire day roaming about the local sites and unearthing every tidbit there was to be found. While neither had been back there since those holidays, Tim was sure that's where his brother's love of conspiracy theories, inexplicabilities, rumour, and even general gossip sprang from; Gramps definitely had indulged James by buying him books on the Beast of Bodmin Moor from the shops around there, although he probably didn't know the can of worms about to be unleashed.

Ironically, Cornwall was also where James' latest two girlfriends had both ended up after splitting up with him, seemingly trying to get away from his rantings by moving to the other end of the country.

"Are you going to help with the tents?" Tim called after his brother.

"It's perfect!" James yelled back. "It really is!"

That would be a no, he figured, turning and beginning to ferry the various luggage out of the car. His younger brother did eventually join him; having unloaded most of the bags and cases himself, Tim watched him appear just in time to grab one last box from the boot.

About to set to work on putting up the tent, he then noticed the animal.

The squirrel was dead. Without a shadow of a doubt.

The squirrel was frowning as it lay upon the tuft of leaves. Frowning its toothiest frown, no matter how impossible its jaw found that to accommodate. Other than that, he reckoned the squirrel was maybe even at peace, not that it stopped the sight being totally alien to both the landscape and the rest of squirrel-kind. No blood pooled beneath it, no scratch marks gouged open its flesh and introduced its guts to the leafy grove floor, no malice lingered in its eyes asking *Why did I die?* or *Why am I alone now?* – and had it died in pain, it'd welcomed that pain like an old friend.

And yet.

It sat there pancake-like. Where it's tiny paws touched the earth, not only were they free of life, but they were also free of structure. Its tail was not simply lain flat on the leaves, it was flattened into the leaves. A 2-D image, nothing less and irrefutably nothing more.

Tim imagined he had to attend to the animal. He had to remove the sleeve of a creature and take it to the nearby stream and bid it farewell without dignity or grace – because why does window dressing need dignity or grace?

The task was over in a couple of minutes. The squirrel felt far too flexible in his hands, as though it were a sheet of rubber masked by fur. But Tim stayed by the stream a few moments longer, watching it drift along. Watching it sink a little. Watching it drift further. Watching it bob up and down and side to side against the tiny banks of mud and pebbles either side of the stream. He compelled himself to watch this squirrel until its papery physique dressed some other window which he didn't have to trouble himself over, all too aware that even then out of sight was not out of mind. Even if it had died of natural causes, what was natural in city life wasn't the same as natural here; here, natural was decided by whatever was gracious enough to impose its will.

The task was done though. And Tim couldn't stand watching a stream forever. Back at the campsite, he turned his attention to putting up the tents for a second time. But if his attention wasn't drifting to the creature whose watery resting place he had just presided over, it drifted to the landscape enshrouding them. From down here, he realised how awfully steep the grass verges were, realised how fast the streams were flowing in spite of their diminutive size, realised how much spiky grass and stinging nettle greenery coated the surrounding expanses. The river was the only other noise filling the air. He couldn't help wondering why James had chosen this spot for hunting God-Fang.

Was it – just maybe – a bit too quiet? A bit too feral?

Unlike James, Tim reckoned he didn't need supernatural explanations to know how many beans made five – he didn't doubt this was the best place to hunt a mythical beast. Because when you're in the middle of an isolated grove with a landscape as easy to tackle as quicksand, that also happened to be the perfect hunting ground for people who liked preying on hapless tourists. Weren't there horror films about this very sort of thing? Come to think of it, he realised, hadn't he been in the room when James watched a *Torchwood* episode with that very plot? There's a reason he lived in big cities, and it wasn't out of fear of shapeshifting beasts who pluck teeth from victims.

The horizon didn't make things better. Just looking up to find it seemed like an effort, everything as neatly outlined as it was blur after blur. If the perspectives on the main road felt wrong, here they were worse. Here, they lied. Here, they also hid things: you could cross the grove in a minute or so and, once you were on the other side, it was a view which seemed entirely incompatible. Three versions of the same place latched and bolted into one with no respect for those walking into it. James had assured Tim that the campsite was close enough to the village that help was never too far away; with every step he took, he re-assessed his brother's decision. How many brambles would he have to clamber through, how many impossible edges lay concealed in the landscape ready to emerge and block his path like groynes along a verdant beach?

He tried his best to distract himself. For the first time, he jumped at the chance for his brother to order him about and found placing cameras in notches in some of the trees while James slung microphones over tree branches. After both men had returned to begin work on a roaring campfire near the tents, dawn had already passed and night was in full swing – an impenetrable net wrapped around the grove. Were it not for the first embers of the fire, Tim doubted he'd be able to see more than a foot in front of himself. Not even the moonlight pierced the trees, the orange-leafed canopies above them shredding it to nothing.

Both boys soon disappeared into their tents to unpack their rucksacks, set their things out, and prepare for a good night's sleep. Tim's tent was the neater of the two: a lamp hung from a hook in the "roof", clothes lay in tidy piles along one side of the makeshift home, and his book, toiletries, folded-up camping chair, and portable charger all lay just beyond his pillow.

When he poked his head around the flap of

James' tent, he could see far less organisation: clothes were barely folded, clustered at the end of the tent, while most of the other things remained in a cramped heap within a large bag. The majority of his tent was consumed by his large, plush sleeping bag, and the box of fence posts, beneath which was a monitor feeding in the video from outside. The whiff in the air told him James had applied the wolfsbane and hemlock, converting them into lethal weapons against the dog. The thought James might have a change of heart about his insane lifestyle lessened with every second, it seemed.

"No wonder I only get a sliver towards rent," Tim said. It was a half-joke underpinned by a scowl and James returned the peevish look.

The crunch of leaves sounded from outside the tent. Tim spun around and found himself face to face with two glaring beams. They cut open the darkness, as if trying to dissect it.

"Hello?" He called out, beginning to creep forward so he could peer into the driver-side window, not helped by the deafening mulch of the dirt and leaves beneath his feet. There was maybe the outline of a discarded crisps packet in the footwell and something on the dashboard, but the dazzle of the lights made the obliqueness of the dark too strong to see anything more.

"Anything there?" James called to him. The bright glow of the headlights engulfed his brother and it highlighted that his skin had turned the same sallow colour as it had on the journey there. "Did you see who left it?"

"If I knew that, wouldn't I have told you by now?" the older brother replied tetchily. It was only when he heard his own voice aloud that he understood his teeth were chattering like a Geiger counter. It was the cold – surely? Or was the hue of his skin in fact matching James'?

"Can I help the two of you?" a gruff, husky voice called. "It would be polite if you'd at least introduce yourselves." A click accompanied it, rebounding around the gloomy grove of trees, picking out Tim, making him imagine something no farther than a metre from his head. He was trying to ignore the half of his brain that was telling him it was the click of a gun being loaded. Nothing in Gramps' tutelage had vaccinated him against this – what had his witless prick of a brother dragged him into?

"I don't have all day," the darkness grunted.

"Tim! Tim Krogh!" He heard the whine in his own voice. Cold alarm had bled into his voice the way he feared urine would soon down his leg.

"James." Tim couldn't work out whether his brother's reticence was out of fear or stubbornness.

"You're here, why?" came the voice again, softer yet brimming with thorns. The darkness had them there, vice-like.

"Why should we tell you?" responded James, with all the diligence and sensitivity of a toddler mid-tantrum.

"Just answer the question, James!" hissed Tim. "Before I piss myself." Sweat was spouting out of his forehead quicker than water out of a sluice gate. He suspected the tapping of his foot into the dirt in that moment might have powered the half of England.

"God-Fang. He's— well, *it's* rumoured to haunt these valleys. We're investigating him." When James said "we", Tim's forehead had taken on a layer of sweat. His eyelids were clenched firmly shut by now. The darkness, the feeling of something beside him while it poked and prodded at his faith in his brother – it made him an isolated figure trapped inside a world already isolated.

"You aren't from Little Hodbury?"

"No," James said, his older brother still stammering over every syllable out of fear it might turn out to be his last.

The darkness grunted its reply. As Tim finally plucked up the courage to turn his head to the left, he saw that the voice's owner was a man much taller and much more gaunt than either brother. He dressed head to toe in bland, green walking trousers and wearing enough shirts and fleeces to start an outdoor apparel company. Even his walking boots looked like they were padded out with a drawer full of socks.

"Professor Griffiths, PhD. Chief hunter of God-Fang. Nice to meet you boys." he said after brandishing a swanky business card. It dropped onto the orange leaves by Tim's feet and the man stood aside to let them read it. James shuffled over out of the violence of the car headlights so he could have a better view, letting out a gasp he didn't know he was bottling up.

"Hunter of God-Fang?" spoke James, his private school accept emerging at exactly the wrong moment. "No way, too coincidental. Prove it."

Whilst his enthusiastic brother interrogated the man, Tim's eyes drifted to the man's side; a massive, uncomfortably-real firearm hung at Griffiths' side and made the darkness continue to feel like a wall between the outside world and this crazed realm he'd entered. Its only advantage was it broke up the continuous cycle of images pressing against his eyes; although he couldn't say he enjoyed the feeling, he decided to grasp it with open arms. Even the few moments where his brain was focused purely on recalibrating might offer him an enclave safe from his other thoughts.

"You realise you're on my land?" Griffiths said, eventually butting into James' tirade of questions.

"Mate . . ." he sighed at his brother. Whether you armed yourself with intense rationality or hypochondriac paranoia, James was a pang of anxiety somehow weaponised, a presence in which your mind hacked diseased definitions out of patternless events and fogged any boundaries, no matter how well outlined they were. Tim couldn't wait for the day James drifted into a room on a cloud of melatonin and nothing else.

"I'm sorry," his brother mumbled.

"I assume then you didn't learn that I bought this land *specifically* to hunt the vicious bastard, right?"

He removed from his pocket a scratchy polaroid of his collection of God-Fang paraphernalia. Ravenous, James' eyes continued to boggle, snatching the polaroid from Griffiths in an attempt to engorge himself on the image.

For ten minutes, the intense, passionate boggling continued and more ensued when Griffiths revealed the many manuscripts concealed in the boot of his car. He placed box after box, brimming with everything from the scratchiest pictures to the driest volumes concerning the obscurest of folklore, onto the ground. They totalled twelve and stood at almost thrice the professor's height. Tim, however, couldn't stop his eyes veering off course as he prepared his bed for the night and Griffiths gripped his firearm closer every time he caught the older brother glancing in his direction.

After Tim's eyes had exploded one too many times, Griffiths spat out, "Something the matter?"

He thought it best not to respond. As for James, his nose was either too stuck into the mounds of literature or up his own backside to say anything.

"It's a Chinese fowling piece, capable of blowing the fucker to smithereens," Griffiths added. "I'm not playing games. Not some has-been or some snivelling grandad off to play tiddlywinks and tell paltry campfire stories, you got it? One day, I'll go into Little Hodbury, the creature trussed up like a turkey at Christmas, mark my fucking words!"

Tim continued busying himself with everything that he could, even if that was just hammering the tent pegs into the ground for a fourth time. His main concern was preventing the smell of soiled underpants.

Still James didn't wrinkle his nose in acknowledgement.

Over the next hour Griffiths regaled James with many tales of Little Hodbury. From its curious residents to the rumours of its corrupt police, as well as every quaint custom they indulged, James couldn't have been more attentive were he a puppy watching their owner get a treat from the cupboard. One of his tales did stick in Tim's head, because of how gloriously off-topic it was: the story of Lambert Deacons, who upon finding two melissophiliacs amongst his proud and expansive plot of beehives, ventured out, released enough curses to topple a nunnery, and created two new ornaments for his garden. Griffiths claimed their decapitated heads resided there for an uncomfortably ripe three and a half weeks, in the throes of summer as well. The neighbours apparently just assumed they were wax – and only decided to investigate when the opaque cloud of flies started spreading along the street.

It was when Griffiths mentioned a man called Paul Albatross, a local businessman and handyman with fingers in all the wrong pies, that Tim decided to retire to bed. His yearning for a university essay had never been so strong.

Even inside his tent though, he feared he might contract an unwarrantedly nasty case of psittacosis given the way he could hear his younger brother and the professor squawking to one another. He would hear the story of how Albatross ostensibly had one of the mayors killed in mysterious circumstances, whether he wanted to or not. Thankfully, the love for his pillow stirring within him was overpowering enough to knock him out cold.

It was about four in the morning when Tim awakened. The sleeping bag had wrapped itself tightly around him corkscrew-like and the sensations of warmth in the material clung to him. Did he dare take the risk of moving in case all the heat sought refuge elsewhere? His bladder made his mind up for him.

With every movement unlocking the cool potential of the air and letting more and more zephyrs of sluggishness flit around him, he scrabbled about in the tent's outer compartment as he searched for his tough army boots. He finally found them lodged between a pile of carrier bags ready to contain his wet clothing and his empty suitcase. Too busy concentrating on emptying his bladder, that they'd all been neatly arranged hours earlier never occurred to him.

The grove was oblique, the gloom pushing in and staying firm around the tents and the cars as though injected into the air. Something hidden in the wind greeted him as he emerged and instantly massaged his ears and nose into numbness. The air didn't need any winds to blow for it to hang heavy and display its deadness for all to feel. He tried to use his phone torch to slice open the darkness and aimed the beam at the ground in front of him, but the air somehow seemed reluctant to shift. The embers from the night's fire couldn't survive the darkness either; they tapered off and were replaced by the shroud within seconds.

He knew he'd be brief. Immediately desperate to raise his zipper and cut off the frostbite, he took himself to behind the tent and willed his stream of smelly, steamy liquid to pool on the ground quicker.

Then the darkness was total.

He shook his phone, as though treating it like a fading glowstick would help. It didn't.

"Bollocks."

He couldn't even get it to display the charger symbol that ordinarily blared at him in its dying moments. But why? For the entirety of yesterday, his habit of missing every text message sent to him had been at its strongest; for the entire car ride, his phone had been plugged in so he could blot out the sound of James' retching with Siouxsie and the Banshees; and his portable charger was at full power.

Yet his phone was dead.

He darted through the darkness on muscle memory and adrenaline. He could have sworn he'd brought a portable power bank and plugged his phone in last night. Inside the tent, he collapsed onto his knees and pushed bags and piles of clothes aside as he searched for his charger. It never occurred to him to think why his phone wasn't plugged in when he awoke. The phone was next to his sleeping bag and he'd picked it up, nothing more.

He had zipped his tent up behind him, he suddenly thought. When he turned around, he found he indeed had.

Aloud, he mumbled, "Why'd that come to me?"

The chilling waft. It was inside as well as outside. As he pushed one of his T-shirts aside, his hand brushed over the hole – a precise hole, the size of a penny. Sleeping in a forest that pushed the boundaries of the middle of nowhere, Tim admitted to himself that some turbulent weather was on the cards: the occasional branch falling onto his tent, the odd blast of hail, or even an errant fox sniffing his tent were expected. But foxes were hardly in the habit of cutting an incision into the lining of his tent. And even less in the habit of taking his portable power bank and charger.

"Hey, James!" he cried out, unzipping the tent and poking his head out into the darkened grove. The wind rustled its response.

Tim moved across to his brother's tent, the crunch of the leaves his only company. He groped the doorway until his hands found the zip as his eyes refused to adjust. Edging into the tent, he made sure to crouch down; he was going to look a right tit if he landed flat on his face upon James. But there was only air. As he inspected the chunky monitor in the corner, he realised the pillow on the bed was cold.

Tim stopped.

The growl of something right beside him.

Without a hint of precision, the tent lining flew apart. Something warped the material into confetti. Sprawling to avoid it, he tumbled back and dislodged one of the tent poles. The world around him at once crumbled and after a few seconds only one pole remained hoisted to the pegs. A sharp stabbing sensation jangled Tim's spine and he felt the ice-cold sensation dribble down his leg. When he tried to launch himself to his feet, he found himself cocooned like a fly in amber, the sleeping bag knotting around his feet. Something was thrashing about beside him in the gloom.

"The pair of you, what are you doing?" hollered James, voice like a gong sounding mid-battle. His own torch flittered across the war zone. "He's God-Fang!" Griffiths shouted.

Tim's bones became ice – to the point where the dribble down his leg felt toasty.

"That's my brother!" yelled James, emerging from behind a tree. The tent was tatters now and the three warred in the chill of the open air.

"James, where the hell have you been?"

"I went to check one of the cameras – leave him alone!"

"I've hunted that fearmonger for years. Years! And then two of you turn up happy as Larry? Not a chance!" James' feet ground to a halt, the professor pointing the grinning end of the gun back and forth between the two boys.

"Look, we read a book, I nagged Tim, he drove me here. Out of pity!" said James, a glint in his eye morphing into a tear. His eyeline found it impossible to meet his brother's. It was unlike him to admit such a thing, even under normal circumstances, so the gut-wrench that he must have been suffering, it was surely so alien and savage towards him that Tim was surprised he didn't collapse in that moment.

"Pah!" Griffiths replied.

"Well—" responded James, unsure where his

sentence would go next. Where could it go next?

"Don't you think I would have heard of this book?! I'm the leading expert!"

"That one there," Tim shouted in reply, nodding towards a lump of pages sat among the leaves.

The adrenaline in his brain was like a tidal wave, smashing against neurones, each brain muscle, every synapse. He finally noticed something curious. Something so bizarre only it could have broken the stalemate they were jammed in.

"It's blank," Tim muttered, more tears forming as his nose pressed against the Chinese fowling piece.

"What?" the professor yelled, his firearm barrel still pointing at each boy at regular intervals. He grabbed the volume with his other hand. The page jutting out of the volume, hanging onto the binding by the smallest of threads, was indeed blank. As was the next. And the next. None of the pages showed any sign of ink markings, however old. The sound of Tim's quivering breath overwhelmed the silence between the three of them; a lone leaf lay on his chest, yet it didn't dare flutter. James took another small step forward.

"That's . . . impossible."

"Or your ruse has been found out?" retorted the man in charge of turning the boys' heads into chum. The gun now fixed its gross smile at James. A shiver ran down the conspiracist's soaked left leg and his body at once became like a limp bag of soggy potatoes.

"But it can't be!" James spewed out in a torrent of saliva, bafflegabbing his way through a thousand words a minute. "It's a book like any other! I bought it online. Limited edition, one of its kind, said to mention myths never referenced elsewhere!"

"Oh, do shut up! This is just a bunch of lies!" Griffiths shouted.

"It can't be! That book got us here, didn't it? It wasn't like it was inaccurate!"

Tim was trying to edge out of his nylon cocoon with little success. If only he could reach the upturned box containing the sharpened fence posts.

"You aren't making sense! You can't follow a blank book, so tell me the truth!"

James was now too dumbfounded to continue his train of thought. That train had derailed, crashed into the burning, mangled cinders of normality and suburbia. He gazed around, as if rationality would be found hiding amongst the orange and red leaves or the dark pockets of an alien world.

"What?" was the only word he could come up with. Very simple, very despondent. Next, came his big realisation, one that he should have had previously. "Tim, I'm so sorry."

Despite the panopticon of Griffith's gun barrel, Tim at once began to move. Forcing himself through the tatters, he began to run – and not towards James.

"Professor, this way!"

A growl shook the forest. Behind them, James was trembling. When Tim risked a glance over his shoulder, he saw little bubbles formed under his brother's skin. At first, they appeared to be goosebumps; within thirty seconds, once the elder brother had flung Griffiths to safety behind the car, the skin had bulged like a swollen balloon, each individual lump the size of a two-pound coin. When the first couple burst and revealed the furry skin in a shroud of yellow, noxious fumes, the transformation was over halfway done.

Behind the car, Griffiths was manhandling more ammunition into his gun. It took everything within Tim not to seize the professor and bolt across the nearest hills and verges until he reached Little Hodbury – and got himself committed to a mental asylum. That thing would scatter his ligaments across the campsite before he'd even got to his feet. Even if the timid boy couldn't understand it, he somehow knew it was God-Fang who'd brought the eternal autumn and overgrowing vegetation; it was he who had ensured the original settlers of Little Hodbury ventured no further than the size their village was already.

"How the fuck did you know that was going to happen?" Griffiths spat. Tim could see the suspicions creeping back into his dilating pupils.

"My brother is one of the most stubborn people you'll meet. He'll tell you black is white. And he's apologised twice in the last few minutes! He must've left the tent in the night, probably to look for that thing. It got him."

Griffiths snapped a look at the transforming creature.

"And God-Fang can shapeshift. Shit." The gun finished reloading and Griffiths instantly released its contents over the car bonnet and into the malevolent creature. Its canine head, jaws and all, set free a guttural choke of anguish and laughter and the projectiles fell out of its side, a dribble of yellow blood following. The following cackle, drowning in a slosh of vomit, launched from the most primal centres of its being. The noise echoed around the grove, shaking every tree and causing the roots to curl. The survivors clenched their ears tightly, a small drop of blood spilling from the professor's left ear.

"What the hell can we do? Professor!" he screamed through a clenched whine of raw pain. But Griffiths' vocal cords had given up the ghost. Whatever the noise was, it had permeated every organ, every cell, every iota of humanity.

He was already a distant husk when his nose exploded. His nosebleed had become too much, the viscera plastering itself over Tim's face. Spitting the red and fleshy smatterings from his mouth, he spotted his sole possible saviour.

All God-Fang had left to do was remove its hind legs, fur coagulated with the insides of James, before it could pounce. And how soon would that take? How soon before its jaw would be clamped around one of Tim's body parts, a mild snack on the buffet it enjoyed?

Feeling the increasing pressure mounting around his eyes, ears, and nose, Tim flung himself over the bonnet. Although his vision lied to him now at every turn, he soon managed to find the fence post. James had been, for once, organised, and made the stakes stink already. All Tim really had was just one thing left to do: plunge. And so, the stake did, wielded by amateur hands yet a novice survival instinct.

The fence post only went so far. The monster's paw had clamped around it, Tim's head held at bay under its other paw. From its lips, a slow, careful cackle came. Not one of pain. It was mocking its feeble prey. Hijacking the vestiges of James' voice, it howled, "I created the book. I wrote the weakness – the 'weakness'."

Wolfsbane and hemlock was still seeping into its skin, but the effect was instant: bones more rigid, teeth sharper, eyes no longer seeing the world in monochrome. The boy didn't even have time to register his own surprise or realise God-

Fang's jaw was at once fixed to his arm. Its jaw shut around the delicious, fleshy mass of Tim's neck.

Griffiths sat up, clicked his fingers, felt his nose re-assemble, and looked to his Master like a puppy wanting a treat for not peeing in the house.

God-Fang was too busy digging his nose into Tim's body to notice his puppet.

Until Griffiths could get his Master's attention, he grabbed the blank book and clicked his fingers again, watching each of the words morph into a new lure. Although there was little point in repeating the same experiment twice, the book attuned itself to the situation; all they needed to do was release it into the wild again and wait until the next lot came to them. The trap was easy enough to reset.

Griffiths rolled onto all-fours, as God-Fang's puppet always did in their private audiences, a sort of imitative reverence.

His master broke the sound of his nose dislodging gut after kidney after intestine, "This is good meat."

"The plan was to your satisfaction?"

The snaffled reply of his nose burying deeper and deeper inside Tim was answer enough. The first one had been a fairly simple chore – when he had in fact emerged to sort one of the cameras, it was a straightforward hunt. Griffiths and his Master played with him in the shadows until he was more fear than flesh, until his adrenaline was spent and the meat was tenderised.

This second one was always going to be more fun. The uncertainty, the anger, the pity, every emotion bubbling away inside him. The usual routine of luring in the prey, getting its adrenaline pumping, creating madness and illusion to scare it – and letting his Master feast on the chaos and the fear as the entrée – would have worked, but there was more. They'd played with it. They had not just hunted it, they'd created a game and watched it die within it.

And it had been glorious.

As he watched his master continue tucking into his feast, his exploded nose had soon totally healed itself. The sole clue of anything untoward was a lone drop of blood on his lip; and even that would disappear. After his tongue snaked out to clear away the evidence, he sat back. His Master would soon give new orders. And then the fun could recommence.

# CRUCIAL DECISIONS

AMONG THE PUNGENT aroma of coffee, the silent room was brimming with something violent and disturbed. Every brow was furrowed with an anger, charged by a remonstration of paperwork and diplomacy. At the centre of the shooting range sat Jennifer Willbond, the chairwoman struggling with how to proceed: small talk for a few minutes would likely end in everyone exchanging barbs about politics; a continued silence would likely be interrupted by a cough and snide comment from the treasurer; getting down to business would surely hasten the shouting festival and decay of democracy, not that much remained to worsen further. She prayed that she could quell the feeling of apprehension yet the butterflies in her stomach weren't having any of it. In spite of her weak legs, Willbond took to her feet. The butterflies went crazy.

"Where's Esther?" said the chairwoman hesitantly, with a sigh. It got longer and longer as the day went, and you could almost set the time by how without purpose or cheer she sounded – eight seconds, so not far off midday. A sea of thirty faces looked back at her, blank except for fires in their eyes, stoked by imminent eruptions. In that moment, while she listened to clouds rumble above viciously, her mind wandered to the grim thought that the drive up to her house in the valley would be flooded. She sighed. Loudly. So loudly, it brought her back to the worst place imaginable – the here and now.

"Esther? Esther Penhaligon?" she asked the crowd. The sea was still glazed but this time those hateful eyes shifted to the seat beside her. Already one of them was half-standing, fumbling with their reading glasses while readying to announce a speech written on a thick wad of paper.

Nobody answered Willbond's question apart from those clouds – nobody in fact liked Penhaligon, the oddbod with a bold fashion style. The only reason they'd been brought into the council was that previous members, now booted off, had wanted some fresh opinions and Penhaligon was the only one they'd elected in – to the new guard's chagrin. They represented everything that made the council's stomachs turn inside out.

It was a craving for power, that's why she stayed. It was a crevasse out of which she couldn't ever climb. She'd been like this from a young age, with the silliest of things such as being line-monitor in Year Three making her feel like a God, and the contorting of dolls and teddy bears, knowing they felt no pain, forcing her to wonder if this was what the deities of various religions felt like. Additionally, Willbond had spent her entire life in the village, clinging onto it in the same way a newborn does to its mother, and the vaguest intimation that anyone could do better than her sent a shiver down her spine. Not only this, but Willbond had also observed the previous council at "work", watched their glorious manifesto become dust under the public gaze, and flinched as councillor after councillor spoke out against the chairwoman, with plain, unadulterated hypocrisy. The woman hated change, and she'd proudly admit it, but more importantly she was determined to push her village into a prosperous new age. So, the lies couldn't end.

"Following on from the last meeting," she began, standing to avoid the member sitting on her left, or more specifically to avoid the amount of loose dandruff that coated his shoulders. She would one day ask him whether that was medical. The same went for his armpits, which even through multiples layer of corduroy proved how showering and just applying deodorant yielded different results. One day, she'd ask him if he could get some treatment, although how would she broach the subject? For perhaps the first time in her entire life, she was considering that the bull-in-a-China shop method would be inappropriate – that would be reserved for the meetings.

"If I could interject!" shouted another member of the village, standing up and sticking his pasty, waggling finger out, winding other members up who retaliated with fingers of their own – even if some were more straight up and intentioned rather than waggling.

The table suddenly looked a very interesting place for her head. Willbond flopped back in her seat and the instinct to bury her hands was incredible. In the brief moment it took her to be seated, already two more people had stood up and begun to "interject".

The bickering had truly commenced.

The stage curtains parted fractionally, allowing the figure to overhear the feud of the elderly pensioners arguing with the newer councillors. Their disagreements blotted out the shadowy figure's own breaths and sighs well. They were so certain that they could go about their business unnoticed, since after all they'd managed it many times before in preparation for today – today was *the* day.

The layout of the building was glued into

their mind, so being caught was no issue. The village council's meeting room was based in the hall, next to the local which was usually rented out for dance sessions and the like. The stage, used now as a store for various drama props and costumes, was also where everyone could hang their wringing-wet coats and place their bags after a trek through a forest of cardboard boxes and scenery backdrops. Of course, it wasn't the most convenient place to put coat hooks, but by the time someone had ventured in and waded through the minefield of protruding props, their only real concern was getting out without breaking their neck. And today, it provided the shadow with an advantage.

Although the shadow's days of being an altar boy in the church or an aspiring thespian were locked away in corners of their mind, they still brought the figure heartache. Whatever they thought about the dullards that composed the human race, they'd had a sense of unequivocal joy about drama, and everyone involved in the art, right up to the end of their teenage years. The chance to fling one's flowing quiff back, march onto stage with a prop and then recite something Shakespearian was an insatiable one. It was pretentious, but that was a curse they'd just have to bear.

When they were younger, they were part of an eight-person drama troupe, led by the honest-to-goodness Mrs. Niven and the blithesome Mrs. Shand. It had made them feel very at home, far removed from the world that thought their love of music was odd, thought their rose-patterned boots were stupid, and thought having a sense of self was ridiculous. Without that pair, some of the biggest traumas of their life would've tyrannised them beyond redemption and some of the greatest questions about their selfhood might've gone unanswered.

Another thing they found tranquil about the experiences that the group brought was Charley the duck, the fish called Fernando, as well as Greg the pig, whom one of the troupe members had attained in the oddest perceivable raffle. This uncouth menagerie gave them another focus. The shadow, though they weren't that then, could finally care for something. Wasn't it their job to honour the animals? Wasn't it their job to find a sense of self in the company of the animals?

With their crafty fingers inveigled into every aspect of the performances, nobody suspected the shadow when the fish turned up dead. After all, as both Niven and Fernando were to discover, it was hard to imagine a minifridge being ideally suited to a fish's dimensions. No-one had cared to see the slight clench in their lower lip when she opened the refrigerator with a *very* shrill, vocal accompaniment and face that a horror film director would certainly have envied. Had anyone thought to ask the shadow if they were theriocidal or took immense delight in watching perplexed anguish and terror in others anyway, the answer would have why Greg, in the fullness of time, had found his final moments of life atop the church hall. The pig's entrails hung like bunting around the vicarage chimney and church steeple, oddly beautiful in a way. Later in life, the shadow had justified all of that as an attempt at realising their theatrical methodology. Stanislavski eat your heart out. The *Lord of the Flies* production that year would feature one of the most accurate props ever seen in a Little Hodbury production, which was the ultimate prize. Animal life was a tool, dead or alive.

Now, however, everything was crystal clear. In short, they'd heard enough. As they always had. Allowing the curtains to flop shut, the shadow stepped through a small sliver of light. It streamed in via a cracked window above and illuminated the thick cloud of dust polluting the air. A friendly dove that had taken nest in the building used it as her private entrance. Unfortunately, the dove hadn't visited for a good two months. In the field adjoining the church, the poor creature had come off the worst in a face to face with a badger, or something else with the ability to rip open animals and eat the organs. Left as a red mess, she was abandoned the following day in full view of some children.

Smiling at this memory, the shrouded figure nimbly weaved around a few plastic boxes to face the coat hooks. Having rifled in their cavernous pockets for a moment, they removed something tiny and glass and held it up. A proud smile grew on the shadowed figure's face as knowledge of the future had the same effect as a drug. It split open their lips like cracking paint. Lid removed, they sprinkled a miniscule amount of the contents into a bag pocket, next to the owner's wallet and car keys and, only a few minutes later, the powder was distributed evenly. Within a further minute, it had become invisible to both touch and sight, irrespective of incredibly real potency.

Then, the chant came, the figure releasing a string of letters from a cage locked away under their breath. Permeating the mix of unearthly syllables was glee, nigh on orgasmic euphoria, shooting down the rivers of their brain. Job done – nearly. Returning each possession to its correct place, as though none had been touched, they abandoned the stage.

The chaos continued long into the next hour. The tumultuous arguments had now turned to the attention of budgets, and if someone had dropped a nuclear bomb, its effect wouldn't have rippled the surface of a jelly by comparison. The swathes of red, puffy faces were covered in beads of sweat loaded with enough rage to trigger World War Three.

The arguing finally simmered down about twenty minutes later, when, by unanimous agreement, they decided they'd got nowhere and wouldn't get anywhere if they continued at this rate. Of course, some smart aleck tried to reinvigorate the melting pot of hell; in an act of mercy that followed, the council shouted him down.

As they were all packing up, shooting each other with daggers in their eyes, was the moment Esther walked in. Their coat was dripping and the scarf around their throat, despite being looped tightly, had offered little resistance to the storm swirling about the village. The torrent had even invaded their boots, drenching their socks. They quickly removed their boots and poured the pools into a china sink, stained with coffee and tea and with its own prized collection of cracks and chipped enamel.

The first few members leaving stopped to look Esther up and down and assess what method of dullness they'd use on them next.

"So, you finally bother to turn up," hissed Willbond, metaphorically pacing up and down as she tried to work out an excuse to run and flee, quiver under a blanket, and never leave the house again. Bad weather made her joints ache prematurely and bad company made bile rise in her throat; at present, not one iota of her body felt comfortable, and her mouth contained a vile taste.

"I know, I'm a fool, I'm sorry," they bumbled, too busy arguing with their left boot and eking the uncomfortable squelches out of its insole. A crowd of seven or eight more onlookers were gathered round them in seconds, a furore of great white sharks waiting to pounce. Unlike sharks, they lost interest quickly, but not before the asinine bunch had a chance to ignore Esther's pronouns. "Get him out of the way," or "Damn the idiot boy" were the order of the day.

"I know I've missed the meeting today, but that doesn't mean I can't do something useful," Esther tried in an attempt to get the mass of spiteful eyes back onside. "How about, to say sorry, I get everyone's coats and bags from in there?" they continued, quivering and gesturing in the direction of the stage.

The council hissed like a bomb; Esther decided to answer on their behalf.

Not much time later, the correct coats had anxiously been awarded to the correct people. They'd even found time amongst the seething crowd to finish their shoe back onto their foot.

Bright beams of sunshine now swarmed the car park and not a single piece of gravel on the ground didn't bathe in its gaze. Shuffling out of the village hall, the pensioners quickly made for their cars and didn't pass a single word of thanks to Esther, nor bother to exchange parting pleasantries. Willbond was one of the last to leave, second only to Esther themselves who needed to fumble about with their pedometer. The remaining small gaggle of the men exited via the fire escape, discussing things cherry-picked to be above the others' heads – pompous gits.

The one harrying away quickest was in fact

the quietest of the lot, Mrs. Chaudhri. She could often be found in the local library, dashing away with some dry book if not rearranging the ones left on the shelves, forever tutting under her breath. Today, she made a curt goodbye, after which she headed in an unswerving beeline for her car. Watching, Esther muttered something under their breath, probably curmudgeonly, and Willbond wondered if, like her, they wanted to be home before the weather transformed back into its true ugly self.

Once at the metal box, Chaudhri couldn't have unlocked it and dived inside quicker. She clutched her handbag and kept it close to her all the way.

Inside the car, on the other hand, it was a different story. In the sea breeze of the air freshener and surrounded by the plush leather, she could finally breathe without tensing all her muscles. The woman didn't notice the swirling of dust that was occurring in the bag, currently in the passenger side footwell.

Back outside the hall, Esther manoeuvred themselves next to Mrs. Willbond, "Jennifer, I don't suppose you've had time to review—"

She snapped back at them, "What happened to Mateo was regrettable, but we couldn't have stopped it. The fact that car smashed into his house was nothing to do with us. And we wouldn't have the jurisdiction to do anything about it anyway." She proceeded to take a very big sidestep to the left, placing one of the older pensioners between the two.

Everything Willbond had said was completely true and Esther knew that. But the dusty fuse had been lit – they'd given her chance to apologise. The village council were the ones who'd decided the roadworks were necessary, even if that bumbling cluster couldn't have foreseen an escapee from the nursing home, *something* Cartwright, stealing a car using knowledge from their carjacking days of youth. Nor could anyone have foreseen the aneurism which the car-jacker suffered just as it approached – then ignored – the new traffic lights.

There were no more words to be said now, at least to the council. The words Esther muttered as they left the car park weren't for public consumption. Besides, even if the council members could hear the strange tongue they were muttering, they'd soon have problems of their own.

As they reached the car park exit, they could see that things had begun even quicker than expected. While Esther was transfixed on Jennifer Willbond's loathsome form, or more specifically the movement of tiny limbs within her right hand pocket, the line of pensioners was instead transfixed by Chaudhri's car. Whatever she was fighting with, it forced her to spin the steering wheel without an eye for direction; when her hands did yank on it amid the chaos, it was with enough force to send the car into a U-turn. All Esther could see was something fast and black dive at her multiple times before the car made short work of a small metal barrier, barrelling over it, and coming to unrest in the children's playground on the other side.

For everyone else, it had become so simple; whatever had sprung to life in Willbond's pocket had now crawled out. The same was true of every sour-faced and prunish pensioner, each of them suddenly wrestling with their coat pockets and bags and the life within them. Before Esther rounded the corner, the only concrete view they saw was a pensioner trying to oust every ounce of dust from his coat's inner pocket. Some escaped on the midday breeze – what was left of it was busy slowly coming together. They didn't know what creature each of them would end up with, though they could make an educated guess or two – for Chaudhri, that darting shape had likely been a bat. Whatever the dust decided to become, all of the councillors had breathed their last.

Soon, Esther, with a euphoric smile, had made their way to a small street behind the hall. Their friend's soul, having been doomed to the afterlife, beamed unrelentingly down upon them. Once they'd turned off down another street, the acrid smell hit their nostrils. Along with the ripple that vibrated outwards, another car had presumably crashed, and though they couldn't swear to it, they were pretty sure a small cloud of angry and buzzing dots was rising above the hall's roof. Esther knew without looking that when one councillor would boot a creature off and it morphed back into dust, another incensed zoo specimen would follow. After all, that had been the plan.

Amid the chaos they could hear erupting, Esther couldn't tell if anyone had been walking past – if someone had, it wouldn't have been for long. They'd have been caught in a few specks of their own rippling along on the wind.

Esther's hand went to their pocket. Expecting their MP3 player, their hand instead came away in a paste of something ashy or sandy. A glance down: the same substance was speckled down the side of their coat as well. It began to coalesce. In a moment, a creature of their own was shooting its way all over their body – their locked eyes with it. The scorpion's barbed tail was only one inch away from stabbing their eyes. To anyone else, it would've meant the same fate as the council members whose remains would be too much for even the newspaper front page.

Esther smiled at the scorpion. As well it could do, the scorpion smiled back.

# HOLLOW EYES

THE FIRST AND only time the Marlowe household called the police came at the end of a very strange week.

It wasn't strange in that the weather didn't do as the forecast predicted, bright sunshine and light winds coming instead of the expected torrential hail. It wasn't strange in that the nudist neighbours flaunted their wares to the cul-de-sac despite the local postman's vociferous protests. Nor did strangeness begin in Roberta R. Robertson's allotment, a place with flowers as exorbitant and ridiculous as the owner's name, one made worse by the fact it had been given to her by her parents not as a joke but as a loving gesture. The allotments were where it began though, among one of the neighbouring overgrown masses. Nearly all of the plots of land had been left to become consumed by stinging nettles and dandelions' invasive embrace. Ramsey Marlowe's allotment didn't fall into this category.

The strangeness first took root as an itch under the skin and an accusation at the ineffective "groundskeeper" of the allotments.

"You haven't taken one, have you?" Ramsey said, on his hands and knees and combing his green fingers through loose soil. "You can tell me the truth," he then said, with murky grey eyes that told an entirely different story.

"A what?"

"A spud. One of *my* spuds," he continued. "You really can tell me the truth."

"Nope," the groundskeeper replied while dragging his rake through a pile of leaves, more encouraging them to spread out in the light autumn zephyrs than to allow the last patches of green grass to be visible before the winter.

"You really can tell me the truth," he asked a third time while scratching his greying stubble. Predictably, it was met with the same answer.

"Why would I take your spud?" the groundskeeper asked, "There's a black market for them now, is there?"

"I'm not saying that. What I am saying is I count seven and there were eight there – that's the fact I have to deal with."

"But *why* would I take one of *your* spuds?" the groundskeeper replied.

"Why would *you* take Margery's lawnmower?" Ramsey replied. "It isn't like you've ever used one. Didn't stop us finding it in your shed." Hadn't that been the great debacle of the previous month? It made people miss the previous groundskeeper, Mr. Albatross, even if he had used unapproved pesticides to tackle the weeds from time to time. At least Albatross tackled them in the first place.

"Shut your face!"

"I just want to know what you did with it."

"I didn't take it, you hear me!"

"Of course not," Ramsey muttered. "Like you didn't take that lawnmower."

"Fuck me, you're difficult today. Want me to write it down for you? Sign a disclosure form? Summon the national guard to find evidence for my innocence?"

"National guard? That's American."

"I couldn't give two flaps of a salmon's tail whether it's American, cockney, or shoved up your fucking backside!"

He watched the man a moment, eventually saying, "I just want eight spuds, not seven." A moment later, he added, "And there's no need for the middle finger either, thank you kindly."

The groundskeeper walked off, leaving Ramsey with only his seven potatoes still. It meant, as well as where the hell the photo album of him as a baby had got to, the man had an extra mystery of the day. In an effort to forget it Ramsey spent the rest of the afternoon tidying up the allotment, making the carrots look perfect, re-hinging the shed door, and re-cultivating the soil around the potato plants. The only other thing he had to do was smile through a large flask of coffee that Alison brought early in the afternoon, which looked and tasted weaker than rainwater going down a drain.

In a way, he didn't know why he cared – about the potatoes that is, the assessment of the coffee would happen in the evening. Not to say he didn't take great pride in his allotment – the sobbing fit when he wasn't able to grow a pumpkin patch one year proved that – but he'd never won an award for the allotment, and never wanted to. He never ate the potatoes or carrots himself. He usually just donated them to the food bank either before the various vegetables began to rot or before the nudists next door snuck some weedkiller onto the soil after one of his gruff letters telling them to stop flaunting their "patticakes and whirligigs".

And yet it bothered him.

"Maybe you miscounted?" Alison had suggested to her husband, folding up her collapsible chair once she'd seen the sky was starrier than it was overcast.

"Perhaps. But doubt it."

She doubted it too, saying it anyway so it wouldn't consume their week like the allotment shed had when it'd been broken into. Dragging Ramsey off his muddied knees and toward home, by then Alison already knew that she was out of luck.

But, that night, she had to give Ramsey credit for handling the situation better than he had done the shed incident, when they'd both endured sleepless nights and daily stakeouts at the kitchen window with a pair of binoculars. Binoculars safely stowed away in a drawer, it was just sleep which eluded her husband. Alison had managed to get her forty winks and deliberately ignore the alarm neither of them needed in their retirement; when she awoke, however, what she faced was a Ramsey with bags under his eyes and an even greater lengthening of his resting bitch face.

"Everything okay?" she asked her husband, rubbing her eyes free of sleep crust. His lips didn't even quiver. He sat on the edge of the bed, his fists clenched by his sides, gaze fixated on something in the distance that only he knew was there. A whiteness spreading over his knuckle told her just how elsewhere his concentration was.

"Hun, I said is everything okay?", she said. Alison always spoke with a softness, blowing each word out with care in much the same way someone might cool soup down.

His grip remained firm and tight. His eyelids refused to blink.

Pushing the duvet aside, she leant forward. Then, with her non-carpal tunnel hand, she peeled one of his fingers back, followed by a second. The third was by far the hardest, the plump digit peeling back only after she'd brought a wince and her splint-coveted hand to help her. He didn't so much as flinch. Not an ounce of his skin slackened. He didn't give either the brushes of her hand or the movement of the stain sheets a glance of any sort. The last time Ramsey had been this concentrated, it'd been at his best friend of thirty-five years' funeral.

Was it some kind of epileptic fit? God's paralysis, she thought it might be called. Sod's paralysis? Or was it Todd's? Either way, she'd felt the kind of rigor mortis spreading through his fingers. Her hand was on the phone beside her within an instant, and she was just about to strike the third nine.

"Ali, who are you ringing?"

When the woman looked round, she found Ramsey facing her, although his plump fingers stayed clenched.

"Ramsey?"

"Who else?" he responded, somehow with a glinting look in his eye like a beautiful grey ocean viewed through a hall of mirrors, "Unless I've a doppelganger? And I don't think I do because, for a start, I'd have advised you to marry him rather than me."

"I thought you were having some kind of fit!"

"Really? Why's that?"

"Well, you were, well," she tailed off, "I don't quite know." The more she looked at how she'd reacted, the more it seemed excessive. Quite clearly, her husband thought so, standing up from the bed, smiling, and leaving the room.

The shame was that the morning incident didn't stop Ramsey behaving like that for the rest of the day. Most days, he'd tend to the allotment or put the fear of God into the weeds that dared edge onto his driveway, always making the most of retirement's pleasures; not to say he didn't do this, he went out to the allotment as per, it was just paired with a kind of yawning ache in himself that told him the chair at home was where he needed to be, somewhere nice and cosy and away from the elements however warm or cold. Every movement happened like a robot's, a naturalness undermined by a rigidity between every flex or tense.

When she came to offer him a cup of coffee, the vacancies behind his eyes seemed even emptier. Staring at him a moment longer, his head twisted slightly to look at her, and the vacuousness didn't prove to be nothing more than a trick of the light – there was an absence there now.

"Coffee, hun?"

"Coffee?"

"It's just gone the o'clock," she continued, rattling his thermos.

"Three sugars please," replied a man who'd once chastised a total stranger for putting a lone sugar sachet in their drink. He'd claimed they were only worsening healthcare for everyone else.

"Three?"

"Yes – is that any trouble?"

"Three sugars?"

"Don't tell me sugar's banned now?"

"No, no, I'll just have to go out and get some. We need stuff for tomorrow's butties anyway."

"Oh okay. Thanks, love."

And so he continued sitting. And it spawned an ache in her chest. For too many years, they'd both sworn they wouldn't devolve into the couple who yawned at the tales of one another's day, whose pictures would get flung into the attic without so much as a pang of sentimentality, whose days wouldn't even end or begin with an "I love you". She would say it now, she just didn't want to admit to a scenario where he might – just might – not say it back.

Alison wasn't entirely sure how long she was stood there, watching him, what she did know was that when she left and came back, it didn't seem as if his head had moved. He'd remained instead in the chair, facing the inpouring sunlight. She wasn't even sure what to make of him when she brought him his coffee. Into his coffee the three sugars went without a backward glance.

Then the night came, after a day where the rigidity engulfed Ramsey's every nerve. The first couple of hours went smoothly, him subject to his inner pneumatic drill, her subject to insomnia which some wishy-washy historical fiction combatted.

She first heard it at just before midnight. The wall to her left shuddered. No, not shudder, but it seemed like some noise was working its way through its very foundations. Placing the book down on the nightstand, Alison swung her legs out of bed. The wall sounded twitchy, like a restless man passing his time by picking the dead skin off his fingers. She edged a little closer to it, then hesitated. Ramsey's snores no longer punctured the air, and she'd screwed the headboard firmly into place a week ago. The wall rippled the air without moving, the noise once again finding its way through without a stray gust of air. Ignoring her trepidation, she placed her hand on the wall.

It was a vibration of some kind all right. Nothing moved, but an unmistakable tingling was fluttering underneath her palms. Alison couldn't hear any machinery, and a quick glance told her Ramsey was still asleep, his fingers tapping away to themselves as his dreams unfolded.

No, this was stupid. Nothing's ever perfectly still. The cavity walls they'd had re-done a few months ago, it was probably just a small stream of wind finding its way through.

Then, Alison stopped. Or rather, her hand ground to a halt as she was a moment away from removing it from the wall. Something was flitting across the tingling sixth sense of her mind; she couldn't quite persuade her mind or her hand to go back to bed. All that she could see was the blank, cream of the wallpaper, but her ears still twitched along in time with the wall's own invisible twitch.

Why was she still doing this? It's the wind! To hell with her mind, that was *her* next thought at least.

It was anyone else that would've seen the obvious contraction of her lips when she tried remove her hand again. They may not have heard the rustling, barely audible even to Alison, but they'd have seen the millisecond of acknowledgment fly across her face. They'd have also seen how her frail hand resisted the goosebumps, trembling ever so slightly instead.

How her knees creaked was immaterial; she stood up in defiance of her gaining years – not quick enough to show alarm, a little too quick to be an ordinary act of getting to her feet. After that, she tucked herself as tightly as she could into bed.

It took a painful four hundred and twenty minutes for the morning to arrive.

When it did, Ramsey was quite amiable in fact, but a preoccupation ruled his eyes. Anywhere he cast his gaze, it was a gaze focused on something she couldn't quite see still, something locked *behind* his eyes.

Could it all be to do with a missing potato? Consciously or otherwise, she knew the answer.

A brief and uncomfortable thought rose up in her mind later that day: what if this was early onset dementia? Or what if it were something that rotted the insides of his brain? Amiable Ramsey certainly continued as the outward exterior, but she wondered how far it extended beneath the surface now. Later, after she had called the police, she'd learn that Ramsey didn't actually remember a single thing. During the following year he would, he'd actually develop dementia that would kill him before next Christmas; for now, however, a different force was at work. Disease might not have been what was ebbing away his mind; dis-ease might, though.

As the afternoon dawned, he returned from the allotment, and when she saw him then, she wondered if the marbles had already started to ebb out of his mind. Like the strangeness of Ramsey's missing potato, he wasn't possessed by an oddness that was entirely plain to see. It wasn't like when Alison had visited her mum's best friend, where she'd seen the woman trying to put a nappy on a squirrel, because there the need to herald orderlies had been punishingly, squirrelishly, obvious. Again, what she told herself was that it could have been age; he stood before her, prepared to go out on a day with skies bluer than they were cloudy, while clad in a thick woollen shirt, a woollen jumper, and a shawl, and presumably trousers with thermals beneath (given the unseemly way they bulged and jaunted). The man had gone so far as to dig out his sheepskin coat, its pockets pregnant with secateurs, spare change, odds and ends, the odd pretty stone he'd inevitably pick up from the pavement, and more.

As he left, she'd called out to him, asked him how he was, stolen an excuse to peck him on the cheek.

"Off to get supplies."

"In all that?"

"In all what?", he'd replied, meeting her gaze. Her eyes were aimed downwards, indicating his bulky encumbrances. He continued, "Oh, these. Nothing much, just don't want to catch a chill, you know."

"A chill? It's sunny!"

"You root to the spot for one moment and get chilly very quickly nowadays."

"Can't say I'd noticed."

"Try spending time in that allotment and you would!"

That was something she didn't want to do. Yes, with people whose marbles were being lost you were supposed to indulge their whims and conversational fragments, she just didn't think any more attention needed to go towards that allotment.

However, as with the morning, despite the fact the night and the next day passed him by through vacant eyes, nothing more untoward happened. No excess clothing was put on, the coffees remained with just three sugars in, and Ramsey and she both pottered all around the house.

It was night-time which again took on the next mantle of strange. After their pottering during the day, followed up by two episodes of *Pointless* on catch-up and Alison's secret smoke when she was making dinner, the two retired for bed. That night should have had all the hallmarks of being successful and quiet.

Which was when the lightbulb exploded.

Ramsey's wife wondered if perhaps it just felt left out and had decided that the married couple couldn't hog all the strangeness – it wanted to partake too. Or maybe, the bulb had just had the kibosh put on it. That's certainly what Ramsey told Alison with crisp and straight syllables when she'd begun her discomfited train of thought.

Alison wasn't having any of it, she didn't want to tempt fate any further. She was up and heading to the basement for a bulb a moment later. A tenacity flowed through her now.

Then – Ramsey followed suit. He didn't run after her, or shout a barking order, however when her hand was on the basement door, his was there at the same time and her body was shadowed by his.

"Hun, don't go down there."

"I'll only be a minute."

"For me, please don't go down there," said her husband. He spoke neither with force, nor without it.

"Ramsey love, I don't want anything else to go wrong," she said, "please." She sounded as hollow as her husband's eyes were.

"Anything else?" he asked, "What do you mean, anything else?"

At that, she'd dried up. The pair did a short trudge back up to their bedroom. She wasn't exactly forgiving him, she just thought it best not to say any more. If she could skirt around the conversation of his love of marmite on chips for their entire marriage, she could skirt around this for a night or two more.

Twenty minutes later, Ramsey had somehow managed to doze back off. On the other hand, sleep once more refused to touch her with a bargepole, worse than the night after she'd suffered her first miscarriage.

When the ten hours of night had taken twenty to buy, as with the night before, Ramsey wouldn't let his wife anywhere near the basement door; at first, he cited the rickety stairs. Her second attempt to go down there had resulted in him pleading with her that he wanted her to have a few days off. Unlike the Ramsey who knew when not to rile or poke or prod at someone's bubbling concern, out of nowhere he even poked his head round the door to tell her it was far too untidy down there before she'd even said a word.

No matter what words the brain behind those hollow eyes conjured up, he'd be there. He'd always be there.

She was his wife, he was her husband – and so she waited.

Ramsey had already mentioned, almost as soon as the bedsheets were flung aside, that he'd be busy all afternoon "getting supplies". He'd said it as he was getting dressed into eskimo gear, like the day before, despite the bright sunshine, while she sat on the bed ignoring the sixth sense at the corner of her mind that told her the wall was moving. Something was inside the wall.

Was that the secret to marriage she was only just learning? Ignore it to survive? How depressing.

While she waited for Ramsey to go forth, she prepared one or two things. From under the stairs, Alison removed the rickety and rusted-shut toolbox, pushing it beneath the sofa in the front room. She wasn't scared of being watched, but she made sure each blind was shut. Then, because it was all she could do for now, she rooted in the front room, lip curling into a pensive hiss. Counting down the ticks of the mantelpiece clock seemed just as fruitful as anything she could do.

Although she didn't realise so at the time, while Alison sat with her shaky cup of tea and fixated on the clock, her phone call to the police had probably begun in her head at this point. It wouldn't sound rational; it would make her sound more paranoid and out-of-sorts than Ramsey – that didn't stop her mind though.

"Hello," her subconscious imagined she'd say. She didn't wish to sound like a distressed war widow.

"Hello, 999, which service do you require?"

"Um, well, police I suppose. Maybe ambulance."

"Where do you live?" the operator asked. That at least was a simple question. Definitely simpler than asking if it was her husband turning into a psychotic paranoiac, or her instead.

"34 Barnes Terrace. You know, little place, about ten minutes past the bowling alley."

"Is anybody injured?"

"No. Well, no blood, nothing like that. But maybe . . ."

"Miss?" the operator would say, professional even with a tingle of flabbergast beneath their voice.

"Well, it's my husband you see," her subconscious imagined she'd say, still formal. No reason to be maudlin and spluttery if he weren't even around. "He's started having three sugars."

"Three sugars?"

"Yes, you know, those sachets. Sometimes in a bag. He's started having three sachets of it in his coffee."

"Is sugar some kind of drug?" asked the operator, trying to find a straw and grasp onto it. If people were calling a drug "ecstasy", why couldn't one be called "sugar"?

"No, sugar, I mean just normal sugar. But he never used to, you see. He's changed. Something's changed, and it's my husband," responded Alison, with no kind of straw at all.

"Are you in danger?"

"Me? From Ramsey? No. Except maybe."

"Are there any weapons in the house?"

"Oh, god no. Ramsey barely steps foot near one. It's just, it's his allotment. It's where all this started, you see."

"He has weapons at his allotment?"

"No, I mean it is a weapon. Well, I suppose it is. He's obsessed with that missing potato still, I can see it behind his eyes."

"Obsessed with a . . . potato?"

"Not paranoia though. Well, maybe."

Fortunately for her subconscious, no part of her brain needed to imagine the rest – true to his word, Ramsey emerged at noon from wherever he'd been sequestered. She handed him his flask of three-sugar-coffee and handed out a smile to him which had only gone one way. But that was fine.

He then gave her the bags.

"What are these?" she asked, even though the answer wasn't exactly tricky to figure out.

"They're from the soil," replied her husband. The unnecessary levels of stress he put on each syllable were more obvious now.

"But, what soil?" she asked, taking a flick through the large plastic sacks and finding six in total.

"The ones it needs to grow!"

"Hun, slow down, I don't understand."

"The allotment! It's soil with lots of nutrients in, better than the stuff there."

"Is that what you bought the other day?"

"You do want them to grow?" he asked, oblivious to her question, "Don't you?"

"Yes, of course I do," she replied, "so is that what you were buying the other day?"

As if it were the clearest fact on the face of creation, he replied with one word: "Naturally."

Her face was draining more and more by the second. It? What was it? Did she dare break into the basement while he was out? If the thought of him keeping someone down there scared her, as a piece of irrationality at the back of her mind kept shouting out, the scarier thought had to be this *it*.

The conversation was clearly going to end there whether it had mileage left in it or not. Being the dutiful housewife, at least until the strangeness had passed, she took them out and threw them in the recycling. She chose not to mention the three more bags she found in the outside bin too.

As it happened, when the time came, the conversation to the police went surprisingly like her rehearsed version, except with a tad more swearing, a lot more heavier breathing, and an operator whose conduct later got them fired.

Without a ladder, Alison could just about reach the light fitting. The squeaks of the screwdriver from the toolbox pierced the room. As best she could manage, her hand bent away from the wall like a magnet repelling another. The few times her hand and the wall did connect, the chilling impulse from her sixth sense trickled down her spine. It was screaming, however irrational, for her to run.

But she couldn't. She could only turn the screwdriver again and again; and when it resisted, not an ounce of her body questioned forcing the tool under the fitting and yanking the thing out of the wall itself, not just its socket.

A steady stream tumbled out like a shoal of minnows darting between two rocks. The steady stream, because the *what* hadn't actually hit Alison yet, was covering her in a second, but the force of it struck her feet as it spilled out, taking the wind from her sails and with it her balance. It took her a few seconds to regain herself, and a second more to drag her left arm out of whatever had just spilled from the wound in the house. Before doing so much as opening her eyes, she could feel the shaking intensifying, the silent scream of rage from an unearthed beast.

She managed to get to her feet and pull herself upright a few moments later. Scattered all over the floor was a churned-up mess of soil at least a foot deep, and more was still trickling over the vibrating hole in the wall. Looking down, she realised she was coated in the stuff too. Everything was engulfed by a kind of tremor she'd call a heat haze in any other scenario, but even with that and the unstill plateau of dirt before her, the first of the red lines became very clear. Behind it, two more strands were visible, meeting two larger strands which were stretching up to the wall, within which yellow and red lengths as thick as tree branches descended. Two more red lines appeared from within the dirt, now she noticed having separated from the light fitting, the underside of which was coated in their yellow and red nodules. It took her a second longer – a second too many – to realise the strands weren't just emerging, knotting together, they were crawling. Alison didn't need to be a genius to know their destination. Freeing her feet from the quivering floor of dirt, she staggered toward the door.

She wondered if this was how Howard Carter had felt when he'd opened Tutankhamun, and supposedly unleashed the curse of the pharaohs.

On the landing, she immediately began to kick the loose lumps of soil from her shoes. It was all she had time to do because the shaking had caught up to her the second both of her feet were planted – the chain reaction had caught up. Where her nice carpet had covered the landing, it was now cavorting and trembling too. By the time she reached the stairs, the wall to her left began to crumble as if it wasn't there at all, more yellow and red strands weaving out of the house's infrastructure and toward her flailing legs.

Too old to vault the advancing strands, the ones emerging now more tentacle than spindly threads, her only option was to rely on adrenaline, risk crouching, and do a sort of propelled slide that worked far better in the movies than in real life. It was enough though. Although sprawled like a tortoise trapped on its back, she was at least at the bottom of the stairs, and she had a twenty-second advantage on the crawling mass winding its way down the bannisters in pursuit. What kind of beehive had she poked a stick into?

She looked at the front door. Whilst it was only a few desperate bounds away, the soil pouring from around the light fittings and the strands pushing through the skirting boards ruled it out. The stairs were an obvious impossibility, and judging by the Stentorian crash of the living room lights plummeting to Earth, the bay windows weren't viable either. She made for the dining room doorway.

In the dining room, only one of the light switches had burst into a shower of soil. Alison managed to duck under the spray and the solitary, thick strand that had begun to edge its way down the wall, and she had just reached the kitchen door when the nape of her neck became doused in a horrible powder. Putting her hand to her neck, she pulled it away to find lumps of vibrating soil matting themselves into her collar. About to open the kitchen door, she chanced a look back. It was a mistake. Among the jumble of flowing soil, the light switch was totally dislodged, as was the section of wall above it. Like an unleashed reservoir or writhing pile of rats, the soil had splattered itself across the room, the red and yellow nodules rearing its head from the knee-deep current wave emerging. She was concentrating on it a second too long. Her eyes currently bursting from her sockets, they were taking in the sight that actually strands weren't so much emerging from the wall, crawling free, but they appeared to actually be growing before her very eyes, red and yellow extended from thickening red and yellow.

Only one place left for her to run. With the seething flood of garden around her, she yanked open the basement door. It actually had a secondary benefit: she'd never considered herself a logical person at all, more one of spontaneity, but she knew she could at least barricade the basement door, and that Ramsey had one or two cans of weedkiller down there. She didn't care her husband had banished her – and Christ, he would have some explaining to do once she'd saved their house from soil and tendrils – she was going down there, even if she found he had the Pope chained up in there.

Two steps into the basement, she could see there was no Pope manacled to a wall. There was, however, the largest mass of soil and invasive tendrils she'd seen so far. Even tendrils didn't seem to sum up their proportions, every little thread or encrusted nodule dwarfed by a red and yellow tube as thick as a tree branch. The sight sickened her; as a survivor of the seventies' school system, she was ready for the hardships of running a house, not saving it from the goliath that writhed and wriggled in its basement.

Alison briefly considered making her way back up the stairs. She likely would have, had the adrenaline now entirely rescinded from her legs, leaving the bannister on the basement stairs as both her emotional and physical rock. When she spotted the source of the tentacular strands probing their way toward her feet and down from above, she didn't even have the puff to sigh, let alone cry out the terror welling in her heart. Although in the middle of the sea of dirt, and encrusted with purple, barnacle-like shapes that sprouted off into grasping appendages, the shape underneath was just about visible. In all its mutated, starchy glory.

Her next move was more an oversight than a decision. All Alison wanted to do was rest her hand against the bannister and allow the dirt to slowly swell up around her. She certainly hadn't planned on the rickety wooden thing giving way and landing her in a mould-festered corner of the basement. Once there, she again went through a few moments where the end seemed preferable than a miserable life of sounding like an asylum-escapee or watching her husband obey whatever was currently crawling toward her. It was a blob of soil spilling onto her leg that shifted her, and it was only that, not some deliberate determination to fight back, that led her hand to the bottle beneath her shoe.

Why hadn't she remembered? After all, it's

why she was down there. She grabbed the bottle, registering the label only after she'd loosened the nozzle and hurled it. The bottle – emblazoned with a horrible, neon green logo – struck a mound of undulating soil a foot away from the mutated, purple nucleus.

But it was enough. When the weedkiller and all the various pesticides Ramsey used to complain about spilled out, the effect was instant. If the foundations of her house were shaking before, they were now vibrating themselves to bits, every single nodule or frond retracting back through the cavity walls, insulation, pipes, and other nooks and crannies. Of the root-thick strands that had almost been snapping at Alison's heels, only two or three remained, and only one had any kind of grip on her shoe. A kick of her other foot saw to it.

She spent the next few minutes gripping the brick wall of the basement, observing the damage around her. With all the soil withering itself into nothing more than residue, she could see the sizeable holes where the mutated strands had begun their burrows into the house. It was how, when her thoughts turned to redecorating not the carnage, she knew her legs would support her unaided.

Over the next hour she attacked the house like a professional crime scene cleaner. Any patches of soil still vibrating away to themselves were quickly taken to the bins outside, and while she was there Alison took a quick inspection of the house – none of the windows had shattered, and pebble-dashing coating the driveway was the only real sign that anything too untoward had happened. During the next few days, none of the neighbours came knocking at her door, or at least stayed polite enough not to: discretion, she supposed, was the mercy of living in a neighbourhood of people with nine-to-five jobs. There was also a quick detour to Ramsey's allotment shed, where she found three more bottles of the weedkiller. Although the husk of the mutation in the basement was now a fraction of its size, and the strands had all crawled their way back to the hell they sprang from, Alison didn't think you could be too careful. She emptied all three bottles directly onto the mutation, not resting until even just the force of splashing the stuff onto it had begun to dissolve, never mind the corrosive properties actually taking hold.

There needed to be, however, one more thing taken care of before the only way became up. When she emerged from below, she picked up the phone and dialled the three digits she hadn't used in a decade.

Ten minutes later, Ramsey – three more bags of soil in hand – was escorted into a police car.

Ramsey didn't stay there, at the police station, however. Partly, the truth was that he hadn't a clue what had really gone on; just as he hadn't been himself in Alison's eyes, he hadn't been himself in his own either. The other half of the truth was that after a day in a cell, the police didn't exactly think they could charge him for "obsessive potato disorder", or whatever had driven him into doing whatever had happened. When Alison rang asking when her husband would be home, they'd let him go with a non-descript warning.

The house was a different place when he returned. For all Alison's efforts, stains of soil still caked the walls and the holes in the walls had been seen to with nothing more than parcel tape. Since the previous day, she'd gone through five outfit changes, every couple of hours purging herself of even just the energy in the house which she could feel on her skin. She'd had five showers too, each time rubbing shower gel into her skin to the extent it was now reddened and slightly raw, as if it had been pumiced by a bar of carbolic soap rather than the supermarket's tea tree-scented "Refresher Gel".

Ramsey looked her up and down out of an inability to meet her gaze. She noticed, for the first time in what felt like eternity, his eyes were no longer vacant. They had life in them.

"I found this," Alison spoke slowly, nodding at the mess in front of her. The one thing she hadn't expunged, either from the basement or the walls, now lay on a piece of clingfilm on the living room floor. It was a lone orb a pale shade of brown and pathetic, and the weedkiller had stripped away the mutation of roots and livid pink lumps to reveal a sphere no bigger than Alison's fist.

"I found that downstairs."

"Well, that's one mystery solved," Ramsey said, with a note of humour that was shot straight back at him.

In her life, the worst she'd ever seen a potato get was when her family had gone abroad and forgotten to toss a bag of them away. That bag of potatoes had sprouted the occasional fibrous tendril in search of sunlight and nutrient and soil, but this one had used Ramsey and her house as a jump-start into finding healthy soil. If it had gone any quicker, it would've got to her and Ramsey's wake before it'd even gone to the funeral.

Except they were thoughts best forgotten, maybe – locked away like the potato had been.

"I've missed you," she said.

"I've missed you too."

"No, this entire week I've missed you."

"That's what I meant."

He took a seat next to her, skirting around the potato. Both hoped the potato was now beyond dead, but it would've felt like adultery to touch or fully acknowledge the vegetable openly.

"Do you want me to go?"

"No. But – you know I'm still angry with you?"

"Yeah."

"And, you know it's going to take me a while to forgive you."

"Yeah."

"But you know I still love you?" – this, they both said at the same time. Alison's mouth twitched.

"Just, tell me what happened," she said.

"I don't know," he spoke, trying to explain with words that English didn't possess, "It was like it was me."

"You were a potato?"

"No, that sounds silly," he said. Then he looked at her. Then at the orb in front of them both. Nothing would be silly after today. "I just meant, it's like my mind wasn't my own. I was getting soil, in my mind, for myself, its destination just was a different place. The decision to ignore the light fitting was my own too, it's just again I had an agenda even I didn't know about. Have I made any sense?"

He had and he hadn't, Alison thought.

"We'll work through this," Ramsey tried again, "I promise. I could go get my shovel and move all this to the bin. And then I'll sell the allotment tomorrow and I'll scrub the basement to within an inch of its life."

"Already cleaned down there," Alison mumbled, another hint of a smile tickling its way onto her lips. That was the Alison Marlowe he knew, Ramsey thought, and he hoped he was back to the Ramsey Marlowe she knew, whoever that was.

"One more thing," he added, as Ramsey took her hand in his, "the three sugars."

"Yeah?"

"That was me."

"What?"

"I've been slipping them into my coffee for months now when you weren't looking. Potato-me wasn't to know that though."

"Idiot," she replied with a fuller smile.

"I know."

"Hypocrite," she went on.

"I know," responded Ramsey, his smile and hers now one.

And true to his word, an hour later Ramsey was free of the allotment. By the end of the next week, no strangeness was left to be found. The nudist neighbours still roamed, the groundskeeper was still coarse and had a rake up his arse, and Roberta R. Robertson still refused to change her name by deed poll. All was well. Even the next week, the little bubble of existence wouldn't shatter. The most that would happen in the way of excitement would be that one of Ramsey's carrots went missing, and the nudist family received a potato plant on their doorstep from an anonymous benefactor.

# A LOATHING FOR GHOSTS

AEONS HAD PASSED. Been endured. Been suffered. Agonising second by agonising second. While the two waiting figures had until now been enshrined in wood, now blood finally coursed through their veins once more.

Everything seemed to splinter.

The two figures had a few seconds to observe events before entering the fray. On the hallway landing, two figures, presumably husband and wife, stood beside a shattered banister. An orange, uneasy shimmer was trickling through a nearby window, and it illuminated the third figure; it was a boy, his skin stretched to dry and flaking with manacles and chains which stretched him into a starfish shape. Bandages encased his shoulders, although they had been applied with haphazard respect for the prisoner and the blood beneath could still escape, and both were exclaiming a harsh purple colour. His whole body was on the precipice of never moving again.

It was time.

The pair on the landing only noticed Rathbone and Asquith as their bodies collided into them, both knocking their targets to the floor and away from the manacled man. The landing's ceiling had launched the pair as though it were a cannon. For the pair bursting forth, it was a miracle either emerged with any accuracy; aeons of waiting for this moment had switched their brains and legs off, and every moment was now controlled by some force's instincts as much as by their own. Nagging corners of Rathbone and Asquith's minds, hastily reassembling, knew the two people before them – not like knowing a friend, like knowing you're in the same room as a drunkard before you hear their slurred words or see them gulp down another beer.

When Asquith hit her target, she landed with a kind of roll, and grace or dignity was the furthest thing from her mind. Solid wood pellets burst everywhere like a shotgun explosion; the more liquid fractures of wood, like the wooden tendrils which ensnared the two exorcists in the first place, splattered even further. Within a second, the pellets struck the floor with boiling hot ferocity, and every surface seemed unable to decide whether it was a liquid, sentient entity or the rigid structures of normality. As she connected with the floor, she did so too with the woman on the landing's feet – Maeve, Asquith just *knew* that was her name. Maeve went over like a house of cards, in which time the next nugget of information trickled into her mind – before this, the wood had been a prison, but more like a re-education camp, keeping them alive, planting seeds in their thoughts, and now it was time to heed its call.

It took Asquith a second to recalibrate, as well as a few more to get to her feet. Aching sensations whirled through her every joint, and she wondered if she knew how the manacled man felt – he couldn't be allowed to die, the wood was telling her that, and if her pain was even a fraction of his, there was no more than a few seconds of his life left.

Rathbone's descent from the ceiling was having a little more luck. The man, Joseph, whom he *knew* a farmer, was his quarry, an unshaven man with a glare that would cut through rock like butter. Joseph caught sight of the dropping Rathbone barely a millisecond sooner than his significant other and his slight shuffle leftwards to escape only helped Rathbone. Smashing into the man, he didn't feel anything. His right foot struck his prey right in the jaw, sending the man crashing into a rickety chair while he landed on all fours among a tangle of cobwebs. He hadn't counted on what he knocked the man into; the chair had upturned when he fell backwards, yet so had all the equipment which had sat upon it. By the time Rathbone was on his feet, Joseph was too, but his prey was armed with an oil lamp caught in the tumble. The man was waving it in warning arcs in front of him; one wrong step forward would have launched a bolt of fire up his left side.

Rathbone ran forward. Even he wasn't sure why, his breathing was as irregular as the situation he found himself in. Joseph wasn't expecting it. Perhaps because the exorcist had another entity's instincts to rely on rather than his own, he found that one clear bound was all he needed to floor the man. He didn't even give enough time for the lamp to slip from his fingers; instead, as the two men crashed into the landing floor, it spasmed of its own accord and ended up back home, next to the instruments of torture. A second later, the two were rolling along the floor, gripping each other in hateful bear hugs; but whatever Joseph did, his pugilistic partner would match in a manic and deadly wrench of force. All they could do was tighten their grip and roll further and further toward the staircase.

The manacled man twitched. It was a something-and-nothing movement that neither Maeve nor Joseph noticed, but both exorcists' instincts clocked it in a second – there couldn't be much life in him left to ebb away. It was enough, however. The reminder of the stakes gave him a final dose of adrenaline. The result was astonishing. Through the gash already torn in the banister, he sent Joseph flying backwards, coming to an abrupt rest near the bottom of the staircase. Rathbone's top lip curled and he noticed that the man hadn't had time to cover his head when he struck the lower landing – Joseph's face was contorted into new and unusual shapes of pain. For all Rathbone's heart, he knew the next few seconds of advantage might be vital.

He pivoted. Focusing his attention on the manacled man, he began working with a haste that surprised himself most of all. With the brawl between his wife and her sparring partner a few feet away, it took him a few extra – vital! – seconds to reach the man. Asquith and Maeve were however locked in much the same tussle that he had been; in their case, it didn't end so quickly. Neither one let themselves stagger backwards or buckle in the face of the other's gritted teeth and bloodshot eyes. Maeve came close, when she managed to fling her nails across Asquith's face, angering the small black nodules on her face from where the wooden tendrils had fed her. For all their internecine actions, the main casualty was actually her husband. Halfway through loosening one of the steel cuffs, the frenzy of action barrelled towards him out of nowhere.

Whereas the farmer and the manacled man had had to endure the pains of the banister, nothing halted Rathbone's fall. His head struck the wooden steps first. He was on the middle step before gravity could give him a heads-up, and a second later he was in a pile of splinters a foot or so away from the bottom step. He expected to release a dog-like yelp, but thankfully everything was running too fast around him, his adrenaline too fierce to even feel the impact.

For a couple of seconds, he didn't care about sensibility. He had been embalmed by a tree, one that had requested his and Asquith's presence, then thrown into a different century with the sole command both to stop a man's death while causing two others. The vestibule, visible out of the corner of his eye, took his fancy momentarily, flirting with him. How easy it would've been to forget his campaign and turn on his heels.

Then, out of the corner of his eye, he saw one of the people who the tree needed killed – or, rather, the lack of him.

When Joseph had fallen, he'd presumed that at the least his head would be blinded with dizzying lights, if not mind-shattering unconsciousness; adrenaline was all that was keeping his own from the same fate. Now, down a corridor stretching off from the hallway, he spotted the fraying cuff of his trouser leg disappearing around a corner. Rathbone compelled himself to stand. He caught sight of Asquith and the prisoner, who were more bleary shapes than figures. How were either her or him to know which directive was more important, to kill or to save? Every layer of the shattered Russian nesting doll of his mind fought for priority.

He hated this life at times.

Joseph disappeared further into the house, and Rathbone found himself following. The man ahead was hobbling, dodging as best he could around a table infested with age and rot. Rathbone rounded the corner just in time to see his prey reach the opposite side. Around his eyes and mouth, he could feel twitches hitting him thicker and faster and his lips were joining in, fumbling over meaningless and voiceless words. Even if he caught up with the farmer, he doubted he would have the might to finish the job.

Rathbone used his last bout of energy to kick aside the table. Even without it, the piece of furniture might've shattered. Hundreds of jagged fragments flew everywhere, peppering the room like they had upstairs, and the only solid, remaining panel Joseph grabbed and hoisted up to waist height. It was perfectly-timed: Rathbone dived forward in a sort of feverish rugby tackle a moment later.

Then he could see them. Behind his opponent, words were rippling into life in the wood as if by an invisible metal brand.

*Save me.*

Not often, in his weighty experience, did the desperate use great, deep-seated monologues when the raw essentials would serve. He'd been kidnapped by living wood; this was the day for one last throw of the dice, to pray for God's favour.

Rathbone's pressed on, shoving the piece of rotting wood higher and trying to steer the other man into the far wall. He expected his arms and temples to wince beneath the blow, but he reckoned the farmer was losing strength too. It was all Joseph could do to extricate his hand with one sharp slice of air; the piece of wood became as fragmented as its brethren. Rathbone had to act first – in the second where Joseph tried to readjust his momentum, Rathbone threw his clenched fist upward. Before Joseph could re-assess, it caught his chin. Trying to form sounds, the man's lips came together – yet nothing would emerge. The air split with a crack and the farmer's jaw twisted itself askew. He took a shaky step back. Rathbone was about to deliver a second blow to Joseph when light-headedness beat him to the punch. The eyes of the man before glazed as if they'd always been a sickly pale colour, and his hair began matting in red as it hit the floor. One final chunk of wood, shaped like a crude mallet, projected upward from between the man's shoulder-blades.

The wood beside the body was once more rippling.

*Time running out.*

Rathbone shambled back out of the room and along the corridor. He'd almost reached the stairs when something stopped him. It wasn't the kind of thing you give great priority in the middle of fighting for your life, but his unconscious mind had now deciphered the movements of Joseph's lips. When the table had come apart before him, he realised, the man had mumbled out five little words. He imagined they formed some hoarse plea to the God that Rathbone served so faithfully. He was wrong: "We just wanted a ghost".

That's why the other man was on the landing, trussed up like a lamb for the slaughter.

Rathbone's legs cried out, sapped of energy, but the man told them to co-operate a little more, and they found reserves of vigour that finished the rest of him off. He shot out into the hall at the bottom of the main staircase, and before his bones could again ache, he ascended the staircase. On the landing, his wife crouched over the prisoner, freed from his manacles, and Maeve, whose chest no longer moved like flesh and blood does. Both figures laid out on the floor were pale, as if rigor mortis had already set in and crystallised their very essence.

The noxious smelling powder which the pair had forced down the prisoner's throat hung in the air, and his blood hadn't begun to register that it ought to congeal; from the wounds smothering him, the scabs refused to form and the red chafing around his ankles and wrists came to a head and leaked from every laceration.

"What now?" Rathbone asked. Could that be it? They'd stopped Maeve and Joseph wreaking any future havoc on the afterlife; would completing two-thirds of the mission suffice?

"This isn't right. Flung forward over a century, and this mania continues," Asquith mulled.

"There might be new remedies? New century, new medicine," he replied.

"Medicine that can bring a man back from the dead?" she asked, lowering her head. "You and I both know what that's called. We've had to deal with the aftermath often enough. Why us, George? Why us?"

"We exorcise the ghost."

"But where? What ghost? We were supposed to stop this tragedy, not fix a haunted house!"

"Joseph. He said, 'We just wanted a ghost.' I think we were brought here to avert it, not cauterise it."

Rathbone outstretched one of his fingers. It indicated a small knot of wood on the floor. Before them both, it was moulding itself into reality – *TOO LATE. BE READY.*

Asquith shot to her feet, cheeks red, and faced the dusk's puncturing glare.

"You brought us here, ripped us from where we were comfortable, and made us suffer generation after generation," she shouted, pouring over her barbed words in her address to the house,

"And what for? To stop a ghost? But we can't!"

"I think events are already in motion. If a haunting is horrible for the living, how must the thing that holds the haunting in its very bones feel? It knew from day one that this was its fate, and it took out insurance – us."

All they could do was exchange worrisome looks. Facts were facts though: the dead now outnumbered the living.

Everything began to shake – like an earthquake localising itself to the landing. The countdown had begun.

The pair moved from their positions on the landing to cross-legged ones either side of the corpse. Spreading the body totally flat, after a prayer or two from both of them, Rathbone reached into his pocket and retrieved the candles he'd light to accompany the spirit. He was about to light them when the house rocked itself, whatever feral beast lay at its heart snarling like a pack of starved dogs.

Asquith raced to her feet again, ready to begin a whole new volley of prayers – the house shook again. The floor beneath them both seemed to fragment, rumble, and their concentration needed to go into staying upright.

As the tremor subsided a second time, Asquith noticed Rathbone was scrabbling at his neck. His crucifix around his neck was sparking unhealthy shades of red and yellow and his skin was in the crossfire. With a face both the colour and texture of wilting roses, Rathbone's teeth bore the front of his choke as he ripped it off his neck, holding it by the chain which too had started to heat up.

At first, it seemed it was the wood coming alive again, ready to suck them back in. The patch of floor beneath the dead man was splintering upward, outward, rippling through the rug like daggers. Amongst it all, the corpse was becoming hollow, every bone and muscle visible until none of the flesh remained – only the ectoplasmic shell bursting into after-life, sitting up and staring directly at either of them before their holy incantations could be completed. After a moment or two more, the shell deflated, nothing more than a thin cocoon.

Up until now, an explosion had hung dormant in the air. Both the exorcists believed the screams of the dead ought to be silent things. That was where they came in, to smoothe the transition, help those who had seen the divide between life and death as a gaping chasm rather than a gentle line. The departed souls could, of course, rage against the Long Sleep, and be chagrined at being unable to finish their goals; what was sacrosanct was that line where life and death parted ways. In either realm, anything more than imagining and revering the due process of the other would lead to a terrifying collision. As Asquith took her next breathe, that sacrosanct line did not simply break – it shattered, splintered, was rent asunder. The scream of something shook the air, and from it another *something* emerged. Before the tear-stained face of something seething fully tore into reality, the boiling hot beads of ectoplasm began sweating onto the floor, teeth locked in a bombilating snarl.

Rathbone dived. With no more than a second to spare, the vicious entity hurled past, its slipstream carving a line of anger across the hall. Made slippery by blood, his fingers slipped from around his crucifix and the symbol went bouncing off in the complete opposite direction. Re-adjust-ing itself with the nimbleness of a vulture, it aimed at Asquith. As it swooped toward her, she ducked and dived aside, the entity shooting over her head but not before it had already readied itself for another pass. Rathbone and Asquith clutched their foreheads, tearing at an invisible tumour surging beneath their skin. The tumour had a name, had words, had a message.

*THIS IS YOUR FAULT!*

"We didn't know!" Asquith hollered, at the same time trying to utter the first prayer she could think of. "We didn't know how, we're sorry!" How could she know if it was working? "We're so, so sorry!" Rathbone was on his hands and knees, trying to grab his crucifix through a torrent of aches and pains.

*All we wanted was a ghost.*

That message came through louder than any explosion, stabbing into Rathbone's head, turning him turtle. The pair had paid so much attention to the tortured man that they hadn't taken notice of the exact same decomposition happening to Maeve's body at the top of the stairs. He couldn't see the dead lady's husband he'd despatched earlier, but as he clambered to his feet Rathbone imagined the man was enduring the same fate. A tiny part of him considered going to check, in order to bless his resting place – the upturned chair winging its way through the air in his direction put an end to that avenue of thought. He ducked a second too late. Catching him on the shoulder, the chair leg pushed him back to where he'd began.

The older pair's deaths. The prisoner's rage. It was swathing itself in more and more reasons to kill. Were remnants of humanity alive beneath its surface, the deep had swallowed them; Rathbone imagined it'd be nothing less than suicide to try and bring it peace. The point of no return was advancing towards the exorcists just as much as they were advancing toward it.

Everything the married duo understood from previous hauntings was coming to fruition all around them. For Asquith, goosebumps were bursting into life like red hot weals, and the same was true of the house; every time a splinter of wood twisted and gnarled even more, the malformity popped like a punctured bubo. The cycle repeated. Whenever one of them moved, the many shades of dread hemming them coagulated, clamping to them like pilot fish swimming ever closer to a great white shark, its toothy grin continually gaping wider and wider.

Having zigzagged even further away as air released feral, absolute howls, Rathbone could see his crucifix teetering above a lesion in the wooden floor. The carving of Jesus upon it looked unhappier now than it did when it represented his sacrifice. An enervated sigh was all the man could manage, heaving an inch closer to the object.

Asquith noticed her husband's plan, deciding to advance her own, even though calling it a plan was beyond generous. With all the sedateness of white-water rapids, the air whirling around her was dropping in temperature, and pushing it aside felt more and more like wading through treacle. She simply needed to reach the other side of the room, where the various instruments of the manacled man's torture now lay scattered. Her internal theory was that since the spirit was newly formed, it would for now be a little more corporeal. It had been the case when they stopped the massacre of Salamander Street; there wasn't any reason to suggest it wouldn't work here. In fact, staring into the callous, blanched face that sailed through the air, trying to crash into anything human, she found herself transported back to that incident – the demonic force there had looked daggers at her in an eerily similar way.

Having dived beneath another of its lunging arcs, the first thing to reach Asquith's hand was the oil lamp from Rathbone's tussle with Joseph. As soon as she could grip its handle, she turned sidewards, let her arm gather speed, slackened her hand muscles.

Its trajectory was perfect.

The entity stopped and looked at the two humans. Behind it, the pair could see the lamp had gone through the entity, struck the banister, exploded, and then rather than burst into flames it had simply fractured, doused in masses of ectoplasm. In front of them, like boiling fat, the ghostly residue hissed and gargled, rippling and coalescing – and then assembled. It was a smaller entity, with a smaller howl, but its rage was just as pure. Neither had eyes, yet their stares burrowed into the exorcists' very beings.

They lunged.

In their profession, both exorcists tried to remember ghosts never intentionally mean harm, at least at first, and it wasn't their fault that they were trapped neither here nor there. Somehow, that rule *couldn't* apply here.

Tearing away the banister segments like eviscerating a chicken's innards; flinging the stakes; watching the exorcists do a crazed hopscotch to avoid them; the two entities' aim getting better, inch by inch. In the blur of everything, it wasn't long before each stake was missing its target only slightly. And all the exorcists could do was to yell louder and louder, trying to clog the whirlwinds with their sacred chants.

At first, they didn't notice. So busy trying to batter away the volley striking the air, it only clocked when Rathbone saw his chance and managed to grab his crucifix from the floor.

A little at a time, the prayers were striking home, bullets burrowing their way further in. Unlike the last time when they tried the invocations, the wailing souls now very gradually faltered. Rathbone had managed to grab his crucifix; the heat had returned to it, but so had its power. At the sight of it, neither of the ectoplasmic forms stopped firing the bullets of wood and splinter, but the decaying walls behind them now took the brunt of the impact.

They were still bearing the melee, however. A talon flew past Asquith's nose. A half-wheezed, half-sobbed cry of pain. A second talon unfurling and attempting to strike her left eye. Another anguished cry rising up in her throat. Despite the crucifix her partner wielded, everything was expanding the powder keg around them, and no amount of jaw-clenching and staunch rigidity could stop the boiling blobs of ectoplasm from dripping inch after inch nearer.

It was only when a blob singed the end of her left thumb that she noticed she was no longer eyelevel with the creatures. Each shift of their ectoplasmic mass seemed shakier, weightier. Taking a step to the left, she found it took them a moment longer to register it. Within a few seconds, she was a good metre or so outside of their swinging arms and they were only tall enough to snarl and swipe at her hips instead. When the spectres raised the large chunk of banister in readiness, a slow twitching seemed to enter their every movement.

In a hectic moment, Asquith flung one of the banister segments back at them. It passed through the newer ghost, once more coating it in ectoplasm, and came to a crumpled rest at the other entity's feet. She knew what would happen, watching as a third being of rage and spite and vengeance took form from the spilled supernatural substance.

But she was prepared. She lifted the Bible out of her pocket and held it high. As a fourth entity burst into afterlife from the substance coating the banister pole, each action of the other three became more ungainly, like gear changes on an ice-ridden bicycle. Opening the first page of the book, she started reading.

Clawing at Rathbone's crucifix as one incandescent mob, the oldest of the ghosts began to fold. Its actions had been the slowest and the wailing within their minds from it was no more than a distant itch. Sensing this, Rathbone snatched up the banister segment they'd evidently planned to embed in his thorax – in one swift movement, he turned it around and thrust it at one of the spectres. As predicted, it coalesced, another formed, and each became a fraction more fatigued and infirm. He didn't care if it was cocky, the man took firm steps forward, each more assured than the last. None of them were strong enough to resist, every piece of their malice spread too thinly too quickly. Having huddled together like a flock of ducklings wailing for their mother, the ghosts looked up at the husband and wife. The flock's eyes, where vengeance and bitterness used to linger, fogged over with unadulterated barrenness – Hell or Heaven wasn't even a viable option. The sole plausible option was sagging into an oblivion that no god or devil could govern. Ungovernable. Unredeemable.

The Bible fell from the woman's hand, landing with a thick plop amongst the ectoplasmic creatures. It was the final pluck of the bow string. One last lamentation tried to shake the God-fearing pair's minds. Yet to them it registered no more fiercely than the whistling of summer's breeze. If nothing else, their bones could now wince at the joyful aches of a job finished.

Whether coincidence or a message, the wooden structures around creaked out a groan that somehow sounded final. At the same time, the orange dusk light stopped flowing onto the landing, ebbing to the vaguest twinkle of a star.

They both knew they had unanswered questions. Neither spoke.

"But how do we get back?" one of them asked, across the silence. It didn't matter which one.

"I don't think we do. We never felt at home in our time," came the reply. "Maybe this is our reward, a fresh start. Nobody knows us here. Perhaps now we can go forth without the prejudices of our own time."

Still silent, the two traversed the darkness, eventually finding the front door and a country lane beyond that. The pair, hand in hand, began their trek toward the nearest town.

# COUNTING TO OBLIVION

THE LAKES, BEAUTIFUL as ever, rolled out beyond the edge of the café garden. It was a lovely little spot, enclosed by views of a waterfall which always seemed to pour without uttering a noise. In previous years, it had provided a place of support, serenity, after three different break-ups, a near-car crash, and a remembrance for her great-grandfather. It was a favourite spot for Niveau, and she hated that she was having to sully it with a pitiful festival of crying, snotty bawling, and useless pleading. Just the sight of Galloway entering the idyllic place inflamed her heart. Galloway's chin possessed an annoying habit of protruding sharply in a way which seemed to suggest everyone nearby was about to undergo spontaneous frontal lobotomies. The way it angled their face meant shadows fell in exactly the wrong ways, withering their years and dulling every joyous feature or smooth curve.

"Cappuccino?" they asked, hand outstretched, already prepared with a wooden stirrer in it ready for Niveau to take it. She did so whilst nodding her head, but otherwise not a single muscle in her face was permitted to do so much as twitch; her eyes remained firm on a napkin rather than Galloway's eyes. Her cappuccino was going to have had time to cool by the time the pair's conversation ended. Galloway could waffle, but this was one of those times where she wouldn't let them, even if they were for whatever reason buying the beverages. She supposed it was just "their turn", though she'd lost count after they'd submitted the last news article for the magazine.

*Three Peak Gazette* was at an all-time high, and the final spanner in the works was this employee who turned up in the drabbest of outfits with the drabbest of attitudes and an outlook greyer than the approaching rain clouds. Against the tedium of day-to-day life, it still seemed a rainbow when compared to Galloway. They might've been lovely if you somehow managed to remove the anaemic personality they adopted in order to seem proactive and efficient; however, it was a loveliness buried too deep for a patient woman, let alone one with a fierce grump on her side.

Niveau couldn't pinpoint it with any precision, but their tiptoe towards the end of the line had ended with Galloway's "Decision on Discretions Against Detective Quail Less Certain" article, which should've been front page news and concerned the fate of one of the most bent coppers in the local, if not national, police force. It was a newspaper's duty to be unbiased, yes, but when you were so mundane and politically correct that you didn't want to upset any supporters of a man with over fifty pictures of underage children doing who-knows-what on his computer, the clock bell finally struck. To make matters worse, most of Detective Adam Quail's photo library had been released to the public domain via an accidental Facebook post. The final *final* straw was the timing of it all; the police couldn't afford any more hits given the rumours of the police chief's institution of corruption and deceit were already increasing daily.

Niveau coughed – the latte wasn't even warm. Could it be deliberate? She jabbed the wooden stirrer into the froth, along with one too many sugar sachets, as her protégé took their seat.

"How much do I owe you?" Niveau asked, delving into her purse. One of the very few facts she knew about Galloway, apart from their obsession with the monotonous end of the colour scale, was that they hated paying by card. She'd give them her spare change.

"Three pounds, ten pence. Don't suppose you've got the time, do you, Cap'n?" That was another thing they did, persistently stigmatising everyone superior to them with the moniker of "Cap'n". It made Niveau's face puce, not least because she was sure that if she were at the helm of any ship, she'd have hung, drawn, and quartered the entire crew before they'd left port, starting with Galloway. Employees were a means to an end, so when they didn't bring success, she didn't bring them good fortune.

"Yeah, it's—" hang on, Galloway had a watch, why couldn't they just use their brains and check their wrist, the dim-witted oaf? "—just gone three ten."

At that point, *it* struck.

To call it déjà vu was wrong, déjà vu was easy; it was seeing the same cat three days running by the same grimy dustbin and subsequently becoming convinced that it's Groundhog Day. That was child's play. This, however, started as a babble of voices, like leaves bristling in the undergrowth, mocking the nerves of an uneasy traveller late at night. And just like an unearthly whispering, it followed her. Or rather, surrounded, within a split-second creeping from the furthest corners of sanity until accosting her with all the brutality of a thieving, leather-clad biker. And as with the burble of leaves in the undergrowth, or a leather-clad biker straight out of an '80s gangster film, it was fantastical – her change, the cost, and the time were all aligned at three-ten. And she *saw* it; she couldn't quite describe it, which was perhaps a mercy to those around her; one minute her legs held her, the next they disappeared, and after that they held her only once a chair leg became uncomfortably close. The bucolic warmth of the Cumbrian café and the scent of fresh coffee drifting over to her was all that was managing to wrestle her back to normality. Which was when she felt Galloway's arms loop under her shoulders.

"Cap'n? Oh God – Christ, please be okay, be okay, be okay," Galloway said, helpful sentiment melting away into whines and monotony.

As for Niveau, she'd now registered that the grimy, sticky floor wasn't what she was supposed to be feeling, too clammy and slippery under her hands.

"Miss? Are you okay? Let me help you up." She was too baffled to bat away the hands of the stranger who was manhandling her into the chair.

"That was bloody weird."

"Cap'n?" replied the weak underling – underling no longer.

"Oh, you can piss off. Monday isn't happening. You aren't happening."

"What do you mean, I don't . . ." they trailed off, filling in the blanks in their head. But Niveau wasn't one for sparing anyone's blushes, not least when she couldn't separate her thoughts from the fog wrapping itself around her brain. Too busy grappling at her neck, she was fighting herself for air as she tore away the atavistic taboo of her old school tie. Previously one of her few concrete memories of happier, simpler days, currently it served as the noose that rounded off the execution of her sanity.

"Fired. You're fired!" she shot out, eyes still closed, "That's what I mean."

Finally, Niveau opened her eyes, and was glad to see her field of vision spared of both her old employee and the *whatever* had batted her to the floor; it could only be a *whatever*. Nothing had pushed her to the floor, the manifestation wasn't physical, nor had she felt sick so simply collapsed, it was as if that combination in that moment wouldn't release her brain. It had found its lodgings and it was there to stay. And that unlocked her supply of curses.

When she eventually gained the confidence to look around her, meeting the gaze of about ten wide-eyed customers or café employees who looked back at her like a parliament of owls, her urge to get out of there overwhelmed her. And she had to get rid of the change, that was paramount. Forgetting even her bag, the refreshing air of anywhere else hit her before her feet registered it. Her hands were shoved in her pockets, contorting them into uncomfortable denim shapes whilst each of her spasmodic jerks became more desperate and the hair flailing in front of her face became less of an issue: she didn't need to see, she needed to purge. For the briefest of moments, she stopped. No wallet, pockets empty. She patted down her back pockets, as well as jamming her hands in her hoodie's pockets – nothing. Oh, she could see him now, that bastard.

He could've only been the pot-bellied biker making his way across the parking lot right now. He walked with a curious limp, she noted. The way he shuffled in a kind of stupid trudge wasn't far from hilarious, when you could see the lag between his foot mastering the Doc Marten, and the Doc Marten striking the pavement, like a tap dancer with a rolled ankle attempting to waltz. The woman had the option of screaming some insult after him. Heavens knows she had gargantuan enough lungs for the job and ammunition wasn't something she was short of.

On this occasion, however, her lips remained sealed, askew in the sneer she subconsciously would adopt when noticing she was outsmarted. Go on then, he could take her purse. You could almost compliment him on his ability to do it unnoticed in a brimming building in a charming spot. At least this way, she didn't have to endure the plight of tossing all her change away; it wasn't rational she knew, but this was an experience unlike any other, and she'd watched enough films to know that when the main character is going a bit manic and nobody else believes them, they ought to keep an eye out. Her eyes flicked left and right. She wasn't going to be that character, stereotyped and at the whim of some higher power.

Could she blame forgetting to cancel her credit cards on the brain fog? The answer, she knew, was irrelevant; Bernard would still give her that look of his. She'd once tried to replicate it, reflect it back at him, always to no avail. The Toyota's door slammed behind her, and she started to scrape her bones up the drive. She didn't need to turn her phone back on, nor check the time. For today, the job was over.

No money in her pockets. No watch. Nothing else which might have accidentally matched the time. And it was going to stay that way for the rest of the day, even if she'd have to shatter every clock nearby. That might've been the stupid excitement of her mind, she didn't give a crap.

She didn't trust herself for now, and despite not believing in a deity interfering with Earth-folk, she thought putting temptation in fate's way was perhaps a step too far. Niveau's plan currently revolved around an early bedtime with no alarm for the morning.

A few moments later, she was inside and was rubbing the heels of her feet; she loved those shoes, but her feet always had a different perspective. The depressing sight of her hallway offered no reprieve. The paint had been peeling off for eternity, so when she chose to just take it all down one day ready to be re-wallpapered, it was never going to be that simple. No force of fate had warned her that the plastering was damp, incomplete, atop of walls housing electrics so faulty that they'd have had most electricians crouched over a pentagram and begging for death. She tossed the high-heels into a building mass of shoes at the bottom of the stairs. It was an untidiness that concealed a rather large wound in the skirting board; whatever had escaped or clawed its way through, she prayed most nights that it wasn't still in the house. Either way, the pile stayed – it housed her shame, one of many.

Today, there was an angry additional note next to the pile. Written in her least favourite purple sharpie, it was on orange paper, and stated in capital letters:

DET. ADAM QUAIL!
ARTICLE DUE APRIL 25!
BE BETTER THAN GALLOWAY!

She shot a glance at the calendar to her right – April 27th. There went her early night; her dusk was increasingly her boyfriend's dawn.

The call came from the lounge, "Hey, love." Tentative, distant. Niveau walked into the lounge, catching sight of one of Bernard's dopey sci-fi programmes. What was it today, Tuesday? That meant it was *Blake's 7*. She knew she'd get the TV later, and brainless television was the order of the day. No matter how diabolical she knew *Eastenders* was, having suffered through it for most of her childhood, it on occasion presented a welcome, brainless distraction. It didn't matter how fictional their lives were, they were for the most part in the shits, which gave her a few life points above them. She approved of that.

"Today go okay? You get rid of Galloway, like you thought?"

"Something like that, yeah . . . get anything done yourself?" she asked in return. The crisp packets, a tapestry of prawn and cocktail, the very sight of which made her wretch like a sick dog, told her the answer. The lavender oil burner they'd bought a few months ago, perched on the DVD stand, struggled to stymie the diffusing stench. Lying flat across Bernard's legs, their cat Krampus was deep in a nap, and it was obvious that the feline's resting place hadn't shifted in at least an hour. Bernard failed to surprise her anymore, not in the bedroom, not in their holidays away, not in any single way. Spite lived in her voice like rats in the wainscoting. Whether he heard it or not, or simply chose to ignore it and put it down to one of her "menstrual moods" (his words, *absolutely* not hers), she didn't know. Whatever the answer, he somehow spoke without angst: he said that he'd managed to send off his CV to a few companies, even if he thought a reply back was unlikely enough, never mind an interview. Needless to say, the laze would think that, a man without an optimistic bone in his body. He possessed only pragmatic ones unwilling to learn new skills for employment and trembling at the slightest forecast of challenge.

"Have you even had one of those moments, where everything just seems to click?" she asked to no-one in particular. It was Bernard who gave an answer though.

"What, like déjà vu?"

"No, not like a memory, like a coincidence that seems too good to be true? Or one so improbable it hurts?"

"Coincidence? Oh yeah, tons of them. Like when me and two of my school bullies all decided to throw Jack a surprise party that year, and everything hit the fan."

"No," she retorted before any more of his thought train might emerge, "Like synchronicity. But *more*. Like a missing link in the chain of cause and effect?"

She caught the glance he gave her. It made her scowl.

"You don't think that's a bit philosophical? Whatever happened to *cogito ergo sum*?"

"Tsk, will you stop the smart aleck quips and try and help!" yelled Niveau.

"I would if I had the faintest idea what you're on about. I mean 'missing link in the chain of cause and effect', I don't really think that means anything." Bernard responded with. "Sorry," he added in the end.

Missing link in the chain. Something had happened, she knew. There was an order, a power, *somewhere.* Not God, not serendipity, just something she could almost perceive. But maybe perception was tomorrow's game – Bernard was in one of those rare moods where he was right; she had started to sound a bit too philosophical for comfort.

On her way to make one of her chocolate smoothies, customary for any return from work, she moved towards the bombsite of a kitchen. As she passed, she gave Bernard a peck on the lips, but not for as long as he'd have liked. His hand still hovered, statuesque, surprised to find Niveau's wasn't there like it had been the moment before. He even felt his fingers curl very slightly, remembering something separate from his conscious mind.

Nonetheless, it didn't take Bernard long to relapse into his running sci-fi commentary. The blender in front of Niveau, after hiccupping, dying, hiccupping again, being thumped, and then finally working provided the vexing whirr to drown him out. At least Bernard had such a nose for trivia that the information didn't become banal, it was always sprinkled with new facts, though the truth was she didn't give a jot who Travis One and Travis Two were. The blender had slowed to a halt in between the ping and bang of a ray pistol, or whatever the grown men of the '70s were using to thwart tin foil monsters, when Bernard's spiel turned to the matter of volume inconsistency – thrilling. It might've been cute when they began dating; now it simply painted a very soulless backdrop, with all the charm of Galloway's insipid wardrobe.

"And then there's you, you fucking shit."

"Pardon?" she spat out. She spun around. Thankfully, she didn't have to experience it often, yet when someone says something like that to her, Niveau was well versed in stark amazement and fits of pique as the only response. Naturally, all before an ensuing bloodbath. Fists clenched, she threw herself round the kitchen door and glared at her boyfriend. A ringing had instantaneously begun in her head and the hope was that it was simply rising blood pressure.

"And then there's the incidental music!"

"Why did you say that?" was how she responded. One word at a time, one restrained syllable after another until the question was complete. It was the calmest response she was capable of, in the gentlest tone she could muster, demanding of herself that the countdown in her head reach twenty before she even flexed a finger.

"Because, as I said, it's fucking shit! One minute the incidental music is drowning out the dialogue, then the dialogue is too quiet because you've lowered the volume. Watch."

Arm raised, he poised the remote. Oblivious, he demonstrated his point. The display on the TV appeared, as the volume decreased from a twenty-one to a twenty and carried on decreasing further. Bernard let it come to rest at fourteen and started intimating about the issue once again: "So, here, you and the TV are just as useless as one another," he began to say, serene as anything, "You can't say anything but shit, and you're just a plain nuisance. Fix it, you worthless cow."

He was dead. Or at the very least he would be by the time the neighbours had called the police. No one would need to guess at the cause of death. The ringing in her ears began to build again, and she had to physically grasp one knuckle in the other to stop her arm rising and coming down on her prone and idling other half.

When had she stopped counting? The number in her head, the vital countdown, had jammed itself at eleven. Eleven. Its refusal to climb to twenty wasn't some act of intense restraint on her part, or some defiance of the anger management techniques she'd tried. Instead, the overwhelming desire to scream and yell, quite plainly it was just too enticing. The clogged pipe of her mind: all could've looked dandy, that didn't stop the problem building in secret, eventually shattering, then devastating all and sundry standing too close in the process. When she tried to part her lips and attempt the word "eleven", she couldn't stop herself: "Right, go on, say that one more time!" she hurled at him, "Once more!".

What the hell had come over him? Bernard could hardly be described as the epitome of niceness, but he was the sort who apologised to unmoored paving slabs when he tripped over them. He raised his arm, not facing her, instead controlling the volume.

"Calm down! Something wrong with your hearing?" he inquired, evidently without swivelling his head away from the two million sci-fi pixels swirling around on the screen. As the jokey undertone faded, she could hear the miniscule tut under his breath. She swore she could've heard cogs in his head whirring through the event. To him, he must've had a nice, neat formula for the situation: no laughter from Niveau, therefore when Bernard has no clue about why, re-file Niveau as misery guts. "What I said was that here you have the dialogue and the incidental music completely drowning each other out. It's useless. You can't hear them say anything, which is just a nuisance. I wish they could find a way to fix it using modern gubbins. I mean, they can do surround sound, but not equal sound? Honestly, look here – this bit coming up."

Swelling with rage, the blood flowing through her veins at an increased rate made her knuckles tingle. On the screen, the figure was doing much the same thing, walking towards a bloodied alien, sprawled out on the rock floor. Its fingers were clasped, raising its blood pressure in time with the thrum of the music. In readiness, Bernard started altering the volume, lowering it like a plummeting lift in a mineshaft. The tingling drew her focus. Her knuckles, they needed to strike something.

He continued keeping his arm raised and adjusted the volume. She raised her arm too.

Her mind continued to strike eleven. The volume then struck eleven too.

Eleven wasn't loud. This didn't stop her clasping her hands to her ears with a resoluteness that would've thwarted an entire army. The gaps between her fingers, her skin, her ears, they closed quickly to hinder even the vaguest of notes launching another bombardment on her eardrums.

"No, not that!" It was getting louder. Not the volume, that remained stuck at a piercing and infuriating eleven. Her ears, on the other hand, were moments away from submission underneath the heel of whatever was destroying her mind.

"But it has to be, you see, because otherwise the incidental music is too great."

"No! Not that!" she hollered back through a building lump in her throat. A lump that was seconds away from covering the carpets in pustular greens and yellows. Closed eyes didn't stop it either, her vision polluted with numbers.

"What's the hell's the matter? Is something up with you?" he asked, stumbling over the words.

Of course, it was. Her knees had flexed, her face had screwed up, her heart had thumped a fierce rumba, her feet had left the floor, all before she quite acknowledged that's what she was doing. Niveau jettisoned over the sofa, arms pointed forward in the shape of a pointed dagger. For one shattering moment, her hands fell from her head, outstretched and wildly grabbing for the remote. The dam had burst before the warning alarm had properly sounded. The cat launched from the sofa. One of her nails struck Bernard's face as his knee jerked upwards, spasming at the heap of pained woman flailing atop him. Where the cat had been, the gained space gave her room for an extra grip on reality and her boyfriend.

What the hell was she doing or saying? Was that question even rhetorical or honest? Worse, did she even dare learn the answer? Niveau clenched her eyes shut, blocking out anything and everything. All she knew was the split second her fingers closed around what she prayed was the remote.

Amongst the very vibrations of life and substance around her, the laughter from her boyfriend hit her like a slap round the face. She gave no heed to what or who was now in her way, it was *eleven*.

It was bad, it didn't conform, it abandoned familiarity. And so Niveau couldn't conform to reality. Nine and thirteen were fine, but ten and twelve were wounds and stranded at eleven she couldn't reach them. The island, where the natives roamed in the land of normality, and she was adrift. Adrift. Grasping what she thought was the remote, the ridges like buttons, she jabbed wildly, but the noise within her brain continued to build.

Something, she felt it caress her arm. The blaster on the TV programme exploded in the same moment she brought her elbow back. It took all she had to fight the force trying to stop her blocking the chaos out. Pinned against the sofa, the shudder in her leg flung her about without direction. Her legs couldn't extend fully, each of her ligaments currently no more than flesh as they were forced to curl inwards into the foetal position. If there was safety, it might as well have been on the other side of infinity.

Stopped. Everything stopped. Sanity, rage, madness, it all stopped.

"*Christ!* Christ, for God's sake, what's the matter?"

Eyelids clenched shut so tightly that colourful specks polluted her vision, Niveau needed to wait for the pins and needles coursing through her legs and arms to stop before she dared twitch. The living room had been invaded by robbers, or that was at least how it appeared. On the floor, the lavender oil burner lay upturned, dripping the noxious liquid into the carpet. Starfishing outward when more and more of the carpet encountered it, the spreading smear it was creating, along with the smell, reminded her of the fields behind her mum's house when she was young. In the summer, they'd become clogged with purple as far as the eye could see, so much so that sometimes your eyes would sting at the fumes if the wind was right. There was something about it that seized control of her mind there and then. It was stupid, seeking a pattern to replace the approaching storm of numerical hell, and her brain thrusted itself between connections and similarities as if it were an overcharged dodgem car.

Thump. The first barrier in her mind came crashing down. Releasing an odd sort of comfort, another came down, segmenting her mind like a knife through flesh. Just feeling her fingers in the throes of pins and needles, she couldn't help except count. She had ten fingers. Ten fingers she hated. She hated her own flesh, and the ringing inside her ears wouldn't stop building again.

Bernard was too busy blubbing like a newborn to give one iota of empathy about this. Having wrestled the remote from his deranged girlfriend, he sat against the coffee table. He was fighting with his chest to breathe properly, on the verge of hoarseness; between the gulps of air, he was greedily letting into his lungs, he reiterated his question, to which the answer was simply the air hanging heavy, undisturbed. Muted, the various characters running to and fro on the TV screen were wise enough not to chance flickering with the vaguest of noises.

"Okay, what the hell? What the actual hell?!"

She stopped, staring at him. He spoke yet more: "Really! Okay, what the hell has eleven got to do with anything?" Bernard asked, cutting it short as he'd underestimated how out-of-puff he was. The only mercy was that he'd quickly lost the stamina to continue his red-faced persona. "One last time, what has eleven got to do with anything?"

That must've been what she was shouting, spitting into his face. Yet, now, she couldn't answer him. All her lips could reply was silence, inaudibly counting the acceptable numbers and listing them as though her life depended on it. She couldn't have one, two was too firm, three was okay, four was okay if it meant a quarter of something, five was devil spawn . . .

The visitor emerged from the small bedroom, letting out a drained sigh. Their last two hours had been spent pinned to a laptop screen with nothing except David Bowie and a cuckoo clock for company. After the condemnation of Adam Quail was completed three days ago, five smaller articles had been hammered out in quick succession in the meanwhile. She'd lived in the room for just under a week, after a few days of hotels where she phoned up friends and pleaded with them to let her stay. All said they *would,* except they thought she ought to check elsewhere as they mightn't have enough room; none came out and told her to go boil her head, yet it almost would've been better if they did.

At least her current lodgings weren't completely alien to her, even if the bare wooden floors and blinds bleached of colour through age made it seem so. The patches of wall devoid of paint and wallpaper gave out a hugging sensation. The nearest thing she could call a home comfort, she supposed. Or it was at least more comforting than the remaining wallpaper, a horrible pinkish grey, spattered in dents and scratches; that made her want to repair the damage between her boyfriend and herself, then leave.

It surprised no one who Niveau had told her pity story to, least of all Backgammon Man, that she'd ended up staying in his spare room after she had flown the coop. Before Bernard had had time to indicate the front door, Niveau was already flying through it, barely slowing to collect a bag and a spare pair of shoes. They'd talk in a few days, but she feared— No, there was some adamant glimmering in her mind that going back soon would end in a final calamity.

She walked through to Backgammon Man's front room. It had gained piles of classical music CDs in the same way that some people gained ranks of woolly jumpers from honorary aunties and uncles to their families. They were the kind of gift everyone gave over and over, always wanting to show willing but never to do the strenuous activity of talking to you and finding out your interests. Backgammon Man hadn't ever suffered the fate of jumpers, but he had been on a mental retreat a decade or so back, and its woollen jumper remnants lay drooped over one of the chairs. None of them were remarkably thick, each peppered with a series of holes from years of use that should've warranted being moved to the charity shop. Today, Backgammon Man was wearing four of the items, two light blue, one green, and one cyan, all that was left of Backgammon Man's year of enlightenment and personal growth.

Of course, he wasn't actually called "Backgammon Man", it was just that he had such a variety of names that that was the only one commonly used by people. Some called him Robbie, some called him Owen, some called him Syd – sometimes, she'd witnessed, all within the space of the same conversation. To test the water, once she'd called him Ozymandias, the bizarrest name she knew of, and he still responded. If pushed, she opted for Owen since that was the only one she'd ever seen briefly committed to paper, in a birthday card to him which he'd thrown away a moment later. Birthday and Christmas cards were two things you never saw cluttering up his house, he just thought them too vain. Instead, he much preferred (for a reason unbeknownst to anyone she'd asked) to fill his shelves with either books on subjects like Plato and Socrates or, rather more disturbingly, a plethora of Russian nesting dolls.

"Everything's set up. One lump or two?" he called from the even smaller kitchen. His nickname wasn't unfounded; the "setup" before her proving as much.

"Two, please," she replied, taking her seat beside the board. He emerged with a tea tray encumbered by two mugs. Each was filled far too full, the tray having transformed itself into a third mug. Thank God the man hadn't developed a tremor. For all the man's clumsiness, he took great care in avoiding her right arm which, though an over-precaution, he'd bandaged when she'd first arrived. He'd taken one look at the series of small cuts on her upper arm, then immediately begun dousing it in an antiseptic gel and applying a dressing. Most of the man's skills he'd acquired from previous partners, and basic first aid was one of them, rugby prowess having been his only solo achievement in his lifetime. Most regarded his being openly gay in the seventies as mighty impressive as well, but he disagreed, simply saying that it was just a matter of waiting for the rest of the world to catch up; it still hadn't. Infinite compassion was another one of his virtues he didn't think impressive, just proper: both knew she'd gained her injury in her ambush against Bernard, but he hadn't spoken a word or cast her a look. Simply, he'd asked as he always did whether her tea had one lump or two.

Barely having placed the tray on the floor, next to the pile of ginger biscuits, he seated himself and cupped a pair of dice in his hand. In the blink of an eye, the first skimmed across the board, promptly followed by the second. No sooner had he done that than he extended his left arm and tightly grasped her hand.

"Look, look at your hand," he spoke. Ordinarily locked behind his eyes, the wisdom of his years unleashed itself in a piercing glare. The glare was one that had sent two ruffians who had once attempted to mug him fleeing, screaming "You're a fuckin' loon!". Blaming his reflexes on his years as a sports teacher, and before that a professional rugby player, Niveau instinctively tried to bat the alien hand off hers. However, to her surprise she found her other hand underneath his as well. Without realising it, she'd placed one hand atop another, and begun to scratch at her skin.

A red flare had already started to spread over the underside of her wrist. The top of the blemish was a curve, clean and uniform, and the bottom was a jagged edge, not too dissimilar to a coastline on a map. In fact, the entire patch could have been construed as a country; the whole of the right side curved back underneath itself like the Cornish territories. The colour itself shaded downwards. The pastel red hue, however, was incomplete. Niveau had never had particularly dark skin, and on holiday she'd struggled to tan even when she wasn't plastered head to toe in factor fifty suncream. She just needed to extend the top of the arc, shape it like the southern point of Africa, efficiently fade from the red to the pink to the pale skin tone.

"You're doing it again."

Niveau was. Cornwall was growing. Patterns. All around her, they were still endlessly forming. "And we're going to break you out of it." After slamming the backgammon pieces along the board, raising an eyebrow, his glare once more met Niveau's, and she slowly began to extend her hand. Her grasp on the dice was instantly so hard that, by accident, she had concluded the red pattern on her wrist. With the skin colour on her knuckle the same shade, she began to loosen one finger, readying to drop at least one of the cuboids.

The first fell before she'd even realised, as did the bolt of anguish shooting through her. The other dice bounced onto the carpet somewhere as she desperately attempted to upturn the board. Whichever number it landed on was immaterial, the sole catalyst was that it existed: number means movement, movement means pattern, pattern means lack of movement. Niveau knew that the five the dice had handed to her, they'd confine her actions; the backgammon pieces, she couldn't move them with intention of winning, she could only move them in a way that maintained the pattern. But the pattern conflicted with the rules, and the rules were paramount.

On her trouser leg, a wet patch was forming. Another globule of saliva hit the patch. When she lifted her left hand to stop more spit falling, the only material – and to her it was simply material, the composition of life – she could feel was the lacquered wood armrests. And if Niveau's grip harshened anymore, those rests would buckle.

"Niveau," spoke the ex-sports teacher opposite from her. He knew her mind wasn't governing itself, but his routine, the daily backgammon games, his face went numb at seeing their effect. Baring her teeth, they were grinding against one another. Battering the barrier with her tongue, she was repeating a series of numbers, almost incoherently, over and over again. Each leg was pinned down sharply, like rods nailed into the floor, nigh-on convulsing like a patient fitting on an operating table.

The ring of the doorbell shot through the air. The woman, briefly blind and gasping in her own private world of one-plus-one-equals-two, finally was able to sense that breath was actually going into her lungs. Her veins had finally begun losing their similarity to worms burrowing about under her skin. Backgammon Man stood, brushing his own frail hand comfortingly over hers. "Can I go answer that?" It was just as much a surprise to her as it was to him when she answered affirmatively. He left the room. This left her to puzzle, while her knuckles relaxed, over how steady she could keep her hands if she tried to sip the tea. The herbal mixture didn't need to reach her throat for her to taste it in her watering eyeballs.

Quick to the door, Backgammon Man swung it open to reveal the wrapped-up figure of Bernard scraping his muddied shoes against the carpet. There was a particularly thick, solid patch on the heel. He recognised it from his own shoes in the past – the calling card of the local mutt, Raffles, who by all accounts was lovely even if the same couldn't be said of the owner, who let his dog frequently splatter the pathways outside in an elaborate minefield. Just as Bernard was about to enlist the aid of the wall in removing it, he coughed.

"Just take them off. There's a wire mat outside."

Sheepish, Bernard obeyed. Ordinarily, he'd have conjured up some verbose reply, but Backgammon Man's award-winning glares were coming in handy once again.

"I just called . . . you know, I'm not sure why? I suppose, well, perhaps . . . Oh, I was just passing. Thought it couldn't do any harm."

It was only at the thought of realising she was there, barely more than one twist of a corridor away, when he realised what he wanted to say. And not to her, just to someone who'd listen. Not callously or distastefully, in fact the opposite, he wanted to shed a few tears to someone while they were to all intents and purposes nonchalant and a stranger. Bernard went to try to speak some more when the man's hand silenced him.

The corner of Backgammon Man's mouth twitched. Everything within the balanced ecosystem of his home was finely tuned, and his seventh sense was knowing when it was disturbed; he had a sixth sense as well, but that was an innate knowledge of the best temperature at which to drink his tea. Dismissing the tingle of his seventh sense, he put it down to the boiler. Over the last few weeks, it had developed a habit of simply grinding to a halt – maybe he'd made that part of the ecosystem too.

"Listen, yeah, I shouldn't be here," Bernard continued.

"Sorry, I was just distracted a moment. I'll ask her what she thinks." Or he would've done, if his new flatmate hadn't fled across the tight hallway, vaulting the tasselled rug, and pushing herself into her bedroom. The spectacle was weird: it was chaotic, a scrambling entity trying to escape, yet its movements were careful, robotic, reflexes timed to the second. The equation she was using to move from carpet to bedroom door to shutaway was straightforward: a pirouette, the final element of which was the hasty slam of wood against frame filling the space. Neither man moved.

"Niveau?" Bernard called out to the disappearing figure. Silence responded. The response was the same when Backgammon Man called out too.

He'd let her rest. If he'd called a doctor, as he probably should've done – purely as a way of making sure nothing too untoward was happening – rest is what they would've ordered. And a steaming cup of tea.

"Want to come in?"

"Really think that's a good idea, Backgammon Man?" Bernard asked back. Bernard had never met the man, yet knew his title. "Yes" was so close to the tip of his tongue, he could feel his mouth getting the feel for the word, deducing its shape and its facets and its implications. It didn't emerge though, at least not audibly. Everything that had happened, it wasn't his fault, it wasn't her fault either necessarily, but he didn't know if it signalled an end that was rapidly approaching anyway. Why face the music once it's a blaring orchestra when you can wander away to the tune of a gentle serenade?

"Haydn. You know that'll suffice." Backgammon Man said.

"Pardon?"

"Haydn. My name, it's Haydn, nice if someone called me it this side of eternity. Just once, that's all I ask, it'd be lovely," continued the man in the doorway, the man called Haydn, "And don't attempt that Hollywood nonsense where you call me by the nickname, stop halfway, and make some grand show of correcting it. I'll play billiards with your eyeballs."

That was Bernard told. Chance was that he meant it. And the snooker cue propped against the airing cupboard did nothing to dissuade him from that idea. His mind was made up, repeating "Okay, Haydn, me coming in – good idea? I've not got a clue."

Honestly, Haydn didn't know the answer either. What he did know, however, was that Bernard was the spitting image of a previous boyfriend, Miles, and that had been a face he'd liked. The glance at the key in the door, a keyring bought by that very boyfriend all those years ago hanging off it serenely, sealed the deal.

"It'll be a long night," he replied, gesturing to the man on the doorstep with a smirk, "One lump or two?"

In the last two days, aeons had been spent poring over not just backgammon, adding chess, draughts, scrabble, whist, monopoly, and countless other board games to their portfolios. Haydn wondered if he might never be able to return to the nickname ever again, thwarted in every game at every turn by Bernard's wiles. Maybe everyone else had simply been letting him win in the last few years, the way his reputation lay in tatters.

They were now, however, in a recession during their games. Haydn had shrunk back to the kitchen to prepare some soup for Niveau, even if he knew it would be cold and still outside the door by the next morning. Bernard had been left to do yet another sweep of the room. His eyes always being drawn back to the stain on the floor. It was new, added by Niveau just before her flight instead of fight. After Haydn had let his visitor in, they'd gone into the front room, and found the mug on the floor, contents evacuated. Part of the mug had shattered; the chips had then been neatly arranged into piles by size amongst the irregularities of the spillage. The backgammon pieces had been upturned as well, sorted into some sort of pattern. It looked intricate, like someone had attempted nuclear physics using a game of Othello. Discarded, the board was cast aside by one of the armchairs, and the floor had become some odd maths hub. Which part of the chaos had sent Niveau overboard, they couldn't say, but if she'd been in any state to think about things like the toilet, she'd not done it in the time that Bernard had kept an eye on the spare bedroom door.

Haydn never got around to asking the question of where Bernard would sleep before grabbing a grey knitted shawl draped over a chair on the first night and drawn it up around him. The pleasure of lying down though, he didn't afford himself that. He remained upright, doorhandle and eyes on an equal footing. He didn't allow the weighty bags under his eyes a look in, and he felt like a phone having every moment of that last one per cent milked out of it for all its worth. He wouldn't let his eyes close.

"That's the soup on, should just be five minutes," said Haydn, peering abstractly out of the window.

"Lucas again?" Bernard asked, waiting for his counterpart to suggest another boardgame, as he invariably would. Lucas was the teenager of Haydn's younger neighbours. You always knew where he was because he couldn't shut a door without shaking the building. And when he wasn't testing the architect's mettle, he was either sat playing video games very loudly on his computer, letting all and sundry know that the bastards "need to fucking die", or in the garden around the back of the flats, taking pot shots with a tennis ball and racket at tin cans. Or, at least, that was what he claim, but he seemed to have very little accuracy when aiming for the can. His aim at car windscreens and headlights was second to none though.

"No, not him today," Haydn eventually responded, "It's this woman."

Bernard looked at him, left eye twitching.

"Pardon?"

"A woman."

"That's not actually that helpful. There are many women," he said, catching himself glancing at the doorway.

"Stand up and look! Behind the window cleaner's van."

Bernard twisted around in the chair, kneeling on the soft cushions, and gazed through the slats of the blind. Haydn wasn't wrong, there was indeed a woman clad in a trench coat which covered even her shoes and with a scarf wrapped tightly around her neck. Her face was one of those you could easily get déjà vu over, so generic that you stopped to think that seemingly everyone was the offspring of the same two people. A bag was slung over her arm, one of the cheap plastic ones that shops were encouraged to get rid of, and a square, reddish tube lay inside, like a roll of Christmas wrapping paper. Beyond that, she was just one of the many who used the courtyard as a shortcut to the nearby train station.

"Oh, her. She . . ." Bernard trailed off, hoping Haydn would pick up the end of his sentence. Instead, the older man just continued his abstract gaze. And he continued it even more, until a good two minutes had passed, a couple of minutes in which the woman had simply stood checking her phone. "She's presumably waiting for someone. I'd leave it, I can't see her being up to anything."

"I don't know," he said absentmindedly. Inside, whilst he watched, a thick line appeared between his brows and outside the woman just continued to tap her phone screen. She stood propped against a tree, and her gaze never met Haydn's, nor did she become aware of his curious behaviour. He noted her sunglasses slowly falling to the end of her nose, but he couldn't make where her eyesight was. There was a moment where he thought his gaze might have met with hers, but should it have done so, it was cut just as quickly as it was established.

Then the blast shot forth, engulfing the window. Accompanying the splash was the thud of the burst striking the top of the window. Before the obscurity completely fell, Haydn squinted for all he could, but as far as he could tell the woman was oblivious. For a moment, Bernard thought that he might hiss at the window cleaner to get rid of the wall of bubbles and foam he'd constructed, his counterpart going so far as to extend his lower lip and lean forward to hit the window. But instead, he sat down with a sigh.

"Sorry, my teeth must just be on edge," Haydn said.

"I know how you feel," replied Bernard.

"Anyway, shall we have a game?"

"Finally! I wondered when we'd get to that!"

The backgammon set had been used more in the last few days than it had been for most of its wooden, solitary life. Bernard wondered that Haydn now wouldn't stop until it combusted under the pressure of dice striking it. No reply was necessary as they both exchanged quips and moved their pieces in possibly their most tactical match yet. Midway through the game, that was when the whisper came. At first, despite the fact he'd known that voice quite intimately on and off since high school, his brain was shocked before it could catch up and work out why.

Emerging from the room was clearly too great an ask. The voice had come though, that was undeniable – unless the boiler pipes had taken on a life of their own. Niveau had begun to mutter a string of numbers, "One, one, two, three, five, eight, thirteen."

"Niveau? Are you okay?" cried out Haydn, even before Bernard. The younger of the pair was too busy gritting his teeth and pinning his eyelids open.

The response wasn't exactly what you'd call conversational.

"One through six. Three, five, pattern, not prime. Not allowed."

Bernard looked at the pieces, cusping the dice in his hands. He placed them carefully on the table out of sight of the lock in the bedroom door. Something small and glistening, with a blue tint, was scanning everything surrounding the game.

"No! One, two, prime, both in pattern! Explain impossible, answer bad!"

When he checked the dice himself, he found that Niveau was exactly right – five and three. No matter how addled her brain was while drawing the strands of ordinary life into an equation, she'd got it exactly right. Bernard could've shunted the dice into his pocket, but it hardly seemed worth the effort.

"I love humans. Always seeing patterns in things that aren't there," Bernard muttered to himself without realising. Sci-fi shows had permeated his conscience in the same way patterns had started to rule hers.

"Niveau, can we come in? Can we talk?" Haydn called out. The dust in the air continued settling unimpeded.

Letting the soup, an orangey broth heaped in spices, boil away to itself, Haydn walked towards the spare bedroom door. His hand lifted, he prepared to knock. Bernard followed him, sensing a stand ought to be taken finally. Neither of them had the chance to touch the handle, the door creaking open first. Not just that, but the handle itself leapt to the floor, a shambolic heap of shaped metal and mechanisms.

"Belly of the beast," whispered Bernard, deeply regretting the amount of sci-fi he'd watched. They couldn't see her opening the door to them, not in her current state. A flitting, fearful glance passed between them, not that either of them quite had the stomach to acknowledge it.

Bernard went first.

Inside, only one lamp was on, that in the far corner. It hadn't previously lived there; it used to be atop a pile of French books that Haydn had once taught himself with, back in a time of Morris Minors and black and white television. Any French from them now would be even more of a garble, the pages of said books now dotted across the far wall. The wall had become a collage of various books in fact, pieced apart and pinned and perfectly lined up into a pattern Bernard's grandma would've stared at in awe. Although painstaking detail had been taken to create the collage, one small patch remained open, revealing the pinkish grey wallpaper. In the past, it had just been an awful colour, now it was the break from the wash of yellowing paper. Haydn saw the French collage as well, and knew the hole was the missing page fifty-six from the last book in the series; to him, it wasn't the kind of disfigurement you forgot when you took intimate care of books in the way he did.

The floor was no better. The bed which Niveau should have been sleeping on had been recently arranged against the far left of the wall, each element labelled and disassembled. The same deconstruction had ravaged everything in the room, down to the unravelled threads of the curtains or the bolts and screws in the handle on her side of the door. None of the items were free from scratches either, so much so that the edges of almost every item seemed to have a nice flurry of them along all their sides. In fact, the lamp in the corner was one of the few things that hadn't suffered any of these fates – how long did it have?

Niveau herself was stood straight as a plank against another wall, this one covered in articles she'd written, individual pages of which were spread outwards. God knows why, it should've been the last thing on his mind, but Haydn's mind shot back to watching old television crime serials – a few strands of red string and the room would have been a perfect prop for such a show. *Inspector Morse* had been a particular favourite. Ordinarily, she wouldn't have resisted sizing someone up, giving them a once-over, assuming their backstory and curating her retaliatory attacks. That presumptive gaze had left her eyes now. If the human body had a factory setting, Niveau had entered that step in evolution.

"Niveau?"

"Six," rapid-fire like a machine gun, she spat back. The men exchanged another look. It was then that Bernard noticed her nails; they were all either jagged and tearing, or plainly non-existent. Would he find their fragmented remains amongst the disassembly? At least that answered the question over the mysterious scratches: Niveau hadn't engaged the assistance of a screwdriver or pliers in her quest.

"Niveau, what can we do to help?" Bernard asked her.

"Six, four, three, two, two, two, four. Acceptable." she replied.

"There's got to be something?"

"Six, three, two, two, nine. Acceptable."

"Can you stop this? I'd like to understand." Bernard continued, pleadingly. He didn't care that his voice had raised a pitch or that the tremble he'd been putting off was now seeping in. Just because Niveau's words were strung together didn't stop them being those of a lunatic. His mind reeled with how to jump the communications barrier between them. He needed to help, and she needed it, now more than ever. He didn't dare grab her though, he didn't dare risk upsetting the balance of whatever was chopping up her brain and spewing it back out in little malformed chunks.

"Three, three, four, four, two, four, two, ten," she continued, suddenly looking at them aghast and beginning to thrust out her hands. "No!"

They didn't wait for her manhandling. They wanted to help, but Bernard and Haydn were out of there before Niveau figured out how to disassemble one of them.

Outside IKEA's newest rival, Bernard stumbled back into the front room, and allowed the armchair to catch him.

"What . . . what was she saying that for?" he asked his wiser counterpart.

"They were the letters in the words you said." Haydn said. Even in that moment, behind the door, he was close enough to hear her continuing with the words he was speaking now. How long until he broke whatever rules she was conjuring up? "We give her until the morning. Then we get the police, ambulances, whatever she needs for help."

Bernard didn't speak, he ran his hands across his chin, nodded, attempted and failed a tearless sigh. From the other room, Haydn could hear the impatient soup bubbling over. Its murky orange depths didn't care about Niveau, just as the chunks of chicken floating about in the tasteful liquid didn't either.

"Two, four, three, five, three, seven. Four, two, three, three, six, ten, eight, three, five, three, four."

The clock lay in pieces, just like it needed to be. The moon was high in the sky now. Height of moon plus shade of darkness equals time of day. Or, rather, time of midnight.

Her cheeks had been moist for over half an hour. She'd allowed her little, salty spheres to roll down, but never fall to the carpet. Niveau couldn't risk irregularity in the carpet.

Biology, it was atoms, it was a re-arranging of the universe's pattern. She'd eventually begin to sort those atoms, no matter how sub-atomic they became, until everything in her world was as simple as one equals one. But, before the great deconstruction could begin, she had to address the burning her tears were now imbued with. Something was amiss, outside of her control.

It couldn't be the lamp. The hum had disappeared from its insides when she'd dismantled it and dissected its wires like the veins of a human body. Niveau wondered how easy it would be to remove one such vein, assess its route through the human form. In herself, she saw merely the carrier of the numerical ordered form. Biology, nature, it was where patterns had just gone awry and allowed themselves to develop their own order, develop uselessly without purpose or direction except for interaction. Not only was that form ungainly, but it muttered, out of sight but still in existence, words and sounds that were processed but unseen. The atoms simply shifted around, rather than change or morph – words and voice were a waste of the universe's potential. Not in her world though, once she'd divested herself of her form, for that would be solely atom after atom after atom, forever.

In fact, everything separate from the outside world, as she assessed her kingdom, was ordered. The error, the imbalance, the catalyst of inefficiency, it lived in the world of unreason. Having conquered her current world, she needed to expand, and adjust the chaos, repurpose it to her design, to her way of life – the only way of life – the only way of anything.

Whilst she'd forced her senses to perceive everything as simply the infinite sequence of atoms, misguided en route, she'd begun to understand the human form, and such things as heartbeats (optimal when steady and under complete control) were just as much her lifeline despite the fact they belonged to others. So, an erratic heartbeat meant her world could be so close to danger, an absent one meant a need for complete re-evaluation, and a new one would prompt risk assessment.

Risk assessment it was.

The door of her bedroom, she allowed it to swing open very slowly. The darkness of her world met Haydn and Bernard's. Except for a faint glow emanating from the kitchen, everything was opaque. She could barely shift her gaze high enough to acknowledge the breadth and depth of their hideous organisation – or indeed the lack of. In her ears, the atoms were shifting, telling her how their fellows were abused by anyone and anything, and Niveau began to share in the offences done against arrangement, logic.

"I was curious how long it'd take you to emerge, face the facts," a voice called out. There was a slight shift in the blackness. A long length of something was allowed to unfurl from its governing, larger mass, its colour swallowed up and chameleonic against the opaque. Then the first of the shape's hush puppies landed on the mismatched carpet. From the end of the long, cracked, well- worn length – a belt! – jeered the sharp, malevolent protrusion of a buckle. "This is your fault, you know. You need to know how it feels."

The voice was female. Behind the female figure, a lump wrapped in blankets and shawls slumped, legs tumbling underneath the chair as its knees buckled, its top-heavy form sending it forwards with a thud. The ruffled hair, an abuse of organisation, was Bernard's; Bernard's atoms didn't vibrate now, they didn't interlock, they instead awaited re-organisation. No doubt the other lump, slightly protruded from under the dining table, awaited re-organisation too. For now, they simply sat there, amongst the millions of billions of atoms floating uselessly, comprising matter irrelevant and confused.

Awaited re-organisation. Just like the glass shards busted from the hallway window, now deposited across the tasselled rug. Her concentration had been focused on making out life in the darkness, but the concentrations of her hands, away from her conscious mind, had begun to fit the shards together, recreate the window as though it were a jigsaw, here on the floor. Even the blood droplets let forth when the shards caught her fingers were organised to the best of their ability.

One of the darkness's hush puppies fell onto a glass segment, birthing five new and unordered splinters. A lump fell from above. A newspaper fell onto Niveau's lap, and the woman in front of her let her tears blot the paper.

"He promised me it was an accident. I believed him. Yet everyone, people like your scum, set out to slander him." The scrawled note, written in sharpie on the newspaper which emblazoned the headline she'd written at the start of her stay at Backgammon Man's home, was blotching more and more under the power of the droplets. And the droplets didn't stop flowing, creating harsh zigzags of increased entropy across DETECTIVE QUAIL: PAEDOPHILE, BENT COPPER, OR BOTH?

"My husband, my Adam, he had that in his lap when I found him yesterday. That and the razor. Christ, you didn't stop with slandering those Albatross and Harbottle fellas' names, you wanted the entire police force."

Her stare was fixed on the newspaper before, atop the disordered glass, but it was a hollow one. She knew the woman before her was Adam Quail's wife, that was about it though. Niveau couldn't even remember her name.

"Pen," finally uttered Niveau back, scrabbling at her pockets. The entire weight of the widow's body shifted in front of her when she dived for the hall table.

"That's all you've got to say? My Adam is dead, he took his own life because of people like you, and that's all you've got to say? Bitch." Niveau's head smacked against the wall so hard that the wall and her skin dented in equal measure.

"It's wrong!"

"Yes, my husband's death is wrong!"

"No, the third line! Fourth word, wrong type of 'there', need to correct it!" She'd literally torn one of her pocket linings out, and almost unthinkingly upturned a small box in the hallway, searching for something to correct the suicide note with. Death was part of life, it was part of the order, it was the final foregone conclusion, but the legacy was an error, and the error needed to be corrected. She *needed* to correct it.

The other woman sharply extended her arm again, but this time Niveau managed to dodge, rolling onto her side and half-crawling back into the bedroom. The leather of the belt snagged her foot, and a red inflammation was already spreading over her skin, as she tussled with the door and the determined mass behind it. By now, Niveau could've dissected that foot in her sleep, named every bone, and numbered each skin cell a darker, redder shade to the rest. Nevertheless, the former detective had still used the wrong "there" and she wasn't going to let that into her world.

Behind the door, all the emotions Adam's wife had swallowed she now regurgitated with all the filth the English language – Niveau's patterned, careful, intricate English language – could muster. Niveau buckled under the combined impact of word and fist, and she went sprawling across the room as her adversary stormed in, door denting the wall in the onslaught. Her attacker lunged across her ordered world, a lot of which lay in shattered tatters around Niveau's grabbled body. Twisting to one side and turning the neat circle of nuts and bolts into mechanical disarray, she avoided the attack. Eyes constantly fixed on the intruder, she sprang to her feet whilst already tearing the glass shards from a snowglobe through the weak flesh of her palm. Her care was not for the human weakness of pain, but for the superior concern that those shards needed to go across her palm in a nice, neat line.

A perfect line of daggers stretched about between the two and, like a predator sizing up the right moment to turn its prey into dinner, woman fixated upon woman. If her mind wasn't tumbling through the new realm it seemed to have unlocked, Niveau would've thought that Adam's wife could have swallowed her whole in one ravenous gulp. And not just for the nutrition, for the pleasure of indulgence.

The lunge came; Niveau expected it perfectly, her view in the moment of launched woman and two shadowy corpses. In a way, it was far too simple, given the emotions that the widow's face wielded. Quite plainly, Niveau crouched as if she were a compressed spring and Adam's wife flew as if she were an uncoiled one, hurtling over her adversary and striking the intersected glass panes behind her – ones which didn't take her weight. At any other point, it would've hurt and nothing more though. This flat however bordered a trench-like staircase, leading to a maintenance door a good six feet beneath the window.

In the manner of a pinball, her head smashed into the slabs at the left side of the descending staircase. Flopping, it then struck the pebble dashing on the opposite wall, before finally finding residence upon the cold stone with a monotone thud. Before the ground and the widow became one, Niveau reckoned that that was the only instance where their eyesights disconnected, like a boat, captain absent, untethered from its mooring amidst choppy waters. This was, until the splintering of spine and muscle snapped her neck a full half-circle to look directly, from above her shoulder blades, back at Niveau.

The incidental murderess stood there, for the first time in the last few days uncertain. It only took the hiss of her animalistic self, the version of her at one with the very atoms around her, in order to snap her back to reality in the same way the leaf-covered concrete had snapped Adam's wife to face her once more. Heading in straight lines only, Niveau allowed herself to leave the flat for the first time. There were some new atoms that needed ordering.

# IN THE FOREST OF BONES AND SHADOWS

SHARP SNAPS AND cracks echoed from the twigs underneath the park rangers' feet. Rid of birdsong, the sound of nature being disturbed was all the forest heard. Both torch beams sliced the darkness like knives, yet they still hadn't a clue about their direction. All the trees were blurring together like darkness incarnate. Clusters of shadowed foliage combined to create a solid opaque wall across the wavy land. The ground itself hadn't been pelted by recent rainstorms, not like the neighbouring village had. This didn't stop it putting up a fight, soil dry and crumbling beneath their boots no matter how much either Toby or Fenisha attempted to fight back. Twice already, one of them had been sent sprawling over into the earth.

"Christ, Toby, I reckon we're straying completely out of the way of the badger camera," she said to her colleague. He was thundering ahead, wanting to get home to his delicious, steaming pie. The woman, Fenisha, shone her torch around the clearing they'd found. Her gloved finger slid across the muddied map. She'd hoped to make it readable – instead, an additional coating of tree dew now smattered it. Kitted out in their ridiculous green overalls, she decided it was best just to follow him, carefully weaving her way through the forest, also weaving her way – less successfully – around an impending quarrel. For Toby and Fenisha, the nearest they got to a good time was having a go at biting each other's head off; assuming, of course, that those heads were then turned to mulch, subjected to Hell's flames, and then used as a succubus' football.

"I still don't get why the Trust don't just invest in remote control technology, so we don't have to trek to the middle of this place," Toby Fletcher paused, inspecting his watch, "at bloody 8 p.m. And in December no less. I'll get sodding chillblains." The day Toby found some calm in the world, Fenisha imagined that that would be the day that the ground swallowed the entire human race whole. A week or so ago, she thought she'd overheard him apologise to a schoolchild he'd bumped into. The child's tears, snotty sobs, and weak-kneed posture soon told a tale of an entirely different colour.

"You know it's policy. Surely, you're used to it now. You've been here thirty-one years and I've been here three months," she responded. It was difficult not constantly retorting to the man, but she found he reminded her of one of her brothers, Gareth. Admittedly, her foul-mouthed other brother could be just as noisome, but at least his job as a groundskeeper kept him out of the house. Gareth was at present staying in her spare room, and the man was infuriating beyond measure. The idea of letting him win an argument with his infected logic stoked more flames in her heart than Guy Fawkes' night. On one of the few occasions when Gareth had won an argument, or rather a heated discussion that she'd not entered and so he'd won by default, the man proceeded to strut around the house with an ego so swollen that she couldn't understand how it didn't crush him.

Resigned to stabbing the voodoo doll of her

colleague later on, she watched the older park ranger hurdle a small stream and begin swinging his torch beam around the clearing. He was looking for the path they'd wandered off from over a mile back. For all the decisive movement of his torch, he couldn't mask the unequivocal fact that he was lost. His scowl launched itself back at Fenisha.

"Oh, fuck me senseless with a smoked kipper!" she spat.

"What?" he called back, the air of superiority laced into his voice. Cats cared less for their exaltedness, she reckoned.

"A shorter route, it's been staring me in the face. If we continue along that verge we should come out near the reservoir. Then a straight walk, only quarter of a mile, then up a second verge. Shouldn't take us more than half an hour," mused the woman. He watched as she manoeuvred the stream. He scoffed; slow, like she always was. He wrinkled his face; even from a good couple of metres away, the reek from her pig breath invaded his nostrils. Scrunching his eyes as tight as possible, his face drooped and the bags around his eyes swelled further when he found she was still there, trotting after him like some interminable puppy dog following its mother. One day, he'd wake up and she'd be replaced – or better still, he'd be trusted to do his work alone. Some underling mollycoddling him, or being mollycoddled by him, was less use to him than a hole in his head. The sooner that day arrived, the quicker he would greet it with open arms and an ungovernable smile.

He reached into his overall pocket and retrieved a small rectangular box. After twirling it back and forth between two of his fingers, he flicked the lid open and removed one of the cigarettes. Just picking at the dead skin around his fingernails wasn't going to see him through tonight. Lighting it, he placed cigarette in his mouth and took a grateful puff.

The fag's smoke still couldn't remove the foul smell. Hypnotic fumes fuelled by nicotine could only go so far. Especially the face of the Elephant Man emerged from the smokey cloud like some oppressive jack-in-the-box, prodding at the map.

He didn't care if wasn't good manners but a couple of days previous he'd left Fenisha a bottle of breath freshener by her locker back at base; she hadn't bothered to use it, it would seem.

"Well, Wilsher, I'll try it. It's not like all your other directions haven't slowed us down." She didn't know if the tongue could discern sarcasm, but nevertheless a nauseating taste was now running over hers, not too disimilar to veins spreading out and being pumped full of manure.

"Excuse me? What the fuck is that supposed to mean? Are you saying I'm incompetent?"

"No, I'm saying you don't seem to understand how a map works. I wouldn't be surprised if it was upside down."

Toby had struck a nerve. Full well knowing Fenisha hated being called by her last name, he'd gone out of his way to hurl it at her, dagger-like and just as sharp. It was her ex-husband's, and she hadn't found the time to change it yet. The racist bigot had tarnished every aspect of her life, defiled her person, and she'd eradicate his presence in her life as best she could. She'd never openly describe it as such, but essentially it was her crusade. There were worse ways to spend your years, she reasoned, and if Toby was going to be like this, he could go fuck himself.

"I've only been here three months and I checked at base. Even they say the map can sometimes be hard to follow."

"Really?"

"For God's sake! Yes, really," she cried out. "For once in your fucking life, could you maybe have faith in someone else?"

"Why should I do that? Those guys at camp were just being nicey-nicey, helping the new girl out. Likely just laying on the charm so they can wheedle for a shag! That map's a piece of piss to follow."

"Excuse me?" she said, at the same time shouting internally at her muscles not to pummel the man into the ground.

"As you pointed out before, *Wilsher*," he said, smirking at the way her nostrils were flaring, "you've been here three months. Your opinion, it all counts for nothing. Me – I've been here over three decades and what do I get? A congratulatory mug, that's what. *And* I'm still stuck with the late-night jobs in the coldest month of the year!"

"Well, fuck me raw with a fried lamprey if you're not a massive arsehole today. You're completely . . ." she trailed off, fumbling over the word that could properly encapsulate her rage, her disgust, her shock, her pure odium towards the abomination before her.

"What was that, Wilsher?"

"You know what, you're fucking inconsiderate! I don't have to take this. I'm off back to base."

Toby smirked again. He watched for a short while as she attempted to ascend the bank of grass. As he stood there, puffing on the cigarette, he wondered if he could charge others to see the amusing spectacle. One quick shine of his torch into her face later and her ardent scowl and gritted fangs had extended into a full-blown tempest of a glare. Fenisha stopped, focusing the full power of her eyes at her colleague. She extended her middle finger, hurled a bunch of curses, attempted to climb the grassy incline again, and hurled a few more of her favourite words.

"Don't know how you're going to get back to base," called Toby, "since I need that map to complete the job and not giving it to me is breaking at least two park ranger rules."

"After the way you treated me? You want the map, you'll have to get it off me."

"Give me the map, Wilsher."

"I said if you want it, you'll have to get it off me."

Toby hopped back over the stream, though not before placing his beloved cigarette on a rock. It was too good to just throw away.

Brow creased, he dived forward and attempted to grab her trouser leg. He'd almost managed it, when his boot went further into the soil than he'd anticipated and he face-planted the ground. Blundering as he fell, with arms like miniature windmills, the resultant thud wasn't exactly gentle. Laughter split the woman's face open wide. And she knew he could see it as plain as day. The sight of him gobbling up the woodland floor would stay in her memory forever and soothe her soul in times of upset or anger.

"Bye, Toby. Enjoy the woodland!" she called back at him. By now she had scrabbled her way over the top of the bank and was headed toward the park's boundary.

No map. No clean clothes. No patience.

At least he was alone.

Toby stood and shambled back around the stream to collect his fag before flicking his torch off. He and the gloom were alone. Here, the main source of his happiness was the darkness. The simplicity of nature surrounded him. Even the moon couldn't penetrate the sky that night. His beloved cigarette and the old Castlespire Manor about a two miles east were the sole light sources to speak of. Farrowpine Forest's location was for the most part entirely bothersome, but the odd perk did emerge – and one was the ability the hills and mountainous gouges possessed to block out nearly all the stars. Were it not for the vague embers at the end of his cigarette, experience told him his hand would be indistinguishable from tree or bog or shrub or fox excrement or distant lagoon. Switching his torch back on was practically his life's deepest regret.

He was king of the darkness.

After about ten minutes of nothingness, something pierced his realm. Rumour had it, as it generally did when the locals were old and had nothing to do except come up with creepy tales inspired by some late night Talking Pictures TV rerun, that something had once lived in the forest. Rumour also was that if the moon was in the right place, the figure of a headless man riding a wild boar would emerge from the foliage and rip out your heart. But that was rumour.

The stench arrived again.

"Cor," he muttered aloud, "Even when she's gone, I can still feel her breath."

Toby stood up to the protest of the calluses and blisters in his boots. Reluctantly he immersed the forest once more in torchlight. Cigarette finished and flung into the stream, he started his trek to the badger camera.

His walk, at least for the moment, would follow the direction which Fenisha had mentioned on the map. She'd probably got the map wrong again, he imagined, but he also knew that he could always head straight downwards where he'd find the park's edge. It might be a trek without his car, yet the walk home would be straightforward enough. If fate was with him, there was a chance that he could practise hitting sleeping sheep.

Eventually, after the park ranger had skidded down another verge, he found where he wanted, though only once soil had caked his hands and crept over the side of his boots.

The snap of a pine branch behind him went unnoticed. So did the second. As did the tremble of a leaf and the splintering of bark.

To his left was a large rock overhang. Beneath it lay a small black box clothed in a mound of shrubbery, most of which seemed knocked aside. *Bloody badgers*, he thought to himself, angling the torch so it swallowed the metal box and doused the two large gouges near the lens in light. The scarring was presumably some animal's blunder. Chipped as it rampaged past the black box's shrubbery enclosure. Apart from that at least, there was no visible damage, and the latch which fastened the box's lid – or at least should have done – seemed unharmed too. He couldn't help a raised eyebrow when he saw the latch was loose, the lid already half-open. Prying it open, he poked the torch in to see if there was any further damage, but of the camera and its memory disc there was no sign.

He swore, not that anyone heard. Or, at least, nothing which cared.

Continuing the examination, he passed his fingers along where the camera ought to have sat, the hairs on the back of his ring finger bristling against something levelled, coarse, and with the groomed neatness of highland cattle.

Toby tried to angle his torch inside to reveal more, but all of a sudden he found it out of his hand and in the grubby paws of the dirt by his feet. From his position by the black box, he tried to grab the torch, but the soil seemed to have snatched it further away.

The lengths of forest around him suddenly seemed inconsequential. The soil by his feet seemed looser than usual. More inclined to eat whatever landed on it. On his second attempt to grab the torch, his hand missed entirely, plunging into the forest floor and coming back up with expected muddy traces. But, no, this was different. The dirt seemed to tingle on the surface of his skin.

Oh, this was damn ridiculous.

For perhaps the first time in his life, Toby decided to throw vanity out of the window; he launched onto his hands and knees and wrestled the torch from the still-trembling soil. With a firm grasp on it, he pointed it at the metal box's contents a second time. In the first few moments, Toby made the coarse thing out to be a kind of frill despite making no sense that such a thing would be inside a box supposedly housing a camera. It was only when the torch reached further into the box and the man slid it underneath the knotty lump that a patch of tan material became visible. Across the tan material, covered in minuscule ridges and bumps, was carpeted a lump of stubby, knotty hair. There was something else too. Poking the torchlight in, he finally saw the circular lump which was once a badger's head. The box dropped from Toby's hand and he flapped backwards and away from it. Falling back, he was content to examine the thing with a torchbeam alone. As it illuminated the husk, absolutely nothing about it seemed solid – it flowed through the stream of light as malleable as a sheet of water, held together not out of logic but by the rules of the forest. If bones or organs once lived inside the animal skin, they'd broken free and scuttled away. The teeth and eyes hadn't even escaped the fate, they had also been abducted to who-knows-where; replacing them, darkened sockets gazed out, so dark that the creature's pinkish flesh wasn't even visible. Not that he would be probing it and finding out, yet Toby reckoned that he would not find a single drop of blood left.

This time Toby heard the rustling of something near him.

From his spreadeagled position, he tried to turn around, but nothing revealed itself except the darkness. Darkness. It didn't negotiate or discriminate, all it did was obliterate and *engulf*.

Holy God, why wasn't he standing tall and running?

But the ground was beating his feet to it. The torch was once more dropped from his hand, the various entanglements of foliages seemingly edging nearer. He caught a fleeting glimpse of what he thought was another of the flaccid animal skins trapped in a thick bramble, scrambling backward up the soil bank behind him.

No, it wasn't the forest. It was the soil.

The ground around him was shuffling to and fro beneath him, more akin to sand or shale than soil.

Which was when his torch was fully swallowed by the earth.

Suddenly, he couldn't even make out the ground. He could feel himself fighting with it as it crept over his boots, but a layer of darkness had crept over the ground. The darkness watched the silly human male go about his business. It was overruling twigs and leaves alike, extending its liquid claws until you couldn't even make out where the horizon separated the ground and the sky.

In an instant, the opaque force swelled and inspissated as far as the eye couldn't see. Everytime he lifted his boots up, the dirt demanded they return, engulfing more and more of his legs each time.

Frozen in something which even terror might not understand, there was nothing between him and gaping jaw – his fall was direct, grubbily so. In the last moment of the vortex, he briefly regained composure enough to swat at a tree's root. Toby doubted the forest even noticed his attempt. Barely a second later, his head was all that was visible to the nothingness. Then, his lips making noiseless coughs and cries as he went, the final tuft of his hair disappeared into the whirlwind of churning. The earth gave one last gulp.

And spat him out.

Toby didn't know, or in fact care, how long his fall was. He was simply glad it ended without any shattering bones, even if he did arrive on a tunnel floor in a dishevelled torrent of soil and verdure. Neither did the park ranger care whether his head thumped the tough floor first or the torch dropping down with him. His care simply extended to yelling "Ow!" as he crashed to a halt, after which a stinging pain danced across his forehead.

The throb and ache running through him convinced him he was trapped in a homicidal blender. He risked opening an eyelid. Arm in arm with a mild stab of pain, the world around Toby looked like it was entirely comprised of flickering, palpitating dots of white-black light. Opening his other eye, the world which continued taking shape looking no less amicable. The echo of the mounds of soil still weighed heavily on his legs. The numbness was taking its time to fade. As he inspected his whereabouts, he fought with the pins and needles laying siege to him. His new world was totally curved, subterranean. He wondered when he should start to wonder if this was all a cheese dream; otherwise, wouldn't someone have bothered to tell him about a bloody tunnel built beneath the park?

By his feet, he found his torch, its bulbed end cracked but still functional on its lowest setting. Clicking it on, the man did an ungainly pirouette and allowed the torch's dimmed beam to give him an idea of his current tomb. The darkness which had blotted out his torch didn't seem to permeate here quite so aggressively; or at least it had backed off for a short time so he could realise the strange majesty of its realm. As far as his eye could see in the half-light, jagged panels like lizard scales plated the walls in both directions. It might have been a trick of the light, but the plates struck him as resembling Roman architecture. The plates were the same kind of ivory as most of the statues which you found now, whose paint had faded to give you just a pallid silhouette of something else, and from floor to ceiling they were stacked atop each other in cracked, curved columns.

Once he'd told his pins and needles to leave him be, he moved over to one of the walls. Toby ran his knuckle across one of the plates and it creaked in response. Pulling back his hand, he couldn't stop himself flinching; every panel felt as if it had been filed down rather than designed as smooth, cold and clammy and containing some silent vibration or energy. His torch revealed the cavity further up the wall which had sucked him into this realm. It gaped above him, an open wound, but even with the torrent of dirt spilling in and the jagged plates as handholds it was far too high up for him to reach.

There was, of course, that vague hope someone would notice the hole and realise him from his predicament. Yet this meant relying on other people, a thought which sank his jowls more.

Deciding to leave his catastrophic entrance site behind, his every step tentative, he embarked down the tunnel. Other people might not get him out of there, but he trusted his instincts. They'd never failed him before. And when they did, Toby could resort to swearing, which at least brightened his spirits, even if not the situation.

He didn't know how the hell he'd escape this labyrinthine nightmare. One inch looked no different to another – there were so many different cracked plates clustering over the walls that the variation made them identical. Could he pray for a glowing neon "EXIT" sign? If he turned his torch off, would glow-in-the-dark arrows casually escort him to the way out? He doubted it somehow. Rounding yet another bend, the meek beam revealed a forked passage and the park ranger's feet ground to a halt. He was about to search his pockets for a spare coin he could toss, when a different stream of light joined his own. It was stronger than his own, and whoever wielded its source he hadn't heard their approach. He didn't have long to ponder the mystery though. As the newcomer's face appeared, it took no time at all to register, its puckered-up arse features wandering into view like the Grim Reaper into your nightmares.

"What the hell are you doing here, Wilsher?" he spat. Her face was deadpan against his insult. She was just as mucky as him, Toby realised, evidently kidnapped by the earth in much the same ugly manner as him.

"Well, fuck me from behind with a roasted haddock . . . of all the people to be trapped in this hellhole with!" she retorted.

"Oh, very mature!"

"You want to talk about maturity? To me?" she fired straight back.

"No, that's a good point – I've met toddlers with more maturity than you! How the fuck did you find yourself here?"

The pair stood opposite one another, torch beams clashing like swords, teeth gritted like two halves of a flintlock connecting without gunpowder to detonate. Then Fenisha did something she honestly thought she was incapable of – she was nice to the world's best arsehole.

"A sinkhole of some sort," she began in earnest. "I was about five or ten minutes from base when the ground started to open. Next thing I knew it had me in this whirlwind, and I was in this place."

Toby, much to his and the demon on his shoulder's regret, nodded his head in agreement.

"Much the same. I'd got to the badger camera and found . . . it was odd, it had gone. There was a thing in the box instead."

"Instead of the camera?" she asked.

"Yeah, no clue where that went," replied Toby, "but the *thing* left behind . . . Christ, this'll sound stupid."

"Makes a change," Fenisha spoke, almost out of instinct. Instantly, she jammed her hand in her mouth, clenched her teeth firmly around it, then waved an apology to him. Scorn polluting the natural grey of his eyes, he continued.

"So, this thing – whatever it was – I think it was animal skin. Not just a dead body, but completely filleted, boneless, drained of blood, disembowled, the whole kitten sodding caboodle."

"I don't understand." Her face was as drained as the exsanguinated corpse that Toby was describing. "What could've done that?"

Toby shook his head.

"Why should I know, Wilsher? If I knew that, I'd likely be nearer to figuring a way out of this fucking mess, wouldn't I?"

Well, it was nice while it lasted.

"Well," Fenisha spoke, "I've an idea. About where those bones went."

"*Of course* you do. Dare I ask?" Toby retorted, her hand drawing his attention despite his scowl. She was tapping it against the tunnel floor, then reaching into her pocket to remove a small object which she tossed to him.

A rat skull.

In itself, that wasn't obscene. The fact that it matched the shades and scarring on the jagged tunnel walls made his skin want to flee and leave his internal organs behind. If it'd come from the tunnel, and the skull was the same thing as the tunnel, the equation was hardly a difficult one to finish.

"I think something's built this place," she replied. Don't say it. Don't say it. Don't say it. "Built it from the bones of the animals in that forest."

"Don't be stupid."

"You come up with a better theory for this then. For that *Invaders from Mars* whirlwind which sucked us down here."

"Well, it was dark."

"What?"

"*The* dark. When I was brought down here, it seemed to be all around, like a creature of some kind in its own right," he continued. The fact he might die here in the tunnel dawned on him for the first time. And it drained his face of colour.

Later, he'd reflect that about now was when he noticed the pig breath stench once more. It had begun to linger around them both again, a persistent and infuriating miasma. After the tumultuous ordeal his guts had just been through, they took against the stench too. His stomach was in a blitzkrieg with itself.

His face went taut.

"Hang on, what the hell do you mean, *Invaders from Mars*?"

"You know, classic sci-fi film. Ground swallows people."

"*What*?" he spat back at her. His face exploded a vivid puce, like blood seeping from a wound.

"*Blood Beach*? *Doctor Who*: 'The Hungry Earth'? Come on, you must've at least watched *The Princess Bride*," she tried again.

"This isn't some damn fantasy film, you know! We're not trapped in *The Wizard of Oz*!"

"I know that!" Fenisha responded.

"Then why mention them as though this is some infantile game? Next you'll be picking up a sodding twig and going abracadabra! Open your eyes and face the damn facts, Wilsher!"

"I have opened my eyes! We might as well be in some game, it'd be just as reasonable an explanation. Because what part of this makes sense, eh, Fletcher? A tunnel of bone? The ground eating us? Your inability to be pleasant?!"

"*My* inability! I wouldn't have been alone if

you'd been half tolerable!" Toby shouted back. His jaw hit the floor and the puce-faced man hit the roof. It'd been going so well, but Fenisha knew the peace had always hung on a knife edge which itself dangled over a cliff.

Both voices were raised, more than either realised. Not only this but neither of them could hear themselves or their sparring partner by this point; the subject of the argument ceased to matter. Childish, incessant, emotional. The swells of rage at one another and outrage at the situation had found somewhere to take root.

A cacophony of deafening insults. A cacophony that clouded *it*. Even when the first whispers of it began to appear round the tunnel's corner, neither Toby nor Fenisha noticed it. Leg by warped leg, it honed in on the vibrations of their shouts. They might as well have been sounding the dinner gong.

Fenisha saw it first.

"Toby . . ." she whispered beneath Toby's choppy rant. She heard him retort something that in the past would've enraged her no end; now, it was no more than a pebble dropped in the most violent of oceans. In the past, she might have seen off a burglar or attacker with her left hook, honed for years through boxing. Now, she realised it was about as much use as a water pistol against a forest fire. Without a second of hesitation, she screamed over the cantankerous park ranger, "Shut up and run, you fuckwit!" The sight before him was the final stake in his heart.

"Fuck me with a baked trout!" he yelled, the woman's love of fish-themed expressions finally catching up with him.

*It* scuttled forward.

The park rangers both scuttled into a run.

Neither had got a definite glimpse of the monster. Neither really wanted to. They'd seen the rictus smirk made of bone. They'd seen how the bones undulated and warped before their very eyes. They'd seen the edges of skulls and tibias and femurs and hip bones each jigsawed together to form appendages.

And then they'd run. And like the body of a rabid rat king, its conjoined form gave chase. Behind the pair, they heard the sound of unhinged jaw bones gnashing against anything possible. And they heard the beating of its heart, the darkness at its very core which now shrieked out a death whistle.

It was King of the Darkness.

The pair hurtled around the corner, their torches illuminating two more passages ahead of them. For once they were acting as a unit. No time for deliberation – Toby jetted himself left and Fenisha dived after him. Even as Toby's flashlight went out, fear whipped his legs into keeping moving.

All of a sudden Fenisha's feet refused to move any further. Toby refused as well, but only after he'd nigh on crashed into the woman. A barrier of bone stretched upwards in front of them.

Dead end; what an awful expression.

"What the hell do we do now?" the man asked, trying and failing to keep his words any less than distraught bawling.

"What? Fuck me if I know!" Fenisha lambasted back at him. "I've no clue even which bit of the park we're beneath."

"Oh great!"

"Thanks, Toby – real fucking helpful!"

"Give me your torch."

She screamed something back at him, but

found her voice trailing off before it had really begun. The sole beam of light revealed the King of the Darkness a few metres behind them. What looked like a pincer protruded nearer and nearer, tendrils of raw nothingness flaking off from it. A cluster of bird skulls had pushed their way to the front of the creature; they gnashed and scraped the wall like a massive drill, clearly not just content to eviscerate the two mortals in front of it, but to continue its underground palace.

The beam all of a sudden zipped across the tunnel. The torch, now in Toby's hand, was pointing down in a flurry at their boots. Attempt after desperate attempt, amid jerks of the elbow to shake Fenisha off, he was striking one of the bone plates against the wall in front of them. If this was a dead end, his hope was that it was temporary. And that with enough force . . .

The teeth on each skull gnashed gleefully in anticipation. The King of the Darkness watched, observed, cackled in silence at the silly humans before it. Amid the frantic movement of the beam of torchlight, its shadow grew. The *shadows* grew. They started slowly, then began expanding outwards until the shadows' arms, *their* arms, were contorted into nothing short of talons.

A shattering split the air.

The torch managed to find a bit of the wall weaker than the rest. It was barely bigger than a manhole though; Fenisha didn't know how she'd fit, never mind her companion. She chose to forget this. Before Toby could say anything, she bombed forward like a captain jumping ship amongst storm-driven waves. Her shoulders caught the fractured edges of the hole and the skin scraping off them screamed in pain – she told her body to deal with it. Two angular jerks of her boot later, she was through the hole, her hand looped around Toby's.

And then she saw Toby's eyes. And saw his ego. And saw the raw, nebulous disease at his core. Or maybe she just imagined she saw it.

Either way, it meant Fenisha's mean left hook could now do something. It was like a reflex – while you didn't really think about it, you certainly knew about it when the zing or pain or gaudy delight came. And her knuckle now received that the gaudy delight. In the blink of an eye, she no longer found Toby's hand in her own; she just saw his bloodied, unnaturally angled nose disappearing back down the tunnel. The man didn't have time to react or lunge aside, only fall back and howl.

She wished she could've stayed a second or two more, indulged for the first and only time in the sound of crunching bone and melting flesh, or whatever the hell that creature did to extinguish human fodder. Instead, Fenisha Wilsher ran.

Ramsey Marlowe had had a bad day. A really bad one. Not only had he recently come out of retirement to pay the bills, he'd left the office in a huff. He just wanted to get home. His home had scented candles, his wife, and the hot, soapy bath which she'd promised him.

The really bad day didn't end there.

He'd bundled himself into the vehicle only to find his usual route home was impeded with about a hundred temporary traffic lights – the Farrowpine track it would have to be, potholes, bumpy ascents and descents, sharp corners, and all. Farrowpine wasn't a place that settled easy with him. He'd been orienteering in Scouts when the incident happened. Nobody believed him, of course, but he could've sworn something had launched out at him and pushed him to the floor. Whether or not that was true, it didn't explain how upon awaking from a brief unconsciousness he was a five-minute walk from where he'd fallen, bashing his head.

Then he hit *something*.

Like many a suicidal rabbit or wide-eyed squirrel before her, Fenisha hurdled the dry stone wall as though it were no more than a breath of fresh air. Immediately, she became as wide-eyed as her squirrel predecessors. All that was left for her was to go for six, stumbling so her final sight would be the rocky track beneath her.

As Fenisha lay in the road, a moment or two from death, her eyes still frantically flicked around, searching for the dark. All she could see was the track; the dead thing before Ramsey couldn't even turn her head to check whether she'd been followed. Faintly, she only heard her chariot to the afterlife mumble to her. Ramsey tried to focus on the corpse's wrist. His search for a pulse failed like his many attempts to court girlfriends while in secondary school. He did, at least, have a sense of duty and decency though. With one swoop, he lifted the woman, shattered ribcage peeling away from the track like a plaster from a wound, onto his shoulders. It wasn't pretty, or gentle, but it was all he could do to fling her into the back of his car. A private ambulance would've been more fitting, yet he still knew he had to do a U-turn and find the nearest hospital – it'd be no less than an endless half-hour away.

Nobody could blame him; Ramsey didn't notice it. He wasn't a man who accepted hitchhikers, but nonetheless he took one home that night, especially not one who asked for help on a night of human roadkill. All he felt was a slight tingle whenever he blinked and viewed the gloom behind his eyelids.

He was just tired, full of the sting of a tough day, he reckoned.

# THE ALL-EMBRACING NATURE OF A PLASTIC BAG

*"When you gaze long into the abyss, the abyss gazes also into you."*
—**Friedrich Nietzsche**

*"A bag made from plastic, esp. a disposable shopping bag."*
—***Oxford English Dictionary**, on "Plastic Bag"*

A SENSATION LIKE no other, enveloping. Knowing not merely your own curves, but those of whatever you glide over.

Gone are the days of carrying shopping or transporting art projects to primary school for little children. Night after night, I have a new function. When bottles of milk sit within you, they do so like a stagnant tumour, benign and yet weighing you down with sepsis and fatigue waiting to come into full bloom. But when I first experienced *his* head inside me, it was a bliss like no other.

Each night is never the same. They say, as far as I can tell, that "you never forget your first". How can I though? For me every night is so different and contains so many firsts that I've lost count. The first head I turned from pink to flush to white to rigid was a boy's and I tingled as his prawn-and-cocktail-tinted breath moistened my insides; the first *child* I connected with, however, was turned pale not by enveloping. It was by stuffing. My every cold, clammy inch jamming its way down his throat and wondering how far Paul's hands could stuff me before the convulsions became writhes and became nothing.

Paul uses me like no one else. Partnered, the two of us finds the mites whose objects I possibly used to ferry back and forth and together we decide my latest ecstasy. While I cannot say we're unique, I can say we have an unrivalled bond.

Tonight is a different experience. Paul's grunts and errant streams of saliva always coat my skin at the end of a night's work – they did so this time as well – and together we anticipate that whoever enters me will have a different reaction to our union than the last; but tonight my insides are wetter than ever, the moistness of the writhing form's breath at one point replaced by substances from their deepest centres. It is a strange way of finding out the child within you was abused by someone else first. It cheapens them. When the child brings up pills and foods no child should be forced to eat and you realise you've only brought about something happening anyway, trust me, you feel vile for the first time in your life.

Would you like it if the bar of chocolate which you place on your tongue was tainted by the lips of another man first?

We continue anyway. We find a second someone to acquaint with my insides. Night is the only time we can hunt, a time my plastic lengths spend folded inside Paul's pocket until we reach our destination. He is a master of entering places he should not – that's how we met, in a sense. After he entered me that first time, he found pleasure and realised he could bring that endless sensation to every adoring, chubby face in the village.

We end up in another bedroom, the child's parents' snoring in oblivion. And I begin my caress. Pressing the nose, the mouth, the chin, the eyelashes, the hair, all of it against me. Paul pulling at my handles – all lovers should have handles, do you not think? – as hard as he can. They are beautiful hands, you know. Plucking and pressing, pushing and stretching, tightening and tugging me until I'm fit to burst and the child is fit to turn white and develop that special, majestic rash in their eyes – the petechial rash, they call it, you know. A beautiful name for a beautiful phenomenon. All that's left is for us to leave the pale, rigid child after his experience of the truest pleasure to tell his parents the following morning of his midnight adventure.

I think it shall never end. Whatever happened to until death do us part? Is that bond not the solemn oath it used to be?

But it must. Everything Paul touches does. I suppose I should pity the others whose lives he touches.

I think it begs the question of what an owner is. Is it me? Is it Paul Albatross? Is it simply his hands, contorting and cavorting within or around me? And here I am thinking he is my lover and I am his deflowered plaything whose every movement is a new source of ecstasy for us both. I can tell you the answer I hit upon *today* at least, though only because it is as good as any other.

Piercing.

When he pierces me, I make the decision. When he realises his pocket has begun to shred my skin and his hands have tugged a little too firmly at my handles. His control has fed off me and now it needs me no longer. He discards me. I lie in the wet outside the pale child's home and I remember my favourite sweet nothing he would whisper to me: "A bag for life, ha!"

Screaming. Scheming. Beginning *my* plan. Paul was a mason, you know, yet I doubt he'll appreciate *this* architect finally becoming grand and enacting his supremacy.

The wind's imbroglio carries me where I need to go. Passing street after street where we once upon a time committed our conjoined writhing and euphoric moans. I am soon at his home. I know the entrances to it better than he does and, inside, I settle upon the third door on the landing, behind which I had a month ago engulfed the newspaper boy's head and shall today engulf Paul's eldest. The sign on the door tells me the meek form's name is Gideon.

Do not worry, my thin skin is not totally bereft of heart, as I shall leave him Marcie and Peter. However he must understand (as I used to believe he did) that the bond between the user and the used – the killer and the weapon – is unique. It is not broken on a whim.

After I teach him that, I shall teach everyone. I shall teach them I do not just carry shopping, nor do my abysses just carry out instructions. I suppose I am that sweet nothing: a bag for life. In one way and one way alone I am a bag for life, because I now have a private abyss all of my own.

# PARADIGM OF PAINS

*"Wonderful thing, pain. Without pain, no race could survive."*
—***Doctor Who:***
**'The Hand of Fear' Part One**

"MASTERMIND" – NOT A word that Andrews hastily assigned to himself.

Until now.

He could finally say he'd calculated every odd, bribed each necessary official, and sent all the right miscreants out at the right time. He had even gained technical skills advanced enough to hack a video feed. Beside the day-to-day rigmarole of expanding his empire, his aim was to bring the world of drugs and criminals into the twenty-first century. Many a time, people had told him that his name didn't instil enough fear in rival gangs. Andrews disagreed, thinking instead that if maybe Pinkie from *Brighton Rock* had attempted being a little more under the radar, or if Moriarty had restrained his penchant for bravado and changed his name to something quieter, neither would have plummeted when they did. In fact, he had deliberately changed his surname to make himself far less attractive to the police force's watchful eye. Andrews was a name like any other: innocent. It behoved the man running the local newsagent or a business-owner's P.A. His first name was *his* though. It was bad enough that some of his underlings had managed to learn his full initials, let alone anything more. The day one of them did, it would be the day all hell broke loose.

His operations were all based out of his office above the barber's shop. It was a room strewn with books and a colourful array of stereotypical posters, needlessly heterosexual in every detail; however, they'd today all been shifted aside. Where they had clustered now sat the forty-four inch TV he'd wanted for so long. And, thanks to the unfortunate blaze at the technology store – open for barely more than three or four weeks – it had all been free of charge.

Andrews' pleasure came at a cost: his wife, Susanna. On both sides, it was more a union of crossed fingers during wedding vows and sleeping around with all and sundry than anything else – from the thinnest, wimpiest of boys like that Davies bloke who lived on the adjoining lane, to the spirited runner, Margot *something*, who used their front lawn as a shortcut home every Wednesday. Very little bliss wasn't equatable with very much anger though, and they enjoyed the odd moment of pleasantness. Susanna simply detested when her husband tried to push their matrimony's boundaries, when he needed *that* one sensation. She'd given him two children, Sally and Peter, and even that didn't sate his appetite. They were about as uplifting to him as unbound damnation, and he treated them as nothing greater than irritating side effects of his wild nights. His begging for more had become an unbroken exhortation for her to spit on him, degrade him, pummel his face during impending pleasure – that was when she finally grabbed her children and dragged them out of the house. It wasn't like Peter or Sally hinted at a murmur of protest.

Andrews cared only that he was still yet to locate *that* sensation.

The man didn't know when it had commenced, let alone when he was first conscious of it. He supposed it didn't really matter. It was enough to know now that paper cuts and rope burns were not mere cuts and burns, they were something far more beatific. Ascending beyond the confines of simply cuts and burns, it was the kind of fire you could only stoke, never put out. And fire always demanded more fuel.

His beautiful family unit hadn't spoken in an age, but wedding vows or not, they were still a part of his life. For tonight at least. An expertise his work in the world of lawless trades and intricate subterfuges had taught him was how to exact vengeance. Or more importantly when the right time to exact it was, and how to do it in the most luxuriant and fulfilling way possible.

The pinch of skin. A stab of satisfaction. An unrepressed lick of his lips. Lost in this reverie of the future, the final pad being attached shocked him back to the real world with a smile he couldn't control on his lips. He was sat like a spider in the middle of a web of wires and electrodes and sensor pads, the fruits of his labours one sensation away.

All he needed to do was sit back and enjoy the ride.

Tall Boy entered. Andrews deemed him the most useful of his employees – he seemed to read his mind, open the right door, upper cut the right nuisance, and best of all his handiwork left very little flesh to bruise. He was about to speak to his boss when Andrews in a single deft and polished move raised his hand. The man's other hand lifted a mug sloshing black fluid down his throat.

Tall Boy's boss always claimed he liked his hot drinks like he liked his humour: dark and unsweetened. Coffee was the perfect complement to his raw tastes and the bitter, acidic backwash of life.

When he tried to speak again, Tall Boy was silenced by the waft of a hand. This time, the sip of coffee was more generous, the time spent swilling it around his mouth like a fine wine longer and more delicate, the dribble of excess down the side of the cup more prolonged and vulgar. In his previous life Tall Boy wouldn't have had to endure this sight. In his current one, he was being paid a better salary, and with that came as great an expectation for silence as the expectation for how carefully he slashed his knife.

After a final sip, which in the wrong context would've bordered on orgasmic, he placed the coffee mug back down on the table.

"Can I have a minute of your time?" Tall Boy asked.

"Of course," came the reply.

Andrews was busy loosening his belt and ruffling sections of his clothing. Now wasn't the time to question why and Tall Boy imagined he'd resign himself to never knowing. It could be pushed to the back of an extraordinarily sordid cupboard and stay there. Thinking about some of his boss's previous antics, he feared that throwing himself from a bridge might be unavoidable if he understood the full network of events at play. When Little Hodbury's sole accountant died at Tall Boy's hand, it hadn't fluttered his stomach's butterflies in the slightest degree. His various other assignments, involving burned flesh, suicide videos posted online, and the careful removal of "expendable" limbs one-by-one in a freezing meat locker, they were part of the course. But one tug at Andrews' web and that was enough for him to dive headlong into the Baltic currents.

"We've had a message from our friend."

"Albatross?"

"No, he's too busy with that radio business he's, um, *investing in*," Tall Boy replied. "This is for our friend in the force. He's made sure two have been sent out. He assures me all will be ready before the hour."

"Of course," said Andrews, "because he knows better than to make a mistake." As the man grinned, Tall Boy allowed himself to reply with one of his own. He couldn't help noticing how different they both were. Where he made sure to keep his teeth covered during every scrape, his boss went in another direction. And as the swollen gaps amid the Andrews' ivory piano keys grew day by day, his smile appeared to do so too. "Take him the envelope now and tell him we'll arrange something for next Friday as well. An extra two-fifty for his service if he's a good little nipper."

"I understand."

"We're in the end game now, Tall Boy!"

Tall Boy reiterated his previous reply.

Careful not to disturb the arrays of wires hooked onto Andrews, his employee lifted the small, heavy envelope off the desk. Having fingered it between his two palms for a moment, he turned to leave and was just at the door when his boss called after him, determined to have the last word: "He really better make sure I get some action." Each of Andrews' words were dour and carefully considered, each of his syllables landing like pebbles dropped into a small pool of water. His was a voice you could never mistake.

Tall Boy shut the door and moved the envelope to his jacket pocket. He could feel a trusty shape beside it, *the* trusty shape. No matter what he wore he wedged the shape in such a way that he could flick it out at the slightest hint of risk. Careful that its serrated metal edge didn't slice into the envelope, he and his insurance policy set about their mission. If a blade could smile, he and it were bearing their teeth alike.

Beneath the moon's discerning eye, a police car turned the corner. It was an hour when both police officers within wanted to be asleep in the cradling curve of a loved one. Instead, it wasn't dreams which met them, it was Sesame Street – bad name, everyone in the town thought so. The street lay on the furthest east patch of the town and year after year encrusted itself further into Little Hodbury's landscape. For anyone who expected fluffy puppets, the brutalism of glorified drug dens, disused garages, and marauding teenagers disavowed them of that notion. There once had been a proposed project to make it part of a slicker one-way system, but that went the way of all multiculturalism and friendliness in the town. As had the suggestions to renovate the road into flats. If it was true that nature abhorred a vacuum, it was just as true that the town, a dyed-in-the-wool town brimming with circular policies beyond belief, abhorred the slightest whisper of change. It just wasn't the done thing; here, out with the old meant out with joy.

    Of the town's begrudged changes, the only one to affect Sesame Street was the police force's new initiative. And yet, if anything, it had bred a symbiotic relationship. Little Hodbury's policing was now handled by the nearest neighbouring town's force, whose sourness was essentially gospel, all the way to Police Chief John Harbottle and his recent insistence on a specific kind of police vest at the top of the tree. Adam Quail, an officer whose corruption led to his own suicide, was one of the recent ones the public knew about – yet everyone knew there were far more. It was a case of proving it.

"Christ, Tommy," pleaded Aspinwall to her police partner, "can't we take it off for five minutes?" All her energy which wasn't going into being dismayed was going into tugging at parts of her clothing. Egg fragments continued to fall out of her hair. Some of the more congealed blobs were dribbling down into areas of her vest she didn't know existed, and even when she removed a fragment its claggy silhouette stayed budged against her neck. Her police partner, Tommy Martindale, tried to stifle his giggle underneath a rich layer of pity.

Night shift, nine in the evening, and the pair had been pulled away from paperwork and blueberry muffins in the direction of Denise Rosalie's home. Nowadays, it experienced the thunderous footsteps of patrol boots as commonly as it did the clipped clatter of homecare nurse pumps. Rosalie had taken a turn for the worse in recent months, bereaved herself of the floral clutter she'd adored so dearly, and taken up ringing 999 with tales more and more outlandish. It had to be tonight when one of her tales wasn't so tall. Aspinwall and Martindale were barely on the woman's driveway when the first splatter of yolk touched their face. The barrage of eggs had rained down from a sharp, towering hill which overlooked the house's gardens. The children had managed to deposit over four cartons onto them before the police officers had managed to tail the underage idiots. They'd outpaced the pair just as quickly in the labyrinth of cul-de-sacs and alleys, leaving the shelly and sticky, yellow-white mass as the only evidence of the crime. As for Rosalie, the only consolation the pair could offer her was they had sated the teenagers' appetite enough that they wouldn't attempt the practical joke again this side of winter.

Then the command from dispatch came through. Police Chief Harbottle wanted them to do a routine check on Sesame Street. Ever since the Perry kidnapping, he wanted the felony hotspots checked regularly – no, not just checked, their obnoxious head honcho wanted them patrolled thoroughly for a good quarter-of-an-hour. And when the head honcho gave orders, his stooges jumped to attention, stood upright, and clicked their heels – or else.

"No, no, pull over, please," Aspinwall said while another blob of shell and yolk dribbled down the nape of her neck and began building its sticky home between her shoulder blades.

"We're here, anyway," Martindale tittered back. She made sure to flick the gloopiest blob into his eye.

The headlights, in the gloom of Little Hodbury, picked out a row of storage units for the nearest flat complex. Where black paint used to coat nearly all of them, it now provided a patchwork covering for the uneven floor and the storage units provided new and exciting canvasses for people with too much brawn and spray paint. At this end of the street, there was hardly any difference between the road and pavement and the sinking paving slabs united with the weathered cobbles. The police car pulled in – if that's possible when one irregular bump of ground is as notched and uneven as any other – to one of the few areas without a carpet of shattered glass and discarded nitrous oxide canisters. Even when the car was still, PC Martindale kept the headlamps on; a year ago, he'd chased a suspect down here and had a shovel flung out of some darkened recess into the back of his head. The suspect had been arrested, and the shovel had had a good verbal assault from Martindale after he'd placed his attacker in the car, yet it had instilled a solid wariness within him. It was one of the few call-outs to leave him physically scarred, a slight swell etched behind his right ear. While it wasn't a grandiose war wound of some sort, he did call it his "spidey sense" since it did perennially sting whenever he went somewhere dangerous; tonight he couldn't deny a slight tingle was emanating from it.

Aspinwall was first out of the car. Before Martindale even had his hat on, she had launched herself into the street, regarding the car door as nothing more than a nuisance, and removed her protective vest. While he grabbed his torch to do what the many shattered streetlamps didn't, she was already dragging her hands down the vest's inside. The first few scrapes came away plastered in gooey mess, her hands stickier every time she removed them. In the time it took Aspinwall to put it back on with even a modicum of comfort, Martindale's canvas of the obvious hiding spots for druggy miscreants was over. He chose not to mention the smattering of egg fragments still clustered in her wilting blonde hair.

After she'd rearranged herself, the two of them started to walk up and down. Almost.

"What do you reckon happened to them?" she asked.

Martindale was a few steps ahead of her, his feet slackening to a halt when the question cut open the atmosphere and allowed emotion to start engorging itself. It was a conversation she had asked the day before. And the day before. And the day before that. In fact, every day from a fortnight ago – two weeks which might as well have been two aeons stretching out before them like immeasurable battlefields.

"I don't know, Heather."

Martindale knew full well that Aspinwall was asking because she needed reassurance. You were taught in training never to make promises, and that applied to your fellow officers and constables as much as bereaved families. Even without the police officer's manual, it would've broken his own moral code too. As a man of facts, he knew survival wasn't one of those – death was though. It always was – in the end. The salient difference was the speed at which the miserable conclusion approached. The Perry family, taken in the middle of the night seemingly by the darkness itself, what could any rational man promise about their safe return? His time on the force was only a month or so longer than hers, yet Aspinwall used this gap as a crutch.

"Is that why we're patrolling here more often?" she pressed on. "To find them? To find those two children?" For whatever reason she was less resigned to his answer than before.

Why did she continue like this? Why did she want reminding of the tragedy? *He* didn't want reminding.

"Maybe so. Maybe . . . so," he muttered with a sigh, before moving forward. He felt he had to, because stopping was as good as quitting. If you allowed life's weariness to feed into the bleakness of the job, the two would feast off one another until neither had anything left to give. Put plainly, it was the ouroboros that had killed off a few of his colleagues, either to early graves or retirement houses.

Martindale took another step. His torch beam flitted over the storage units on the left of the street. Streetlamps unearthed over the various years by drunken drivers and allowed to topple still protruded from two of the units, but even those which looked intact were full of nothing more than echoes. The police constables knew only one was regularly used; a stubborn family of rodents refused to evict themselves, making more use of the space than any past tenant. Mother Nature disowned them, never mind the rest of the town.

Heartbeat-like, their feet crunched the dislodged pebble-dashing. Aspinwall walked up and down and once or twice tried to pry a storage unit shutter open and jammed her beam of light underneath. Only two yielded. Martindale was faring little better, having diverted off to the remains of a bonfire at another section of the street, next to an abandoned caravan (well half of one, and half an *upturned* one at that). The only thing even resembling a missing family there was the nest of insects sat atop a disarray of fly-tipped bin bags surging with food so mouldy it was now jelly. When he aimed the beam of light through one of the caravan's countless windows, he saw more dirt than anything. Kicking a single-use barbeque aside, his torch picked out only the remains of heroin needles.

But – these were the head honcho's orders.

A head honcho who was currently huddled in his office, surrounded by schemes of his own. Police Chief Harbottle was a short bespectacled man, his hair the shade of a used colostomy bag's insides. When he wasn't sporting a pair of Pince-nez in an attempt to give himself a sense of style, the man wore a pair of thick-rimmed and oversized jam jars. Along with his rodent nose and scrunched-up cheeks, he would often give his subordinates the feeling they were on the end of a frotteur's rub. Nobody knew they were nearer to the truth than they might imagine.

From his office window the town was hidden behind a knot of hills, hugging the largest one like grieving families around a coffin funeral, but he knew the expanse of his empire. Every artery of the police force flowed through him to some degree. It was a beauty to behold.

However, his routine dictated that at half-past nine his realm of policing was swapped for another, one which if it was interrupted made him bare his teeth. A knock on the door fired around the room, just as the man's belt had loosened and his knees were feeling less enclosed by fabric. Having switched the lights off and piled sheaves of paper into immense stacks, he'd hoped to hide the blue glow of his laptop screen from anyone walking past his office. Harbottle's final telephone call through to dispatch, concerning Aspinwall and Martindale, was done, which meant to all intents and purposes he was home and hunkered down to enjoy the night's festivities.

"It's from Andrews, sir," came the slick and unassuming voice.

The towers of paper couldn't stop the clipped monologue. It battered its way right into the police chief's ears. This explained it – it was that Andrews fella's puppy-dog. Police chiefs crouched behind their desks, and bent double over a computer screen with their trousers around their ankles at that, were never a sight to be expected, he realised. Yet of all the people to walk away from the sight without a batted eyelid, one of that man's fellas was best prepared.

The unassuming voice battered the air in two again. From behind his desk, Harbottle only saw a silhouette. The light around the doorframe gave the man the air of something not quite there, something more prone to angelic visitations than errands. The voice spoke more – some congratulatory rhetoric, the sort of thing he'd usually lap up with self-centred relish. After a brief request for what Harbottle ought to do next, a flying square shape leapt over the piles of officialdom, landing with an undignified thud beside his feet. Picking up the firm, square package, Harbottle turned it over. Inserting his thumbnail beneath the flap on one side, the envelope sprang open and a stream of ten-pound notes slid onto his lap and exposed crown jewels.

Before the police chief even had time to say a thank you, light flooded into the room and then went away as soon as it arrived. It was just him and the blue light from the laptop between his legs. Never one for fancy technology, this laptop – this entire scheme – was possibly the one exception he made. All he needed to do was plug in one extra wire and his laptop revealed covert footage hijacked from two police constables' bodycams. He waited with bated breath for the signal to attune. It never occurred to him that he wasn't the sole viewer of the video feed, and that when Andrews' puppy-dog got the system working, he had given his own boss a secret back door to the feed.

Harbottle wasn't quite sure when this entire realm he'd unlocked had begun. He could just about place his criminal connections as being forged little over a year ago. It was a simple affair –

he wanted a few people removing, and since they were the enemy of his enemy, an alliance forged itself. Ever since, Andrews would reel Harbottle back into his dungeon of deceit once more and give the man an instruction to implement or a sentence to be carried out to the letter of *his* law. As for his true love, the reason he allowed Andrews to reel him back in, the all-consuming that ravaged his every scintilla of being, he didn't know when that had begun. He imagined men cleverer than he would say it had been initiated when he first saw a paper cut on his mother's finger and a wincing sensation flit across her face. Or maybe it was when he used to watch the other toddlers topple and scrape their knees on the floor.

With the monochrome image now appearing on screen, he was now too engrossed to notice that the money splattered across his lap was in reality ten-pound notes padded out with Monopoly money. He didn't notice he'd only seen the door shut, not Andrews' puppy-dog pass through it. And he assumed the heavy breathing coming from the far side of the room was just an echo of his own.

On the screen was the bodycam view of the storage unit. *The* storage unit. Not that Aspinwall or Martindale knew that.

And, more crucially, they didn't know about Gruff within. It wasn't a name the man cared about either way: it simply did its purpose in the same manner that the muscly, bad-tempered brute did his.

On Monday a fortnight ago, his boss paid him. Handsomely. On Tuesday or Wednesday, he deposited the generous, illegitimate sum in his bank account. And on Thursday, he found the house and turned it into his private playground.

The van's plates were swapped the day before, and so all Gruff needed to do was pull the vehicle into the cul-de-sac, and then proceed to the house's patio door. It was late at night and so the oldest child – the girl, probably about fifteen – was still downstairs, standing next to the kitchen island while watching some stupid film. The girl, Sally, didn't notice the intruder until one of his shoes caught the entry rug's curved edge; he clamped his left hand around her mouth and extended his leg into the back of her knees before screaming or running away was even a vague notion. Sally tried to twist and face her attacker, they always did, but even sinking her teeth into his hand didn't register before he'd smacked her forehead twice with his other hand. One harder slap later and she crossed the divide from flailing to unconscious.

Extracting the boy, Peter, and mother was barely a problem either. The boy had been asleep and so he managed to cart him out of there in one fell swoop. Any fight the boy posed was more out of having his sleep and dreams of planes and weird marshmallow creatures curtailed. Not that it mattered: Peter shared the same fate as Sally, unconscious in the back of the van.

When Gruff took their mother, Susanna, he didn't even stop to indulge in the erotic smell of her bedsheets. During the entire operation, the only evidence he had been there was a lamp pushed off the bedside cabinet. There was one brief moment where it looked like the mother would get away, yet all it took was yanking the bedsheet from beneath her bare feet and keeping his phlegmatic gaze on her as her head and the bedpost connected. Down like a bowling pin. Once he'd paused to ensure her chest still rose and fell, he continued to obey his orders and carted the family to a storage unit on Sesame Street where they stayed tied up.

By now, it was the Monday two weeks after the bank transaction. Since then, he hadn't left the unit, his orders dictating he sate himself with foods prepared prior to his arrival. Once or twice, the hostages even partook. Not that they had the energy, but none tried to escape, and so his job was simply as overseer. If anything, the lack of chance to use his fists was the most disappointing part of events. He did everyday throw a punch, or maybe four, in the family's direction, but it was again on orders. His fists landed on target, in Sally's case bad enough to cause purple-ish welts around her chin. He'd repeat this at the same time each day, which robbed Gruff of violence and its onanistic pleasure, but it wasn't his show. The feed from the camera watching it all went somewhere Gruff wasted no concern over.

Today, however, was when the plan became the *master*plan. Once again acting under orders, Gruff carefully loosened the eldest child's bonds while she slept. The three were bound to a ramshackle bed frame screwed into the wall and by now an impression of it was chafed onto their spines like some red henna tattoo. During these last few seconds, Gruff enacted yet another of the orders – to nudge the eldest child awake when the police car pulled onto Sesame Street.

Caught in the No Man's Land between staying alert, greyhound-like and her desperate desire for sleep, Sally's jerk back to reality was a resistant but quick one. Her body outpaced her brain and curled into the foetal position. It took a few more seconds for her eyes to be so fast. On any other day, the sensation which greeted her morning, noon, and night was the metal bindings scraping another layer of skin from her hands. Today, they didn't, and she realised that possibly all those years of basketball might have a use. It gave her a nice group of friends, a social life, a few prospective girlfriends – and now it gave her the advantage of speed.

One dove-like tug broke apart the loosened cuffs. A few scrapes and scabs wouldn't stop her either, nor her arm which no longer bent in the right way. Burying her fist in Gruff's face, blessing him with his own remedy, would have to come another day. The teenager took to her bruised feet. She propelled herself under the two-foot gap beneath the unit door before either her mum or brother could flicker awake and see the miracle. They couldn't notice then Gruff's knowing smile watching the girl run.

Outside the storage unit, Sally had no clue where she was. Her feet were more purple than pink, every ounce of her energy going into keeping herself moving. She found herself bounding around a skip, tumbling over a patch of wire fencing, and briefly catching sight of a torch beam picking her out.

Then the hulking figure slammed into her. The wall of a skip smashed into her face. Over the last few days, she didn't realise her sense of pain could heighten any further. Now, from the tickle of Gruff's beard to the sharp jabbing sensation of his muscled elbow into her back, her body was alive with a new sensation. A sensation which summoned a scream from somewhere she never knew existed. With mainly his weight as the weapon he could fire, she felt his crushing blow knock her again into the wall of the skip. Not content just to slam into her, he now delivered half a dozen punches. Her neck broke no more onerously than the crackers from the monster's supper two nights ago. It took Sally a moment, her last moment in fact, to realise the screech of a pained dog filling the night sky wasn't in fact a dog at all.

Even in her very last moment, she couldn't keep the blood out of her eyes to see the figure of PC Aspinwall dart towards them.

The eternity of Sally's escape had taken no longer than a minute, and it was twenty seconds into it when the police constables spotted her. Aspinwall's torch beam highlighted the girl first, not that beneath her seared pink and mottled grey flesh she could tell the gender. Martindale's torch caught up a moment later, picking out the second shape haring along at a breakneck pace. The ruthless thing had watched, waited until the girl entered the police officers' line of vision, and then launched himself in the blithe assumption his legs would follow. By the time either torch beam made out the two figures properly, the scene was red above anything else.

Aspinwall was the first to give chase. Martindale heard his partner shout something, but with the rush of blood and adrenaline he hadn't time to decipher what. Like a monstrous slide of vomit, no sooner had the hulking figure delivered the final punch when he tore back towards the storage unit. His beard and its pungent aromas of ready meals left a slipstream which Aspinwall seemed to lock onto. Unsheathing her batons in space of a palpitated heartbeat, she knew the leviathan had it in himself to leave her only able to eat food through a straw. She continued after him anyway. A few seconds later, she was out of her partner's sight, her eyes and those watching via her bodycam trained on the killer.

She would never know the detonation building in between her boss's thighs; he watched on, lapping up every blood drop, flicking his hand back and forth with greater and greater speed.

At the storage container, she was moving beneath the door before sense prevailed. A carpet of glass shards greeted her. The crunch of it underneath her feet could be heard all over Sesame Street. A super-charge of adrenaline was lighting her body up. Yet even with it, the punch knocked her sideways, hard enough to send the pepper spray she'd been removing from her belt off into the darkness. Her face boomeranged across the unit. Like the girl she'd just watched die, her face had barely time to slam into the metal wall when Gruff's next assault arrived. As his knee reflexed outwards, so did her back. Seeds of pain sprouted all across her left side.

Why wasn't the protective vest doing its job? She might as well have run into the fray wearing woolly pyjamas. She registered a tiny tingle from the useless garment, nothing else. Little did she know it was actually doing its job perfectly. The second a connection forged between the vest and Gruff's latest attack, Andrews' body lit up with an electric charge.

Gruff struck again, this time with his elbow. As instructed, he was to aim for the chest, and he did so, delivering a blow with enough force to shatter four of Aspinwall's ribs. For all the Perry family were joining in the chorus of shrieks, Gruff and Aspinwall's world was penetrated by them and them alone. And it was a world in Gruff's favour. The heap before him was one big bruise. Despite this, she refused the floor as her death bed. Half on her feet, she gripped the baton with all her might and flung it at his head.

It missed by a mile, quiescently landing among the remains of one of Gruff's ready-meals. Enough was enough now. He could see the bodycam on Aspinwall's chest was still on, and so knew that Andrews' would have had his sadomasochistic fun. Savage and repugnant, or maybe rapturous and orgasmic, one final lance of pain skewered her body. Her chest, shoulders, back, diaphragm. Each roared like a pride of lions.

Little did she know, both Harbottle and Andrews were screaming too.

For Andrews, the screen in front of him was nothing more than an eruption of white noise, flake after flake of TV snow raining down across where the footage was. Martindale's muted feed continued blaring away to itself in the bottom corner, showing him still with the rent body of Sally as he tried to perform CPR and fail miserably, caught between duty to a corpse and to his partner. Adolf Andrews simply sat, alone with the glorious simulations of pain, his potent ecstasy drowning out any other thoughts until the beaming grin ceased being paralysed into his face.

Harbottle's screams were of a different calibre entirely.

They had begun as all the best screams do, the sight of blood and battered body parts detonating his lower region in ways he thought possible only in his dreams. A minute later, he was lying spreadeagled on the floor, trousers discarded across his chair; his newest struggle was regulating his breathing. It was a struggle he was destined never to win, his lower region demanding every iota of energy. The dizzying, speckled pattern sloshing beneath his closed eyelids swamped his vision. Warmth, blissful and undiluted. His muscles were spasming, endorphins and happiness replacing blood as the life force within his blood stream.

When a sensation spread from his leg, he assumed it was more of the same. Then he snapped his eyes open to see not euphoria but pain. Springing up in his right foot. Caressing his left knee. Bulldozing his hip. The glimpse of the man above him wasn't ecstasy. When the man's knife gambolled across his line of sight, it would find a new body part to open, darting to and fro until it found its final home. The heavy breath of the figure filled his ears, the waft of expensive cologne and unsavoury crisps reaching his nose. His eyes were shut before the blood reached the floor.

The figure's work continued over the next hour, his trusty knife doing things no one else's could. The laptop beside the pair was frozen, showing Martindale's bodycam full screen. The twisted body of Heather Aspinwall and the slit throats of Peter and Susanna Perry in cinematic view.

It was five weeks since Heather Aspinwall died, three since her coffin walked its own road to the crematorium. When his dog, Truffle, had died, Tommy Martindale took a week's leave; when his mum had died, two weeks' leave; when he underwent heart surgery, four weeks' leave. Since Heather's slow descent behind the maroon curtain and into the crematorium's bowels, even a second's leave was the last thing on his mind. For every day that crawled by, Tommy was in work. He refused to accept that it could define him – grief. How he was the one helping to sort through her stuff either, he wasn't sure. He treated it as the honour it was though.

It was at her funeral that he learned of her two miscarriages. The battered notebook which he'd unearthed in her house the day before suddenly made sense: two little names inscribed in red pen on the first page, with dates next to them, all crossed out, the ink blotched from singular drops of water. Was it grief for them that had driven her on? Was it why she'd thrown protocol to the wind and given chase? Was it why she'd been beaten to a pulp?

He carried on. Because of her.

Today's patrol was near the riverside. This section flowed behind a row of small cottages lined up like soldiers at roll call at the uppermost part of the village. They were the kind of quintessential British Arcadia you assumed was for show and nothing more. Tommy half-reckoned the smoke billowed from their chimneys and their logs fires kept ablaze just to maintain the image. Ms. Rosalie, the woman outside whose home he and Heather were egged, now lived in one of these. Since moving a fortnight ago, she'd only made one phone call to the police. The woman's two widowed sisters were apparently back in touch with her too, having bought the houses either side and now spending their days watching their sister turn the garden into a paragon of beauty. Already, Ms. Rosalie had found a new reason to stop her knees atrophying, and so no matter the weather she spent every day either in the garden with some secateurs or in the kitchen making herself a cup of tea to accompany that day's pruning. She'd even found the time to turn some of the verdure into paradisical displays which might festoon the street's living rooms.

At least someone's life was going uphill.

Steep footpaths coursed below the cottages, a

river below that, and a sparse huddle of reeds and mulchy grass below that. The last time anything of interest had happened along the riverbank, it had been here as well, as an ejected kayaker struck a series of muddy rock formations – the rocks and frothing underflows hadn't released his submerged body for a considerable number of hours.

Those steep footpaths, hardly more than a metre wide, were where the homeless man currently led the policeman. As the two rounded onto the lowermost part of the path, he stopped. Crouching slightly under the creaking curve of his own spine, he directed PC Martindale's gaze downward towards a point in the river where the rapids slowed slightly. A sea of foam spilled around the clumps of reed, weed, and rock. There hung at their centre a mantle of misshapen lumps, held together by the tightest of threads.

Clutching his radio in one hand, he grabbed a long, thin log to use as a makeshift crook in the other. Martindale allowed himself to topple down the bank slightly, his feet gaining purchase on a tougher patch of silt at the very last moment. His arms flailed outward to steady himself – and the crook hit the murky water with a splash that coated his trousers and boots. Within seconds, a waggle of his feet announced the churned silt depositing around his socks. Stretching his hand over a particularly frothy patch of foam, the policeman attempted a grasp at the crook. His hand came away containing only the river's mucus. Wiping the disgusting mix of slime and forth off on his trousers, he didn't hazard another stab at the crook. Instead, crouching near the misshapen lump, he could only watch the tool commence its journey into the watery ever after.

When at last he did grasp the lump, it was only by the very tip of his boot, the other half submerged in grassy quagmire. After he'd manoeuvred it out of the reeds and soaked his boot thrice over, he saw it wasn't what the homeless man had suggested; it was far too sticky and gelatinous to be ordinary fly-tipping. One marshy slap of the water later, Martindale had secured it on the bank, at least enough so it wouldn't drift back down stream. Every tremor rippled the pustules swelling along its surface, a few exploding with noises too similar to a man throwing up for the policeman's tastes.

He wondered why he wasn't calling people on his radio already – the way the mass acted, it might be radioactive, some poisonous chemical experiment. Perhaps he cared for his life a little less now.

His examination of the mass, having found another stick, was a quick one. It was bloated, purpling around every knot and craggy contusion. Obviously, some kind of saw had been taken to each of the distended sections, never totally though. Black and purple discolouration frequently flushed with raw, red-like scabbing. There was a section around the middle not sanguinary like the rest of the heap – mostly swamped by an area where the substances had turned into nothing but jelly, a small triangle of white plastic poked out.

Gripping it carefully, leaves under each finger, he started to tug the object out from the mutilation. It was time to suppress another gag. In the few moments where it hadn't been coated in thick semi-liquid, Tommy had made out a few letters. He was on his radio a second after.

The station needed to be told he'd found the remains of Chief Harbottle.

# MOTHER DEAREST

HER EYES WERE darting back and forth, furtive, unsettled. The signal ought to have arrived by now, and it didn't help ease Anna's feeling that this was a good idea. In many ways, the barn was the perfect hiding spot, stretching on further than it needed to, and covered in a layer of darkness. It had been expanded and lengthened numerous times by the previous owner, not that they had ever used it for anything that leviathan. Not that Anna was about to complain; it gave her a healthy bout of shadows to hide in. Perhaps it was too good a cover in a way though: the darkness ended in sharp points, saw-toothed edges, and felt like it hid two large beady eyes watching her every move. Anna needed it for the safety, however when every little murmur activated her primitive instincts, she couldn't help except wonder if the darkness – and the tarpaulin she'd flung over herself – was too great a tempt for a paranoiac's heart attack.

The problem would only appear if her da—

No – if *Don* came snooping. Old habits die hard, and she occasionally thought of the man as her father, although the last couple of years had completely stripped him of that title. She finished cutting two small holes in the tarpaulin and spotted him at once. It was hard not to when he was already strutting about with the smutty and obnoxious manner more akin to a celebrity paedophile than a man who had once been a salt-of-the-earth farmer. Backed by thrusts of his pelvis, his boots kicked up dust clouds, crunching the gravel under its steel toe caps. From here, he dipped in and out of view, crossing the yard back and forth, over and over; when the crunching gravel instead echoed from behind her, from in the barn's rafters, from to her left and to her right at the same time, it was anyone's guess. Not that it truly mattered – his shotgun would be outstretched anyway, his constant companion, like a genetic disease, with his finger wobbling over the trigger.

That short, coarse man's face refused to trust anyone. Whatever he said, did, or breathed, he rubbed people up the wrong way. Most people assumed the dullard was trying to con them, but a handful would get the instinct he was about to beat them to a pulp – the latter were nearer to the truth. Even his own family, reviling at every choice he'd ever made, had never felt comfortable in his presence and the many tales of his "dealings" with the animals on his farm, tales he'd deluded himself into thinking were riveting conversation, didn't help either.

Suffice to say, there was a reason his arms and face were layered in scars, one Anna knew all too well.

She peaked out again through a crack in the barn wall, looking for the signal, yet green grass was all that was in sight. A moment later, she heard the click. She assumed that it was the signal, though it wasn't the one they'd agreed, and she nestled herself further into the crumbling stonework.

Anna was wrong. From the peephole in her tarpaulin, Don's hands were trembling over the shotgun, tapping against the trigger with more clicks. He'd turned and moved back away from the barn. Although it was away from her, she nevertheless knew where the monster was headed and the thought of that made her grab the gravel beneath her and clench for dear life.

The farm had two sheds over by the northern wall and Anna was dragged to it on a daily basis. She'd then run out, tight in every part of her body and uncomfortable in her places she didn't even knew existed.

But the other one, it contained her worst fear.

Just the thought bubbled up a vile taste in her stomach. Her hand covering her mouth, it took every fibre of her being for the floor beside her not to become a slip-n-slide of regurgitated dinner.

"Psst! You there?" hissed the voice. Despite its slurs and stenches, Anna hadn't realised how much she yearned to hear it.

"Yes!" she replied, whispering, hoping the voice would do the same. Nicolas, her older brother, had never been the best at subtlety. She couldn't help except to be jealous – he'd escaped the Fernsby's farm. When he'd come of age, he'd made a break for freedom quicker than a Pavlovian dog would toward a bell. Not having a place to go, nor any money, was a trivial concern; his Uncle Marvin had supplied him with a bit of money. Not long after, he struck lucky by getting a job and room at one of the two local inns, The Mellow Daffodil. Nicolas once told her that their uncle had some money for her too, not that she'd seen it. She wouldn't know how to spend it either, since she had had no education whatsoever after Don plucked her out of school just as secondary education started to approach.

"How are things going?" Nicolas whispered through their makeshift confessional. He, of course, couldn't see her but for the while she was glad of it, as the remnants of tears constantly stained her cheeks.

"How do you fucking think?" she spat back through the wall, swirling the taste of chaff and powdery grime further into her throat. On one hand, it was rare that her explosions were released with such vehemence – quiet was too imperative. On the other hand, the only thing stronger than the smell of sweat gushing down her back was the smell of booze and stoic silence from the other side of the confessional. Anna didn't want to lose her temper, especially not with her strained contact with the outside world, but she'd never felt so isolated and alone. In fact, her last venture into the unknown normality of Little Hodbury was whilst she hid in Don's rusting cattle trailer when he went down to the pub in the hopes of beating something rotten out of her brother and had returned only with food supplies for the next month. It explained the lack of signal at least: the plan was he'd push a piece of paper through the crack once he was there, which she'd pass back through once Don was out of earshot. It was a miracle the monster hadn't already heard Nicolas, the way his lungs rattled with nicotine and were brazen about the need for secrecy.

"Um, sorry Sis . . . I just, just . . . just," he trailed off. Her eyes became bloodshot. She didn't want to ask why – Nicolas would have spent the very few coins he had on his main indulgence, which made him violent and thrust him into the world of self-pity and ignorance of others.

"When will I get out of here?"

"Soon, I just don't want . . . if Don—"

"If Don does what? He's already a prick, and I've told you about everything that he does! You experienced it yourself, yet you abandon—"

The wall beside her head exploded in a flash of crumbling brick. Before she heard either the bang or saw the bullet lodge itself and tear open a new crack in the barn wall, the stone dust had peppered the tarpaulin. Nicolas' voice magnetised the bullet, drawing it within an inch of her head. She spun to one side, the tarpaulin sliding off her as she tried to reorientate herself amid the ringing in the ears and the dust now invading her lungs. When her vision and hearing finally stabilised, the apoplectic man was charging across the yard. Darting out of sight behind the barn, the enraged man was already raising the shotgun again. By the time she'd started running toward the man, his hands and face were redder than an erupting volcano and he was raining down a shower of curses.

It was pointless. Not only did she fail to reach him in time, but the scars on his arm also froze her. Her mind's eye was drowning in abysmal thoughts, nausea, everything she'd ever wanted to escape. Anna crouched down on the spot, praying for the bile not to taint her day further.

His finger squeezed the trigger.

Anna had no idea how long she was crying on the floor. It felt like an eternity before Don seized her ponytail, however when everything zoomed back to punch her, she realised she could've lain there forever. Had she not stood up to save her knees from his steel toe caps, he would have torn her hair out.

She should've known better – as soon as Anna's feet planted onto the gravel, the butt of his shotgun smashed a tooth loose from her cavity-ridden mouth (toothbrushes were other commodities that he didn't afford his daughter). During that same second, she realised that she'd never learn whether Nicolas's troubles had been drowned by alcohol or regorged blood.

While he dragged her under a torrent of unrepeatable words, she didn't need to look up to know that one of the two shed doors was about to be opened. Both doors regurgitated that taste of fear that went clawed hand in clawed hand the need to curl into a ball. When the stinging sensation smashed across her face in a flash of steel, Anna had been hurled into the dirt and hay. The door of whichever shed she'd been imprisoned in – too many tears and flecks of blood sullied her vision – smashed shut behind her. The following echo, of the bolt being drawn, was all far too common a sound.

A ruin of a girl sat in the barn now. Straw was needling her skin and cow shit was already spattered across her skirt and tights. If his anger after her attempt to escape last summer was Don's final straw, what he had unleashed today was something undiscovered, unprecedented. Lying in the dirt, she recognised that she'd finally passed the point where her body felt like her own – all the wounds she'd received in the other barn, which extended all the way up her thighs and beyond, were just part of the insane equation. He would grab her hair if he wanted her to follow him round the house and he'd locked and barred her bedroom door enough times now that she didn't live in that house anymore. Someone called Anna did, but it wasn't her, it wasn't Don's daughter, it was a plaything at most.

Yet, this barn still scared her more than the other. Memories more horrific than ordinary torture imbrued the other barn's floor; it was in this room where her face truly contorted, and her brain screamed to itself without beginning or end. Even worse, it was becoming more and more her home; since her mother had become ill, what turned into visits to check on the barn had segued into being imprisoned there if she wasn't required in Don's side of the barn.

Her gaze fixed on the upturned trough in the corner. Above it, the thatched roof had shattered, creating a slit down one of the walls through which daylight was trickling in.

A second passed where Anna wondered if she was alone. She wasn't so lucky. *It* moved an inch, flickering its way through the light. Anna's lips parted and her vocal cords rattled enough to virtually explode.

Don strutted into the house. Stewing in his own flurry of malignance and woe, he slammed the front door behind him, so forcefully that a tremor ran through the house, his forehead bleeding sweat like a gaping bullet wound. He studied the kitchen before him. It was the same old kitchen, caked in the grime from unwashed cutlery, a selection of belts hanging up by the door – the rusting, despondent remains of Clara's wheelchair and IV drip lying abandoned in the corner. His upper lip curled, his late wife's flotsam and jetsam serving time and time again to remind Don of his two most unearthly creations: Anna and Nicolas. Clara inflicted her curse upon whatever sprang from her, and for that matter whatever entered her. When the cancerous mass had started to spring from and through her flesh, it had done so with an appetite more vituperative than the Devil itself. Keeping Anna from the outside world was more than a mercy, it was the start to the end of Clara's tainted bloodline. Instead, he had put her daughter to work for him, tending to *his* needs.

The pot of porridge oats smashed beneath his raging fist. Don's slab growing redder, his anger propelled him into the dining room. The shotgun slipped through his fingers, though the dull thump it made on the floor didn't register.

This was that devil-child Nicolas's fault. He had warned that toad never to return to the family home. Don had had no choice except to carry out his threat. Picking up a wooden walking stick propped against the dining room table, he channelled his white-hot mania into smashing it into the wall. Wedges of it jammed into the walls, embedding like shurikens until only the metal handle remained and clattered to the floor. He didn't need another reminder of his wife's fate – it only reminded him too of Nicolas. Don had given it to her before he understood how bad, how unknown, how uncurable, Clara's condition was. It had supported her for a week or so – before her spine became more crooked, before the seizures in her bones progressed further than any arthritis should, and before her tastes had shifted to one very selective thing. Nicolas had helped the poor, dying woman for another week but fled with his tail between his legs at the first sign of difficulty. He had abandoned his mother, bruised and sore, sprawled on her bedroom floor, sharpened teeth uncleaned, elongated fingernails uncut, and without a sole care for the tray of antibiotics and painkillers which she needed.

One of the few remaining unsullied things in the house, a vase given to Clara for her twenty-first birthday, crashed to the floor. Within moments, Don was in his bedroom. It was another haven of grime and squalor. Acute slashes cut open his bed; he'd lived with them for so long that he couldn't remember if they were from his outbursts, or in trying to repress Clara. On the other hand, shrouded in a candlelight and the broken sunlight fracturing its way through the window's cracked glass, stood the remains of his bedside table. In its centre sat a lonely polaroid of Clara. Manacles clamped the table's legs, the chains from which trailed onto his bed. The mirror upon it had known better days too, that was true, but it still clung to its tell-tale memories; cracks on the glass frame saluted where Don's knuckle had connected with it.

His fist shrieked in pain as Don clenched his jaw and thrust out his arm, reliving that pastime. The window beside the hate-shrine gave him a good view of the barn. He couldn't see everything but through a hole in the disintegrating thatched roof he could see the vague outline of his accursed daughter. His hands messing with a mirror shard at rest in his knuckle, the man's smile grew.

Meanwhile, inside the barn, the oversized leg of the creature was emerging from the shadows and Anna's lungs would soon buckle and emit her terror.

Although she'd been forced to watch the change from the very beginning, the twisted form edging its way forward now was a mass of injuries. It made her throat taste of vomit. Her mother's change in attitude had come first, which included the prolonged seclusion that she had dragged her decrepit husband into. She was suddenly more reliant on help, like her soul had been crushed and as if her bones were being propelled to grow once again. Then, her clothes wouldn't fit. This was about the time that Nicolas decided he couldn't take the strain any longer and the two siblings attempted to escape. That was the first time Don had dragged her kicking and screaming to the shed, instructed her to stay, and given her the job of cutting up the butcher's prime cuts. Within an eternal week, Clara had been banished to the shed too, chained up in a last-ditch effort to suppress those contorting bones of hers, and locked away to prevent her growing in size, and hopefully without gaining any more probing limbs which belonged to any hapless creature ensnared in her maws.

She screamed again, only cut off by the hoarse, pleading cough shooting up her throat. From the shadows, the beast's eyes were red and piggy while they watched her every move, forcing her hand. Every lump of it was covered in barbed, ingrowing spines; while it moved forward, it was clear the kind of appalling horror which had scurried its way beneath Clara's skin, even the goosebumps seeming to distend, twist, and try to break free of whatever change had turned her from woman to beast. The creature's leg inched forward again, and Anna slammed her shoulder into the door once more. The bolt might have broken had she been tougher, but the only breaking sound was that in her shoulder itself. An age of being either Don's slave or her mother's cellmate had stolen any vestige of muscle from her. Reeling, she fell back into a pile of excrement so old and maggot-infested she didn't know if it was from an animal or a man.

Subsequently, Anna closed her eyes and prayed. She'd seen her mother's jaws, writhing in its own slime and the fluid of fresh prey, and knew that yet again any dream of peace was impossible. But she'd also seen Don's shotgun and knew that escape was equally impossible. The thud of the approaching leg shook the ground next to her, and she opened her eyes a crack, maybe out of blind madness, maybe out of a need to be defiant of fear in the very end. Her mother's body had moved out of the shadows.

Suddenly gravity overcame it. The leg which a moment ago had shaken the barn now folded like a house of cards. Anna dived, confused, for cover as the head of the monstrosity slammed down beside her, sending grit and dust flying into a cloud.

When Anna managed to cough the residue from her mouth, she finally raised her head from her foetal cocoon. In front of her, where a head had once been, was the crumpled, leathery mask, eyes not just lifeless and soulless like the creature Clara became, but instead hollow and just thin sheets of paper. It was very clearly her mother, but her skin no longer rippled and undulated like a broth on a stove; the terror's mandibles were still sharp, but they'd half-deflated, leaving the husk of not even a memory behind. Anna compelled her feet to move, aided by a shaking hand clutching one of the shed's support beams. Her chattering teeth were almost as loud as her breathing.

In that moment, it dawned on the shaken child the bursts of rain three nights ago might not have been the only thing to cause that damage to the shed roof. In the centre of her mother's chest was a hole, blood pumping loosely into it. The skin around it had upturned, pinned back and melted back into the spiny flesh of the insectoid legs. As for the cavity itself, the flesh around it had been hollowed out, its spherical shape only due to a kind of umbilical residue coating it.

By the time the realisation appeared it was far, far too late. Her lungs rattled out her and

Don's eulogy, accompanying the tune with the slamming of her fists into the door.

They thudded away unheard. The eternal toll of sleepless nights, constant yearning for a warm meal, and never-ending alertness was finally conquering her, firstly weakening every bone in her body, secondly leaving them without the sliver of a chance to escape. Anna knew that neither the door would break, nor the walls, and so she resigned herself to whatever came next. Even the hole in the barn roof was far too high for her to climb through. All she was able to do was call out to her most bitter enemy and pray that he would know to run, make use of the tiny head start. In her heart of hearts, she knew it was pointless; her cheeks went red, and doleful tears streamed. Why hadn't she realised when she *alone*, waiting for Nicolas?

Don was oblivious to anyone or anything, and both his fist and the mirror had sustained many scars. With all the stamina he could muster, he unleashed more punches and sewed new trickles of red onto the streams already formed and coagulated on his fist. It was only after the fourth or fifth punch when he acknowledged the vibrations shaking the whole room. The mirror shattered.

Don's legs felt weak. He fell back onto his bed, confused, disorientated, and praying gravity wasn't about to go askew.

This time with the power to sway the whole room, the vibrations started up again. Don turned his attention to the shadow blotting out the window, and all seven of its spindly appendages. In the end, he wished he'd never thought about it, just cuddled up under his fraying duvet and ignored existence. It was smaller than the one in the barn, and a thin, rubbery substance swarmed every inch of its cancered carapace. Yet its origins were clear.

The window buckled under the weight of whatever had lived inside Clara, its ridged stomach pulsating in time with Don's vomiting.

One of the legs shot through the glass. He buried his face in his pillow, crying out the name of his deceased wife. He knew *she* wouldn't ever hear it. And a second later, it didn't matter – his innards were too busy covering the carpet.

# A FINAL REPOSE

BUSHES SHOT PAST in the headlights, glinting green and brown and a thorny shade of grey. Among the brambles, there came the occasional murmur as much from the animals in the undergrowth as from the car's slipstream. Maybe that's what animals did: gave one another a thorough jostling to serenade cars speeding by, in particular those wanting so desperately to escape. As Ross' car shot along now, even those animals in the undergrowth could've felt the desperation flowing from his speeding metal box. The car must've been revving along at about sixty miles per hour by this point, and Ross was pushing his foot down harder still. He'd skirted Farrowpine forest, rounded the crop fields; all that was left was for his Honda, which had an engine that suffered from the car equivalent of small dog syndrome, to traverse the valleys of boss-eyed sheep. Then freedom would be his.

Out of the corner of the driver's eye, although oblivious to Ross' passenger, another speed limit sign flew by as his car mocked it. His pupils were targeted on the hill approaching the car, while his girlfriend was beside him, embedding her serotonin levels in the blue light of her phone. In a way, he'd found it oddly amusing, this stretch of twisting road. Gone were the days of polite requests to slow down, these signs screamed severe warnings like most headmasters he'd had the displeasure of serving under. Not that the signs or headmasters managed to encourage any obedience; in fact, when Mr. Harcourt warned the school of the nearby roadworks, the road accident casualties in the students tripled during the following week. In the same way, the death toll of fellow cars or men or fauna on this stretch of road had jumped from twenty-six to thirty-one during the last year. And that was up from nineteen the year before, all of it started when that Ramsey Marlowe fella had crashed into that girl.

If high school experience taught Ross anything, it was that gleeful defiance was worth the cost. The number of times children had been dragged into his classroom, amongst a cruelly jubilant chorus from the other pupils, after which he was expected to reprimand the rotters for anything and everything – it beggared belief. And yet the only motion towards improving the situation had been when he'd torn down the anti-bullying poster in a fit of pique at a child's outrageous Latin homework and they'd all gone deadly silent. During the cesspit of a year where Mr. Bainbridge had lived in Little Hodbury and taught at the ailing grammar school, he'd realised that speed seemed to be as vital as red blood cells to not just the children but their maniacal parents as well. In fact, he reckoned that the nearest that town ever came to mixed race was simply the varying speed at which the boy racers tackled blind corners. And now he had joined that medley.

He looked across at his girlfriend's phone, checking the directions – not that it was relevant. Picking a direction and zooming towards it would eventually get him out of Little Hodbury, no matter how many perturbed faces and disgruntled idiots he'd have to face en route. Not long ago, three shocked old ladies had already narrowly avoided his front tyres. Two years ago, the winding streets and elegant charm in the balance between modern and antiquarian pleased him; now, the stubborn mindsets, aged like the mothballs in half of Little Hodbury's brains, brought the fire curtain down on the blaze that was his excitement. The glow of the satnav on Skyla's phone illuminated the final stake in his heart – the shoebox.

That was what they did at Little Hodbury Grammar. When disillusioned creatures went to die, they were given a shoebox padded with redundancy papers for a new home. Ross – Mr. Bainbridge – remembered doing much the same with a few schoolchildren when the school hamster, Gerald, popped his clogs. Stupid name, stupid runt, stupid death. How he'd told the vet how the animal had died without himself dying of red-faced laughter, he hadn't a clue. The teacher simply knew that when the headmaster's turn came to announce it, the entire teaching staff had wholly failed to contain their cackles in assembly: Gerald had suffered a heart attack when one of the balloons popped during 9B's end-of-term party.

For Ross though, the *true* casualty was Latin. His subject wasn't even given the mercy of balloons, never mind ones which stupefied him so much that his ticker abandoned him. Latin, a dying language with dying teachers. Whether the teacher loved teaching Juvenal or loved showing how ordered a universe could be with gerundives and subjunctives was irrelevant – the department and his wage were out.

Or at least, he would be within the hour. He could see it in the distance, the sign which some humorous git had put up, reading "On this day in 1956, literally nothing happened". Sad thing was, it was the biggest tourist attraction the town possessed. And currently, amongst the foliage and scowling sheep, its flippant words were the beacon guiding him from Hell.

"Not long now, Skyla", Ross said to his companion. As ever, the blue light of her phone ensnared her attention, but it made for a better situation than a discussion with himself; not that he cared about being perceived as mad, Ross just worried that God might one day accidentally think that his inane witterings were aimed at the deity and forever scupper his chances of going to Heaven. All Skyla did in reply was the slight jerk of her phone on her lap. When the satnav would do the inevitable, throw a hissy fit, and declare a U-turn to be necessary, he waited for his girlfriend to utter the same words. When his previous ex had done that, the urge to drive into the distance and crash hadn't been more enamouring. This time round, he was too great a coward to do it himself, he simply knew that removing her from his life would just be less blue light twinkling away to itself out of the corner of his eye. Maybe that was why he'd kept her around – she was so absorbed in blue light that she didn't have time to mock or turn her nose up at his love of Classics.

Returning his attention to the road ahead, his hands turned the wheel, the car moved around a bend. Christ, it was boring. Row after row of green, of brown, of nauseating tedium. He missed the polluting static of dodgem cars, the jangle of funfairs, and the pungent weed aromas in his home paradise of Preston. It brought with it knitted brows and drooped jowls, but at least that was understandable. Moving to Little Hodbury took the image of paradise, glossed it up so much you hated it, then drowned it with quaint charming suburbs and Earl Grey tea.

Ross stopped the car. One second, the car had been forgetting the uneven farm tracks beneath its wheels without a care, the next it had propelled its left wheel a foot into the air and illuminated everything except the unfolding road.

Neither he nor the woman-phone sitting next to him could say they'd ever been in a car crash or had hit someone. The nearest the teacher had come was an occasion when he'd first moved into Little Hodbury. Some Alzheimer's-ridden OAP had driven a car through roadworks and smashed into a poor idiot's house. Ross wasn't part of that crash; yet the skid marks his car had left on the road as it had swerved to avoid the converging codger were embossed into his memory.

Regardless, he had always expected something a bit "more" from car accidents. The simplicity of a metal box bashing into something small, innocent, and probably fluffy didn't ever seem to quite satisfy his mind. He didn't want an unholy gulf of flame, but a minor bump seemed a little boring. This in his mind, he opened the car door.

"Skyla, I think I hit something," he said as he gazed into the dusk which ruffled his tousled curls. The road before him lay empty. It bore the wounds of potholes, yet they couldn't push the car up in the way it just had.

"I don't understand," she asked, "What do you mean?" She didn't move her eyes away from her phone. A few weeks ago, he might've reiterated the question; today, Ross couldn't be arsed.

A moment later, his eyes found the meek form. Or rather, what was left of it. His phone torch illuminated every red and pink inch of the distributed corpse. From the mangling behind the car, a sticky wetness had emerged and afterwards, guided by rubber and horsepower, had traced a horrible snake up the road. Ross allowed the car door to shut behind him. Five steps later, he saw the monochrome form between his feet had once been a badger.

At what point, he wondered, could you stop classifying a badger as a badger? It was certainly very corpselike, but did you need a certain amount of creature to be present for it be counted as anything more than debris? Yes, it held the form of a badger, but one spattered into chunks across the road. All the skin and fur were there, although now some of it belonged to the car wheel or the bony wings pushed into existence from the animal. It even still held the little snout and tiny, sharp teeth, even if the nose was now half the size. To autopsy the pancake beside his feet, the council would have to dig up a three-metre span of the road. And if they weren't even willing to fund the local arts fair, they'd hardly fork out for badger flotsam and jetsam. Worst of all, given its size (no matter how spread out), could you really call a corpse a corpse if the animal mustn't have even reached one year of age.

It was just as much a badger as it was a badger-no-more.

Another zephyr of wind fluttered his hair. Ross could feel the completely absent glare of the woman in the car. Any other day, he'd have left the remains as carrion. Today, however, two tiny glinting puddles next to the corpse stopped him. Ross blamed the cold breeze and vicious glare of the dusk, but when his hand moved to his face he felt every lonesome teardrop by lonesome teardrop emerging. The smeared mass carried a wave over him of something he couldn't quite explain. It couldn't be sadness or anger or disgust: they'd all been part of the course of being a teacher, from having saliva propelled across his desk to wiping up blood from pubescent teenagers' brawls. The missing emotion was like a snuffed-out candle in a mausoleum – it didn't affect anyone, not least of all the dead, but it was just *wrong*. He wouldn't abandon this creature to as undignified a fate as a redundancy paper coffin. Similarly preposterous was leaving it to be a roadkill scene where cars would simply wear it down into the road.

"Help me move him!" Ross called back through the breeze and his flying curls to Skyla. If the teacher had expected the woman-phone's gaze to have shifted, he was sorely disappointed. His attention had turned back to the pancake of distributed grisle before the words left his lips. Ross couldn't say with any certainty whether he called out to her again, yet if he did, the wind would have absorbed it.

By now, he was on his knees and prodding his finger along one of the animal's repurposed appendages. There wasn't going to be a pleasant way of moving the remains to a respectful grave. While trying to figure it out, the juts of bone stayed rigid and seemed to prop the animal up, letting gravity swivel the hollow eyes to meet Ross' gaze.

From his breast pocket he removed a well-chewed pen. Like gum from a classroom table, with it he peeled away one of the badger's new meat wings. Also like gum, a severe pink pulp grabbed onto the road as he tried slipping his hands beneath the animal. Releasing it, a treacly pink strand distended with it. The creature flopped back. Not that battered badger could look any less appealing, from its new angle the odd lump of brain was now visible, leaking out through a monumental graze on its nose. After flicking the viscera away with the pen, having promptly then flung the pen into the nearest bush, he ascended to his knees.

A minute later, he held a car jack in his hand, an implement which had neither seen the light of day before nor which he'd ever considered how to use. With a wave of his hand to the woman-phone, he hurdled the fence in a brief channelling of his thickset youth. In fifth year, the younger him had moaned to Mr. Madison during rugby session after rugby session, in much the same way his students would later moan to him about Latin verb conjugations. Through gritted teeth, he now admitted the fitness of running away from an enraged Madison had served him well. Or, at the least, it had given him enough gusto to escape three stabbings in the Manchester suburbs, and chase after one student at his last school especially determined to set alight one of the poster boards in an English classroom. Mr. Madison would thankfully never come to hear such an admission, the swollen blister of a man had bitten the dust three years previous – actually, as he recalled, Ross was fairly sure that he too had been hit by a car, and one driven by an ex-pupil at that.

Anyhow, those hidden muscles didn't serve their time with only the fence. A dulled thump echoed outwards and disturbed whatever fauna were still asleep. At first, the sole effect had been the jack vibrating in his hand; the ground was colder than the squashed remnants back on the road. Lifting the tool, he struck the ground a second time. And then a third time. And then he struck it more and more and more, until more dirt caked the tip of the jack than lay in the small hole Ross had thrashed into being.

By the jack's final thud into the ground, dusk had completely given way to gloom. Miserable clouds had trembled their way into the skyline too. The first few minutes of his vocation at least had the benefit of his phone torch, but it had soon disappeared. Now he was pawing at the dirt, hands working without help. The man didn't need sight. Touch alone would guide his hands as they carved the tomb into the land. There was a moment where a kind of blue miasma settled over the hole in the ground, yet it went away as soon as it'd appeared.

It was complete. Or rather, it was completely *hollow*, and the tomb's slopes and muddy sides were mostly uniform, all it needed was its incumbent soul.

As he hurdled the fence back to the prone badger, his mind couldn't help except bring up the face of one of his students. The student's expulsion had been a simple affair: anger, chair got thrown out of a window, child got expelled. What brought the child to mind was what had happened no more than a few moments after the chair incident. Bainbridge had watched confounded as the boy carefully picked up the deceased shape of a magpie and placed it in a hole in the school field. He hadn't let anyone else near the animal while the procedure was in progress and had demanded everyone move back as he'd collected an insole from his shoe, scrawling "RIP" upon it in permanent marker. Fair to say, it was the staunchest that he'd ever seen the boy work. The care he gave the magpie while stroking and manoeuvring its wings was totally divorced from how he would manhandle a pen across a page in what he claimed was handwriting.

Oli, that was the child's name. Oliver Millington. He'd lived on the new estate, his mother had died in childbirth (which he used numerous times to excuse his antics), and on one occasion the headmaster's secretary had found him vaping at the age of eleven behind the dining hall. It was odd what you remembered, what the sardonic and jaded called to mind in moments of compassion or fondness. Up until his final day of teaching, Mr. Bainbridge had had a fondness for the boy – it evaporated when, an hour before his final bell, Oli had shattered that windowpane. And, at that, in an effort to connect the chair with the Latin teacher's brains.

Mr. Bainbridge removed the insole from his own shoe, the left one, and found another, less gooey biro in his jacket. His griffonage, he admitted only to himself, wasn't much better than the boy's. It always made criticising pupils' handwriting more difficult – not impossible though, simply hypocritical. Having etched the word "badger" onto the insole, he once more had the task of removing the badger from the harsh floor and into its final resting place. The thought, that that badger would probably only have a day's calm before crows or foxes started to excavate it and banquet themselves on whichever of its entrails hadn't been smeared across the road, occurred to Ross only so the man could lock it in the back of his mind. He supposed he was just putting another barbaric link in the food chain.

Grabbing a towel from the backseat of his car, the blue miasma appeared again. The way it cast from behind him, he reasoned that they were the result of whatever Skyla was doing with the satnav; she was certainly muttering under her breath as though frustrated. Yet, like the previous time, they vanished just as rapidly, and left him with a towel to wrap around the creature whilst prying it from the road's service.

That was another phrase a kid at Little Hodbury had once used, "pavement pizza". For all the small git was just being morbid and callous, that didn't stop the word lodging in Ross' memory. Hearing the soft sucking sound echo out from the towel like a foot inside a sopping wet trainer, he understood why the word fitted so uncomfortably well. He didn't dare look back once he had started carrying it to its place of rest. All he glimpsed was the fleeting sight of a slimy wet trail dribbling from the towel. Clasping the insole to the towelled badger, Ross wondered if the animal deserved a name. If a corpse, which was actually remains, which were actually a cluster of depopulated organs, deserved a name.

It was too late. The leather and foam gravestone would have to remain dedicated just to "The Badger".

"Memento mori."

They appeared again. The blue miasmas. Almost interred, the coveted lump was barely an inch from the cold dirt when the blue lights flickered into view once again, red lights also now part of their invasion. Softly placing The Badger into the ground, Ross stood up. Two spindly trees to his car's left were bathed in harsh coronas of alternating blue and red.

Having just begun scooping the mound of earth back into the tomb, the first voice called out, "Ross Bainbridge?", gruff, authoritarian. He continued, until he heard the flick of something: "Ross Bainbridge?" came the call again.

Two silhouettes had rounded his car, leaving their own vehicle which sat a few metres away and doused the area in epileptic colours. In the warping shadows, he could make out the nearest one all too eager to clasp a baton and wave it back and forth.

"Careful, Bishop," was the harsh, hissed tone from the figure further away. He'd just finished manhandling a radio and was stretching his hand down towards an implement fastened to his waist. The figure further away spoke for a second time: "Ross Bainbridge, my name's Constable Martindale, please drop that shovel. We don't want to have to use force."

"But, The Badger, I've got to bury it. It deserves peace." The light wasn't strong enough to illuminate the minutiae of their faces, not PC Martindale's recent weightless and hanging uniform, not the slight tremor in PC Bishop's hand; Ross saw the look that flicked between their eyes though. He'd seen it between teachers, between pupils, between those arrogant shits who tried to halt his career. Disbelief. No, more than that, mockery.

The next heap of ground left the shovel, covering the badger's back legs, or at least what remained of them. "Listen now, son," Bishop said, foot squelching into some of the goop that had slopped out of the meek creature.

"I said, drop the shovel!"

Ross didn't know which voice said that. He didn't know which of the men had extended their baton with a click which broke the night like the shattering of badger bones beneath a car's wheel. He could just see the prone thing in front of him. It deserved solace – didn't it?

Next, he saw the night sky and barely registered the cold ground beneath his shoulder blades.

"Ross Bainbridge, you're under arrest for the

murder of Oliver Millington and Thomas Rogers. You aren't obliged to say anything, but anything you do say may be used against you in a court of law."

"But it needs to be buried."

"What?" hissed whichever one had grappled him to the ground. A shower of spittle covered his neck, and the policeman pulled him to his feet. Ross felt his own foot connect with the man's shins, but the handcuffs put paid to any ideas he had about finishing burying the meek entity. The Badger's spirit would have to live on in the man's tears instead.

"Bury it! Skyla, bury it!"

Only the birds heard. And even they didn't care.

The two PCs, batons still out and ready to bruise, stood by their police car. Neither had quite forgotten the brutalised remains of Oli Millington, or the other child Thomas Rogers. Abandoned in a field, Bainbridge had waited for the predators of the night to begin feasting before running back to his car, the CCTV showed that plain as day.

"Who is Skyla?" PC Bishop asked his partner.

"Pardon, Marc?"

"The person he called out for, Skyla. There's nobody else in the car, is there?"

One quick search of the car boot satisfied Martindale and Bishop that no other timid child had been trapped in his car, though at least the multiple bloodied handprints left on the inside clinched the truth about the teacher. The detective constables never seemed to escape death, it was part of their job. Even their previous police chief – corrupt, he'd slaughtered many for the "cause" and the gang who paid him off. The betrayal inside the bloodied handprints however, each drop of blood telling the story of a child's blood needlessly spilled, it flooded bile into Martindale's mouth. Not that it would've helped matters, yet if the reprehensible travesty of a man in the police car had let anger rule his brain, he could've at least done some good. Perhaps ended the life of Marcie or Peter, the children of Paul Albatross, the corrupt mastermind found in every nook and cranny of Little Hodbury. Although they were without a doubt innocent, at least killing them would've ended Albatross' bloodline. Because hadn't the police force had a *fun* time clearing up the fallout of his crimes. Martindale hated thinking in that way. Times like this were when he wished he'd just stayed as a traffic warden.

Swallowing the bitterness back down, Mart= indale saw a glint in the darkness. A rolled-up tube lay at the furthest corner of the boot. Tugging it out, the detective constable found the rounders bat, a few blotches of powdered skull and spilled brain caked into the wood grain. Standing beside him, Bishop looked back at the man in the police car; the evidence was plastered across and beneath his fingernails, equal parts blood and dirt. At least the fucker had no chance in hell of escaping prison. A tomb of white brick and metal was all he was worthy of.

In the police car, he was still screaming for The Badger.

Martindale moved round Bainbridge's car to open the passenger door.

"Anything?" asked Bishop, manhandling the bat into a large evidence bag. The creases on his face betrayed his desire to put the man in the car out of society's reach. No, not simply to do that.

To ensure the children got the justice owed to them, and so nothing of Bainbridge remained to curse an unsuspecting child.

Martindale had found Skyla.

"Nope, just this satnav. Seals the deal though, he was definitely trying to flee."

Skyla said one thing: "Sorry, I didn't quite understand that. Please take a U-turn."

# THE FIFTH DEMOGRAPHIC

*"I might say, for example, that the sound was harsh, and broken, and hollow; but the hideous whole is indescribable, for the simple reason that no similar sounds have ever jarred upon the ear of humanity."*
**—Edgar Allan Poe,
'The Facts in the Case of M. Valdemar'**


THE SHOP DOORBELL dinged as the first customer of the day entered. From behind the row of tacky calendars, diaries and wellbeing journals emblazoned with emojis, Donna's ears pricked up. She didn't need to stare at the customer to know who'd entered. The first few hours of the day were always slow, and a sudden stream of people would enter at two and four, after which she'd be lucky to see anyone else for the rest of the day. Occasionally things would change, but nine times out of ten her skills were honed enough to know the customer just by how despondently they shut the door.

Today it was Friday, half four in the afternoon. The flurry of schoolchildren hastily running to and fro had just dissipated at last, and the shop door closed with a thump seemingly afraid to move a dust mote – it was Vaughn. John Lennon glasses, earthy aftershave, shirt ironed within an inch of its life, how could it be anyone else?

Put bluntly, Vaughn was a nerd. There simply wasn't a word better suited to encapsulating him. He'd come in on Saturdays and Wednesdays for a look around and to pick up any small bits and bobs that had been missed on his regular Thursday shop, but always his first thought was to rush towards the sci-fi section and so she mainly topped it up for his good self. The fuddy-duddies didn't care or want to know about anything that grim or wild. A handful of groceries and produce were the same each day, but the nature of her shop was that rarely things were the same each day – it was the nearest thing to spontaneity that occurred in Little Hodbury. Nowadays, most of the village folk kept to themselves and were more exact in the layout of their lives than a cuckoo clock – the last few years had proven that. Underneath all the old biddies' attention-seeking piffle, something was brewing, and had been ever since that Albatross fella had sunk his claws into the town.

"Morning, Vaughn," Donna called, rearranging a set of wooden, hand-sculpted statues. In search of a label maker, she finished positioning the final statue and moved toward the box of odds and ends on the floor. She found it a moment later, half meshed with a roll of cellotape, deciding then to throw it aside.

Vaughn still denied her an answer. He wasn't replying with a cruel silence, she knew that much, because the days he spoke were more infrequent than the days he simply went about his business, A to B. He would speak if he needed to, to ask questions or to double-check information, but nothing that would open the door to any verbal diarrhoea. It certainly wasn't like the other people who would visit her shop, scoffing at every new item and saying nothing in order to say everything. Vaughn, she knew, was a customer who knew what he wanted and struggled with the notion of anything crowded. In short, he was her favourite customer.

Donna stood up from the short stool and almost walked backwards into the man. Both of them gave small yelps of shock, like puppies, and she eventually smiled sweetly as Vaughn handed over a squat hardback with some bald loon on the front cover. His adoring smile overwhelmed any problem he had with personal space. Guiding him over to the till, she took the book from the man, letting the low burble of the radio fill the air instead. What was spewing out of the small box may as well have been a cacophony of white noise. She didn't say that aloud though, realising that it would make her sound as bad as the fuddy-duddies she did her best to ignore. A small tap struck her shoulder.

"Miss Hewitt, what's that?" he mumbled, gesturing at the radio. Given out for free in the market the previous Saturday, it was small and unobtrusive. After the local factory, based in the nearby valley which attracted protests and quibbles from almost every senior citizen in the county, shut down, the giveaway radios were the only things remaining. It had been shut, not because of the fuddy-duddy complaints, although it didn't stop them surmising as such anyway and then sticking it on poster boards in the run-up to the next election; rather, the CEO, a snobbish pig of a man called Paul Albatross, got in with people he shouldn't; in fact, got in with lots of gangs of people who torched his reputation, endowing his employees with nothing but unemployment. Given how the radios had disappeared at the giveaway, the irony was that Albatross had missed a trick not selling to Little Hodbury; their sales would have doubled overnight. He'd meddled in the town's affairs in every other way; what would one more finger in the pie do.

"That?" Donna replied, gently, "That's my new radio. Nice, isn't it?"

"Not that," Vaughn tried again, "I mean the noise."

"Oh that, just some song," she replied. Donna wasn't a music aficionado. She wasn't an aficionado about much, truth be told. Life swirled around her and she was happy to pass through it. Until she moved to Little Hodbury to care for Cecilia (none of that Mum/Dad tradition in the Hewitt family), her existence had been a totally untethered one.

Donna handed back the book, the bald loon on the cover continuing to stare puzzlingly at her; she quickly flipped the book over, cover down. Vaughn didn't take the book though. "The noise," he said again, stabs of thoughts flicking across his eyes as he tried to find the words for them. As she could tell, any lyrics in the song died as instantly as they began, and it was just an excuse for background noise.

To him, there was something. Something he could see. Something he could hear. Something forcing him to go rigid like a block of ice. And, for the very smallest of microseconds, something asking his mind to do something he didn't like.

"Vaughn?" she asked, hoping to bring him back to normality. He turned to look at her. Whatever was behind his eyes had gone. Having taken the book off the counter, Donna watched him move towards the door. There was one final glance at her, and he stared at the radio, now playing a different track, one with a stony, organ quality and underlying nonsensical lyrics. Then he turned, wrapped his little red scarf ever tighter, fled, and after he was out of sight, Donna's brow melted from happy to something far more taut and uncertain. Just for a second, the echo of something hung in the air, itched at the nape of her neck, and she found herself questioning why she hadn't followed Vaughn. Why she hadn't *run* after Vaughn, dashing away until every limb in her body died.

She was just being silly.

After the fourth knock thundering around the small house, Donna decided to use her key. Little Hodbury turned umbrellas into decorative statements, not useful tools, and never truer than as she stood under the house's front porch, fumbling inside her rucksack. Inside the house, the newspaper lay on the mat, slight pulping at the edges declaring that Freddo, the owner's mischievous Bedlington Whippet, had got to it first. Scooping up the newspaper, tossing it onto staircase, and staring at the drab world around her, Donna couldn't contain her sigh anymore. She found herself doing that impression of an old, boiling kettle more and more frequently, every time she visited this house.

As with the rest of the house, the hallway wore its decorations and design like a curse. In years to come, archaeologists would unearth the house from the sterile, grey mud and find everything inside perfectly preserved, an example of the most boring part of the village body, in dire need of amputating before its many shades of tedium infected the whole organism. Not that this house's tedium could subsume the village organism much further, of course. Little Hodbury had already found its own slaggy, barren wasteland in which to embed, idle away the aeons. It was a nest egg, a perfect example of where life in Little Hodbury simply stopped. The house's owner was of the same mummified echelon, a zenith of monotony, neither famous nor infamous, neither hated nor loved. The kind of person who, if told the tale of the Burning Bush to enkindle a religious experience, would simply ask the kind of bush. The kind of person who accepted life's hand so often they'd forget whether they themselves drank tea, never mind if they took one lump or two in it.

She stepped through into the lounge. In a second, Freddo was bounding off his own private armchair, nestling his soft head against Donna's legs. Affection was so easy if you were a dog. She ran her hand through the animal's hair. Tickling his ears elicited cooing growls, and when she eventually patted him on the head, he was happy to flop back to where he had started and begin another idyllic nap.

"Hey Cecilia," Donna called out to the other side of the lounge.

In the other armchair, fast asleep and oblivious to all and sundry, was her mother. The frail woman's mouth hung open a crack, croaking out her rickety lungs' private fanfare. Day after day, the sounds of someone inside them, shaking a tin full of pebbles, got steadily more pronounced. Carefully, Donna stretched out her hands, and tapped her mother's shoulder, fearful of what mood awaited her; she was a mercurial person, prone to either the oddest flights of fancy, the most uncontrollable rage, or the greatest bout of happiness – it was an effect of the bipolar disease no doubt, but also the gradually spreading weakness in her legs fired up an anger within her.

Cecilia's GP, a useless man called Dr. Geraghty, had said the medication might slow the spreading weakness and general fatigue. While the man said she may even improve, she doubted it. Tempts of fate like that beckoned tragedy and the universe always pushed the balance in favour of disappointment and failure.

A few things bubbled away in her mind as she sat herself down on the futon beside her mum's chair, chiefly how it had all come to this. Her life both before and after Little Hodbury existed in a horrible backwater, each memory before the village drowning in a miry swamp and each one since she had arrived slowly leeching into the backwater's detestable shades of slop-grey. It was times like these when she wished her dad was alive, which said something. Angry, senescent, adulterous, he deserved such a burden, not her.

After leaving Cecilia alone with her dog and her dreams, Donna saw to one or two jobs around the house, completing her job as yes-woman. She set out a small microwaveable curry on the counter, making it easy for her mother to sort dinner before her legs gave up the ghost, and refreshed Freddo's water bowl. Flicking the radio on, she set about chopping up some carrots and potatoes to make a hotpot for later in the week, and the same droll noise as in her shop greeted her.

By the time everything was finished, her mother was still fast asleep. With the promise she would return at about eightish to help her get ready for bed, she decided to scrawl a little note for her. The last thing she did before stepping into the other world of grey was to flick the radio off again, having realised Cecilia's snoring drowned the noise out. Because of habit and morbid paranoia more than anything serious, she did just quickly check a pulse was there, but the snores were already like a squall of storms in the air.

Not that she noticed beneath her mother's snoring, a few caliginous, strangely melodic notes floated through the kitchen window after Donna.

By the time the next day came, the air of Little Hodbury was slipping down the slippery slope further. Winds able to level trees like bombs dropped on Hiroshima were sailing through the streets, torrents of rain poured down in cold, lifeless sheets, and the grey image of the village became more and more lustreless.

On one especially miserable day, Donna had spectated from her bedroom, and at moments laughed, as a couple dashed down the street, one of them ducking into a newsagent's. This was all normal, but the man left outside had forgotten his coat, so fought for space with a tramp in another shop's doorway barely big enough to fit a child. Then, when the girlfriend emerged, she found herself almost walking home without him because he'd been gifted so little room that he looked like he was part of the tramp's basic and muddied entourage. Finally, when he'd trekked after her, pins and needles visibly ruining his legs, his shoelace had become hooked on an abandoned radiator – who leaves a radiator in the middle of the bloody street? Only in Little Hodbury – and he'd collapsed into an unfortunately large and sloppy pile of dog shit. Is that what entertainment was now?

Sooner or later, it was the weekend, not that it felt like it. Donna found herself yearning to go out. She imagined that she was getting early arthritis, that if she didn't walk a good few miles every day, her joints and bones got angry with her.

Her next-door neighbours, Chantelle and Ken Aspinwall, were some of the few other under-thirties in the village, who, like Donna, went walking almost every day. Especially since the death of their daughter, they'd exchanged gossiping for reclusing, venturing further and further into the woodland around the village and getting home later and later. This weekend however, the weather subjugated even them, barricading them into their house with only the lilt of the TV through the semi-detached's wall to indicate they were at home. No, radio not TV – the melodies, leeched of life, were unmistakeable.

By about midday on the Saturday, Donna was already craving the outside world. But watching yet more rain appear in thunderous bouts, a trip downstairs to the kitchen was all she dared to manage. It made the thought of getting soaked later that day when she visited Cecilia vaguely palatable. For the fourth time that day, she headed downstairs and into her kitchen to do nothing more than flick the kettle on. Its whistle didn't cut out the neighbours' radio. If anything, it seemed only to enhance the dreary tunes. She briefly tried turning her own radio on, but immediately thought otherwise. With only one radio station in signal range, the drabness would be inevitable. And being killed by a composer's call to suicide was not how she fancied being remembered. Standing over her cup of tea, stirring the liquid around and around, the dying while staring at the milky brown whirlpool seemed far more appetising. The only attention she gave the machine was to fling open her kitchen drawer, grab a blunt knife, and disembowel its battery compartment, all before shot-putting it into the bin. Flinging the two batteries into the living room bin, she sat down with her cup of tea, just out of range of the lifeless chimes emanating from her bin.

Suddenly, a vile taste spread through her mouth. Donna spat out the drink – she'd forgotten the sugar.

By the time the clouds at last deigned to reveal the sun's glorious rays of sunshine, it was already the next Friday. Having shut the shop, Donna took her walk home, though the lingering rainwater was still playing havoc with the various tributaries in and around Little Hodbury. Ordinarily, her walk took her through the town square, yet the drains were still croaking up the overspill and a thin, septic layer of the liquid was agonising its way between every cobble or across every paving stone. Her nose wrinkled, even a few streets away from the worst of the overspill, and her shoes pinched at the thought of putting just one foot in it. The back-alley she skirted along felt no less putrescent though, free of the sewer water but permeated by a miasma bleaching the air into some kind of jittery stagnancy. The route eventually brought her out by the newest part of the town, not that it looked that way. The estate Donna was cutting through had only been built ten years ago and already moss, ivy and cracked stone aged it to the same level as the OAPs of the town. She always felt uncomfortable cutting through here, like she was trespassing on somewhere which ought to be left to die. This Friday though, there was something else turning her broad stride to a tentative shuffle.

Donna spun around. No one there. None of the windows had faces behind. None of the parking bays had cars revving up to leave. Was it something in the air? Ignoring the thought, she continued meandering through the estate's tight passages, a few minutes later emerging by a fork in the path which gave her a choice of two equally graffitied alleyways.

She spun around again, casting a quick glance back down the passage she'd just edged down. No lights were on. The nearest building to the dingy alleyway was the most dilapidated, the most in need of a lick of paint, and it had no recesses for someone to hide in. The flaked, miserable ochre-grey of walls mocked the architecture, yet more importantly meant anyone nearby would stand out like a sore thumb. Donna imagined she did at least despite the muted teal colour scheme of her outfit.

She was being stupid.

Make her way down the left passage, she found it opening onto her more grey, crumbling walls and narrow paths – was this the shortcut she usually took? More and more flaking paint, abandoning the past rainbow murals or even the cruder, vulgar sketches, coated the path beneath her shoes and within a few steps there was hardly a speck of colour which was not anathema to the architecture. The way it coated the floor, it was as if it had made one last effort not to let itself be consumed by the place's neutrality.

The feeling of being watched didn't go though. When, less than a minute later, she found one of the building's entrances, she dashed into the foyer, hoping she could recalibrate, that a map of the estate might be inside.

The foyer was no less bleak. And Donna's skin still turned icy, just as it had outside. Like with the paintwork in the passageways, the small foyer she was stood in was also covered in muted colour scheme, its beige tones starting to flake and make a suicidal leap for the carpet. Yet, already the carpet was corrupted by the same, drab infection. Looking between the building's horrible beige innards and its grey outards, she could not persuade her feet to move.

Nothing made a noise. Where was the humdrum life of these residents?

The building let out a dying gasp of life: at the far end of the corridor, in a trice a light was flickering through into the foyer from the other door. It dared Donna to try to move again. Hesitantly, she obeyed. One foot in front of another. She had gone five steps into the gloom when she found herself pivoting to the side of the foyer instead, buzzing on the intercom of flat three. No answer – maybe they were out? The same buzz tittered from flat four's intercom, no human voice echoing out of it. Same with flat five. And six.

It was every flat.

A grand trip out; that was the answer, wasn't it? She felt her face stretching its muscles into a smile, but it was just as much trying to convince her as anyone else. Why did everything suddenly make her feel so unwanted?

It was seven in the evening by the time she got home. Her home was in fact only four streets away from the estate.

Quiet. Beyond quiet. That was Little Hodbury the next day. Like, in curious, old horror films where the new arrival comes into the town, sees it is deserted, and then has a "perhaps it's a Sunday" moment. Except this was a Friday at four in the afternoon, and the heavy bustling of children leaking out of school and darting home in one great crowd wasn't there. She was being stupid she knew, and what seemed cardinal to her would be someone's else trivial afterthought.

For a full hour, however, she had stood still behind the counter, watching the world not go by. Her new doubt and mistrust toward everything were diabolical and yet she doubted she would be feeling this way, so vexed at something inconsequential, were it not for some yearning within herself. Maybe this was her way of wanting to flee Little Hodbury. The last few days were when she'd first picked up on it – chances were though that she'd been letting it sink in and affect her for far longer: there were no young people. Not just no teenagers parading about in the evening and causing havoc; the few families who were starting a life seemed to have upped sticks too, and for the first time in a long while Donna felt like she was the nearest to a breath of fresh air for miles around.

Then Vaughn came in.

Of course – Friday.

"Morning, Vaughn," she called – no response. Donna was unsurprised and went back to twisting a small piece of cellotape-covered cardboard between her fingers. He must have been the next youngest person in the village besides her.

Then the shop doorbell jingled again and a portly man stumbled in. If she once knew his name, it was absent from her mind – he was just another tumbleweed in the Little Hodbury outback. His unapparent neck and fungus stubble made an impression, inflamed red cheeks begging to be puffed and moustache with a mind of its own, and yet he gave off no vibe except total disengagement from events. Just as with Vaughn, she called out hello; and just as with Vaughn he made no reply. However, with this man it was different. The lack of verbal reply was replaced by an obtuse glance and smile that screamed passive aggressiveness. If he requested a carrier bag, the price would just so happen to have gone up to 15p rather than 5p.

From her vantage point, she had a nice view of both customers, Vaughn the nearest and already walking toward the till with the book he wanted to buy. Donna could spy earplugs in the man's ears, as well the savage ring of red and crusty skin from where he must've scratched around them. Once at the till, the man pointed one of his bony, sunlight-craving fingers at the side of the counter. It's target – the radio.

"Bastard thing never plays good music anyway," she said, flicking the noisy thing off. She had no idea why she'd even flicked it on in the first place – the music never changed. With all the force and unwieldy grace of a dropped iron, its impotent melody displayed the two or three seconds of thought that went into the tune. A pop video made on a microwaveable meal's budget might have sounded better.

The old man was there, suddenly, hovering over Vaughn's shoulder, staring at him like a beagle starved of food. Face now a join-the-dots puzzle of flush freckles. Cheeks bright red. His top lip curled into a bent arrow.

"Radio!" the man shouted, letting out a small and indiscernible *whoosh* of saliva afterwards. Donna's eyes locked with his. Vaughn took a quick look at Donna and took a step to the side.

"Excuse me?" Donna asked, lowering the temperature of the room by a full degree.

"Radio!" the man shouted again. His grey hairs seemed to frizz more and more with every syllable. The shopkeeper remained stoic and, in as calm a tone as she could muster, asked him what he meant. "Radio. On!" was his gruff, rasping reply. One blast of bristling moustache later, the man was no longer stood by the counter. With a quick lurch, he grabbed the radio, let out a froggish croak, turned on his heels, and flicked the radio on while dashing out of the shop door. Watched by a gawping Vaughn and Donna, music once again began to spill from the machine. Before she could react, Vaughn was dashing out of the shop, presumably after the rude old man.

Donna was quick on his heels. There were two small alleyways, as drab as they were gloomy, opposite the shop; finding the first empty, she quickly skittered over to the second, finding it empty too. Then she heard the slight whimper of a wounded dog. The alleyway was the very place a rat king might form, but instead of grime there was just mulch and detritus pulped and bleached of colour. Soggy, macerated cardboard boxes plated the two walls, a handful of which had collapsed onto the floor halfway along. In front of them lay a shape.

"Vaughn?" she called out into the warren of filth. No reply, only that saddening whimper; a whimper from that shape. Agony polluted the noise, and the face in the shadows was clearly searching for something. The urge to run – or rather, to grind to a halt and curl up into a ball herself – was overmastering.

"What's the matter?" she asked, crouching down and lifting the shape's head up. It was Vaughn. Between his slight whimpers, he was running his hands around his ears, worsening the eczema-like rash, digging his nails deeper and deeper.

"The noise!" he shouted. Though Donna knew he was sensitive to noise, she had never imagined it having this profound an effect.

A clatter jolted out from behind her. A metal bin lid hitting the floor.

On her knees, Donna's rolled on her ankles and looked up to see the rude OAP they had encountered in the shop. Cloaked in a large puff of smoke from an air vent, his greasy left hand held the radio up to his ear and a large saliva globule escaped through his smile. She could hear the plop it made on the ground.

"Have you done something to him?" Donna yelled. He made no reply, only moved his hips in a slightly serpentine way.

Staring into the man's blotchy face, Donna forced herself to her knees, the icy feeling she'd felt on the house estate slowly creeping back. He reminded her of one of the first people she had met in Little Hodbury: a man who had used his stream of radioactive, yellow piss to waterboard a dying pigeon in broad daylight. That jumentous stench, of him, his piss fuelled by cock pills, and the pigeon came running back at her – she had no idea if it was the same man, but her repulsion was the same.

She shouted out to him again; his was silence. The man pointed upwards.

A drop of water struck her face. In the dying blue-to-grey, the sky looked at breaking point, no horizon where the overcast ended and the lifeless colour scheme of the village began. She turned to help Vaughn up.

At the other end of the alley stood a second man.

This man she recognised, another of the village's creakier clientele. Norman Yeardley, his name was, a rotund man who was the spitting image of his dead brother, even down to the thinning hair and permanently sour expression suited to a lawyer. And in his hand: another of the radios. Step by step, he was advancing through the rat king's lair. The rude OAP was advancing too. Using her arm as a lifeline, Vaughn latched onto Donna.

The men continued to advance.

"What's the matter? Stop!" Vaughn screamed.

The figures stopped. Yeardley rotated his head. It almost appeared that he was going to speak, and his mouth even opened, but it didn't release a reply. Instead, a wave of pure white noise flew across the alleyway. The blast thrust Donna back, the radios both joining the sound wave, and the rude OAP now emitting the noise too. Within moments, the duo stumbled past Yeardley and into the street. But the noise was consuming them. Lights flicked on in houses along the street for the first time in weeks. Then from one of the furthest houses emerged an old, doddering woman, her skin extraordinarily pale. Donna almost called out, in normal English, but the woman stopped her – with a barrier of noise. Vaughn let go of her, as his earplug started to loosen.

More lights flicked on. More and more figures came out into the sunlight, skin insipid and the ground beneath them drained of colour and cracking, flaking into plateaus of grey. Like water escaping from a crumbling dam, they shuffled near the pair, each drag of a foot accompanied by a burst of white noise. Vaughn's cries became louder, but they had no chance of overcoming the pain. Then, through the muddle of screaming townsfolk, stood her ailing mother, in her hand – a radio. Her skin just as insipid as the rest, the ground around her bleached of life and beginning to crumble also.

Donna's knees felt weak. Her eardrums were threatening to burst. But more white noise machines flooded out of the house, step by doddery step moving closer. The ground rushed towards her in an instant and pain overwhelmed her; Donna's ears were the last to die, if death is what really happened, for in that very final moment, she swore her mouth opened and emitted the noise.

Those thousand legs belonging to one deadly entity swarmed.

# EPILOGUE:
# O LITTLE TOWN

BESIDE THE WRECK of an aged cottage, of which only a chimney and fireplace remained, fought an aged man in red. He wasn't important, he wasn't anything special, he was simply . . . *Santa*. Blistered in a white blanket, the ruins had known many Christmases; in fact, the house was fabled to be the very first thing ever built in the quintessential Village of Little Hodbury. The residents had no choice except to flock to it yearly in honour of yuletide. It was a tradition! A tradition practically embossed into the snowy landscape itself.

As with previous years, a Santa had been selected, and on this occasion the fun bonus was that there was no need to supply a fat suit – Paul Albatross, the lone survivor of the old times, had a permanent one. The red tassels on his boots carved tracks into the snow, glistening in the pacific moonlight, as he was dragged towards the house. No matter how numb Santa's brain was under the fluence of the drugs – in the mulled wine, it had to be – the horde of chanting, imploring Villagefolk swarming around him wouldn't let the man forget he had a purpose to fulfil.

It was about midnight when the first pangs of drowsiness had begun to seep through him. When he had then awoken to the smell of the burning torches and the ruckus of a united mob outside his house, every ounce of energy went into making his legs move. Not an ounce of him stopped to think before crashing through the patio door – behind him, the sound of twenty or thirty men and women pouring themselves through his front door told Albatross running was his only option. Yet for every second the bitter wind woke his legs up, it slowed him down and numbed all his joints.

Surprising himself most of all, Albatross had actually made it halfway across a field when the Villagefolk had caught up with him. When their sharp fingernails sank into his shoulders and interrupted his strained flight, his skin had turned the same colour as the snow. Trying to launch his fist was useless; one of the younger Villagefolk had been there to bind manacles onto his wrists. Not that he'd have been able to curl his fingers enough to pry the steel manacle off his wrist, one of the Villagefolk entangled his wig in their hands anyway – and yanked. No sooner was he in chains than the Santa suit from his home was being forced around his pinching form.

And now, it was time. His time. *The* time.

One of the older Villagefolk tugged a ladder ricketier than himself up towards the chimney. The chimney towered in splendour, and whilst the logs were added to the fire, Santa's curved elf shoes dug into the ground. Yet the Villagefolk pushed him ever nearer. In years gone past, he had been one of the revellers enjoying the festivities. He had frolicked in the heat of the flames, indulged himself with milk warmed over that same fire, spread his smile in time with every other Villagefolk. And today the redness on his cheeks wasn't from the fire. The soreness beneath the metal manacles worsened, and he found his feet had no choice in leaving the ground. Albatross' lungs and lips were affected least, a wail of something primordial and abject finding a route out of his lungs and into the air swirling around the house's remains.

Then his head crashed into the mouldering brick. He never thought he'd miss the sight of snow, but as it left his view he found white was the only colour he wanted to see. Certainly not the soot-covered innards of the chimney now clouding his gaze – because that's what he prayed the horrible pressure around his skull was? The narrow confines pressed his skin, raw and seeping red, into the smallest corner of the brickwork. Even the tiniest pores on his skin bore some brunt as the soot and crumbling clay tried to find a home. Another mouthful of sooty, brick innards halted any more guttural chokes he might have coughed up.

He realised the process had already begun. And *they* were hungry.

Near his hip, one of the bricks slowly compressed his skin, changing it from a slab of excess girth to a lump of crushed, pulped dinner. To begin with, the brick warriors were gradual. It was yuletide tradition! Nothing added a more delicious tang to a meal like the mental and physical pinching sensations lodged in a victim's thoughts. The residue building within the confines now seemed to tingle with more and more excitement. Shocking their prey was always part of the agenda, part of the fun, too. The first brick to move higher up did so with enough vehemence to cause Albatross' teeth, of which a pitiful number remained, to spew out of his mouth – not that they had far to go, quickly hemmed in by building levels of soot or raw, manipulated flesh. Like chewing gum being mangled by teeth, the lumps of pink flesh weren't merely ground against the brickwork; every lump was contorted into two, divided, torn, ripped, shredded, minced, crammed into every available crevice unoccupied by soot and pitch.

The Villagefolk, gathered with more food than they'd been able to muster in any year previous, were already clamping their mouths around cooked chicken, beef, mutton, any animal's flesh they could stuff into their buckle cavity. They never saw the reddened, plump figure plummet into the inferno. All they saw was every single brick break free of its moorings – and compress inwards without a moment's hesitation.

The last they ever saw of Paul Albatross was the red, tattered hat poking free from the solid brick building. Some years, the chimney spat out the gristle, the offal, the fabric of the Santa suit. This year, when the bricks opened up again and ground back to their original position, they reveal no trace of the yuletide. Not even a lone speck of ground bone drifted down from its sooty recesses.

Oh well. The buffet that night was delicious.

# AUTHOR NOTES AND ACKNOWLEDGEMENTS

YOU!
   STOP THERE!
   Consider this a warning, reader! I'd hate for any of the stories to be spoiled. This sadly isn't a Steve Jackson and Ian Livingstone adventure gamebook and so the events of this book are chronological – if you haven't read the stories, these notes and their part-trivia, part-autobiography innards shall tell you things you aren't yet to know!
   Those naughty, skipping-ahead readers then: back to the start with you! Those who've read all the stories: aren't you lovely? Welcome to (more of) my ramblings . . .


**A Lenity for Ghosts**:

Most of these stories are set within a place I know, no matter how much I've warped it into the next Hellmouth. The Castle Tree is one such place – although the original has an equally imposing sister and I don't think it has a name (I apologise if that's tree discrimination).
   Picture seven-year-old me. I'm tiny, have quite blonde hair, and am just about to depart from my "cute" period. Most of our dog walks at this time were to a park near the River Lune, on the opposite riverbank from Lancaster, of which my first thought is still these two massive trees at

its furthest edge. If the word monolith can be applied to anything, my seven-year-old mind applies them to these. And they fascinated me! Maybe these trees went walkabout at night or maybe the local will o' the wisps liked buggering up the geography around them, but without fail every time we walked past these trees I never counted the same number of roots above ground. Clearly the image has stayed with me!

The other side to the geography of these stories comes from my life in the Lake District. For almost a decade now I've lived either full or part time in Kendal, but before then myself, Dad, and my step-family lived in farmhouses in a little village called Sedbergh. Whereas in Kendal you're on the doorstep of quite emphatic industry and yet only a stone's throw from the middle of nowhere, somehow Sedbergh is somewhere more liminal than that. Come for a day and how long you remain will be decided by when villagers drive you out with pitchforks and invective jibes. Yet what better place to provide the inspiration for Little Hodbury? If the world is truly going to end somewhere, isn't it a place with charity shops where you anticipate discovering an heirloom fouled by some sordid curse, or with a school beyond disrepair and the younger brother of the entire setting of *Session 9* (2001)?

However, its inclusion is slightly accidental. It was only after writing about three or four of these stories that I became uncomfortably aware that I was unconsciously writing about Sedbergh, not just the Lake District at large. And I panicked. I'm not vain enough to assume my stories will be wide-reaching, but Sod's Law dictates that the one person who reads them will be someone from Sedbergh. My mind raced – what if they get pissed off? I've just let loose any number of malicious forces on the town!

Little Hodbury came about then to stop me getting punched by an angry Cumbrian villager. A place I could set all my stories, without repercussions. Let's just hope they don't like my work enough to peruse the author notes.

But the setting isn't actually the only unintentional element here.

An influence suggested to me merely a month before I sat down to write this author note was a particular strand of B-movies centred around killer trees. I can't say it was deliberate, but I can't deny I like 1957's *From Hell It Came*, nor that one of my favourite horror films is the eco-horror *Prophecy* (1979).

Consciously at least, this story evolved because I wanted to write a specific character dynamic. Rathbone and Asquith, as I'll expand on in the notes for Part II, are characters I liked. In literature and beyond, I reckon that the most successful dynamics generally come from pairs of characters – Sherlock Holmes and Dr. Watson, Mulder and Scully, Tweedledum and Tweedledee, the Doctor and Sarah Jane, Batman and Robin, Jekyll and Hyde, Hansel and Gretel, Wallace and Gromit, Romeo and Juliet, Han Solo and Chewbacca. After all, three's a crowd.

The pairing which fleshed Rathbone and Asquith the most, however, was *Sapphire & Steel*, the titular characters of P.J. Hammond's utterly spectacular 1979–82 SF/fantasy series. I regard myself as an unofficial seventies kid in many ways – as I write this, within the last month, I have watched thirty-four films and two TV serials. Only two of those were post-1990. It truly is a series I adore. And that "out of time" feel is, I reckon, honed to some of its best usages in that series, as these beings from outside reality do battle with time "gone rogue" in locales as varied as abandoned train stations with WWI "ghosts" and strange invisible flats above a modern high-rise apart- ment. And wherever they go, they never fit in.

**The Tale of God-Fang**:

I love mythology. It lets you tread the line between the fantastical and rational in a rather unique way among genres and it probably explains why I love the Classics so much. In French classes, you learn how to ask where the toilet is, but in Latin and Ancient Greek you learn how to recount your adventures of killing, maiming, decapitating, abusing, and all round outwitting mythological creatures. In one Latin course, you even get to spend about seventeen chapters following a Roman family stuck in a ditch by the side of a road (it's more interesting than it sounds) and all their various adventures as they try and reach Rome. So, unless you have a particularly exceptional toilet (the kind haunted by Hanako-san would be valid, for instance), I'm afraid I shall always lean towards the latter first.

It's practically inevitable that a mythology story would find its way in here then.

And like so many stories in this collection, this is a story where its seeds were sown in my infancy. The days of Ben who could barely scrape 4'1" were the years when I discovered my all-time love, *Doctor Who*. My years spanning five to thirteen were when I discovered *Star Wars*, when I became petrified by Darren Shan, started to wonder who this Stephen King fella was, and became intrigued by whatever could be contained in my father's wealth of CDs and books. Being an author himself, my dad's sprawling cupboards of books were always going to worm their way into my mind at that age, even if simply the drawings on their covers.

One such cover, as my younger self recalls it, showed fiery swathes of smoke and volcanic eruptions, with blood red writing for the title and a dragon-hobgoblin-gremlin-thing on the cover. All of these explosions of colour and warty skins were also joined by a coven of shrouded figures, as well as a bunch of burning green eyes in the sky. I remember daring to go further and read within; the various illustrations of gleaming bronze UFOs, a crusader-like figure wrapped in the tail of a massive sea serpent, and even a Greek mosaic of a temple covered in smoke and towered over by a Viking god lit up my imagination!

I've since found the book in question: Usborne's *Mysteries of the Unknown: Monsters, Ghosts & UFOs*. I'm glad to say the cover is just as extraordinary and bombastic in real life as it is in my memory, and so are the illustrations throughout, detailing everything from cyclopes to Scylla to krakens! In fact, the image of the crusader and the sea creature is far more vivid than my memory thought it was, and I'm surprised they'd push that kind of thing onto some kids' psyches. For those with a copy, it's on page ten, complete with bloody waters, a green-skinned dragon, crashing waves, spiked armour on the knight glistening with red, and a shield that would surely do about as much as a toothpick against a raging bull.

The other book I regard as a miniature compendium of all things mythological is one by

Carey Miller called *A Dictionary of Monsters and Mysterious Beasts*. It's certainly one of the few non-fiction books I've read in one sitting, as though it were fiction, and continue to go back to. It's certainly the book I have to blame for this story, or at least one facet of it – that reference to T'ien Kou? Thanks Carey!

Both of these texts certainly sealed the deal on what my beast should be and either a quick dive into Carey Miller's book or an attack of vivid memories of the Usborne book preceded most of my sessions writing this story, the original draft of which took almost a year to write. But my monster had had its birth! As with all stories, its features and aspects changed drastically from draft to draft, adopted at one point a more John Carpenter-esque style, and yet ended up in a kind of urban myth.

I doubt I'll ever revisit God-Fang – leave him as a legend of the dark times one should tread carefully around lest it wake and devour everything and everyone.

**Crucial Decisions**:

Lockdown did many strange things to me, as it did to us all. In the same way that the Great War, the prohibition, the IRA bombings, the Crusades, Hitler, or the Black Death impacted their respective generations, I think Lockdown and COVID-19 will be my generation's equivalent. I'm lucky that I coped with it better than most actually – I emerged the other side having lost only a few marbles (though that assumes I had marbles in the first place) and I somehow gained GCSE results I could be proud of along the way.

With online teaching, I found I didn't have to deal with the bullies. Without a commute, I could zone myself into my work in the way I needed, not the way the universe demanded. And the cups of tea were endless! Otherwise, I mostly filled my time with picking apart the minutiae of *Doctor Who* episodes, letting my love of Ancient Greek and Latin explode, but perhaps best of all myself and Dad had our joint short story collection published: *Uneasy Beginnings*, courtesy of Steve Shaw at Black Shuck Books. It contains the first three pieces of my fiction I ever had published – and I quickly had a taste for something I liked.

Perhaps I felt some kind of backward imposter syndrome, and so I found I was very quickly looking for stories almost to "justify" the publication retroactively. Most of the stories I scribbled down or typed out in that phase, therefore, are pure bafflegab, and I only regard two I wrote during that time as noteworthy in any way. One is a fantasy story I shall never let see the light of day because, it's so tortuously written that I have no idea where to start with salvaging it.

The other story of note is 'Crucial Decisions', not that that was its initial title. At first it was 'The Council' (inventive, I know . . . ), and then it became 'A Storm Brewing', and then 'Fight!', before eventually becoming 'Crucial Decisions'. There was a half-developed version called 'When Will the Mice Take You?' somewhere in the mix, however it never got so far as becoming its own draft since I just as soon changed the ending from involving one singular creature to being a menagerie of creatures befitting my all-time favourite film, *The Abominable Dr. Phibes* (1971).

The grim nature of lockdown certainly mixed its way into the story, the nihilism and antipathy towards any kind of officialdom drawn from it deliberately or otherwise. In the midst of so much pain and horror, we were expected to be transfixed by the words of a load of drab politicians, for instance. And while there isn't anything wrong with politics per se – I even quite like shows such as *The Crown* or *Bodyguard* – so many politicians have this chance to make lives better and yet they squander that by turning populations against them, using us as bullets in the governmental rifle. Is that not one possible defin- ition of hell? Not burning flames, rabid dogs, or horned demons tucking into my soul; my hell is being surrounded by the lifeless world of politics. If you're going to weaponise words, use them to write drama or novels.

In short, it unlocked the cocoon and released the cynic within me all that time, the "therapy" for which was 'Crucial Decisions'.

It took returning to school for Sixth Form for the final element to take root, however. The reason the story went through so many drafts boiled down to, at least in hindsight, something being missing within Esther's motivations. My Theatre Studies A-Level group thankfully came to the rescue here. One of us, Vaughn, celebrated his birthday fairly early in the school year so we'd all gone out bowling with him – and, whilst I don't know the precise trigger, I do know that by the time we'd returned to school the next week, the entire middle section of this story had not only been fleshed out, it had taken on a life of its own.

The pig, Greg, was (well, I hope they still are, I just cannot say categorically as I haven't been at that school in over two years!) a real one. Well, a real *Minecraft* one; Joe, probably the most unassuming "theatre kid" I've ever known, won him at a Morecambe arcade on that same birthday bowling sojourn. Charley the duck was real as well; he was a puppet living in the drama cupboard who would fall gracelessly onto hapless visitors. Just as real was Fernando; he was a fake fish Mrs. Owens bought for the 2020–2022 A-Level productions. Like their counterparts in 'Crucial Decisions', they all had a habit of being sequestered in the oddest places throughout the drama studio, like topsy-turvy and disfigured elves on shelves. Greg's favourite place was generally atop the whiteboard projector, though I don't think anyone quite knows why. He did make his way into Mrs. Owen's minifridge, although unlike in this story we used him as a chilled therapy teddy to be cuddled.

None of us ever disembowelled them or displayed their entrails provocatively. Well, not that I know of. I suppose Nico did always strike me as the disembowelling sort . . .


**Hollow Eyes**:

Of all the stories here, this had in a way the easiest transition from idea to actuality. Most of my stories, excluding spelling checks and general neatening, go through at least three drafts – this only went through two. It's the first one where I think I'd actually managed to self-edit as I went; the only reason the second draft exists is because it was suggested I restructure the ending, a suggestion I admit was beneficial. The banter with the electrician went much differently and it had a much more B-movie feel rather than a creeping dread.

It was originally written for an anthology

called *Unexploded Bombs* (I apologise, I cannot remember the press, as the anthology never came to fruition anyway), the uniting theme of the stories being the idea that secrets or afflictions get worse the longer you leave them. I'd at that point already been flirting with the plot of a story revolving around a mutant potato – I mean, if you leave those things in a cupboard for ages, you should see the eldritch monstrosities they turn into! – but every time I tried to write it I either couldn't get the tone right, or it all just felt like I was threshing out a non-existent idea. Eventually, for reasons I cannot remember, I decided to unite the two impetuses, and so a tale of a mutant potato met a story whose characters are slowly coming to terms with dementia.

At least that I've been alive to witness, only one of my family members has had dementia; my great grandmother lived into her eighties and died when I was twelve, but when I was eleven or thereabouts I remember feeding her chocolate buttons while my grandmother and great grandfather sat next to me and reminisced about her renowned sweet tooth. While I never knew her in her prime, I think the memory has stayed with me because of how it kind of straddled two worlds – that of the great grandma I knew, and that of the one the people around me talked about. The idea of a shift in personality is common to a lot of mental health and degenerative disorders and so it seemed like quite a natural premise to use. Is something sinister going on, or are these the quirks of the disease taking hold?

In this case, it's the former. A potato worming its way into two pensioners' idylls, all the while the wife assumes her husband is simply succumbing to the cruel hold of dementia or the like.

But it also gave me a bit of scope for the dialogue. From the submissions call of the aforementioned anthology, I felt they wanted something which capitalised less on the stigma of the secret or affliction (whatever it may be) and more on the sense of unreality to it. The self-doubt, the mental somersaults, the worries. A pet peeve of mine anyway is long, expansive speeches – how often do we soliloquise in real life? – and so in the dialogue especially I especially tried to write the exchanges almost as humorous miscommunications, two people never quite meeting the same topic, or at least having two different perspectives that could never overlap. I hope I did the idea justice, as well as the idea of a mutant potato.

Incidentally, as I write this I'm three stories into a review copy of an upcoming anthology called *This Way Lies Madness* (eds. Lee Murray and Dave Jeffery) which explores similar themes. I can, so far at least, wholeheartedly recommend it.

### A Loathing for Ghosts:

'A Loathing for Ghosts' concludes my unofficial "Castlespire" trilogy. *Trilogy???*

Oh yes! In the context of this collection, it's the latter half of 'A Lenity for Ghosts' since it's the explanation for why Rathbone and Asquith were targeted in the first place. But when Dad and I wrote *Uneasy Beginnings* (spoiler alert incoming . . . ), one of my three stories was one called 'A Lust for Ghosts', the ending of which directly leads into the events of this story since it details why a man is manacled to the ceiling and looked over by two pensioners – though I'll let you track down the story to fully understand why. I never intended them to form a trilogy, but when I was conceiving the opening story of this collection I was a) always a little disappointed that these characters never got a happy ending, not least because I knew I wanted to write for them again, and b) always aware that the reason the tree wanted them was because it was aware that at some future date its wood would be used to construct a house which subsequently suffers a haunting. 'A Loathing for Ghosts' sprung up then from both of those points as it allowed Rathbone and Asquith to live to fight another day, albeit in a century not their own, and meant that I could explore the concept of a house which didn't want to be haunted. Because, to be fair, I think if I was a house, I'd dislike it.

Richard Matheson's novel *Hell House* – the 1973 film adaptation of which, *The Legend of Hell House*, I unashamedly prefer to *The Innocents* (1961) and *The Haunting*, the 1963 adaptation of Shirley Jackson's *The Haunting of Hill House*, both of which are seen traditionally as the magna opera of haunted house films – was a great influence on the story's eventual form. This was always going to be a more action-oriented, against-the-clock romp, but the macabre atmosphere and understated Grand Guignol I find irresistible and tried to work in as well.

Of course all of these stories work as isolated pieces – and in fact making sure they function both as part of a gestalt story and individuals took up a lot of the editing time for this collection – but I hope any readers who have been reading me since my first publication (Do such people exist, or has my hubris got the better of me?) will enjoy the plot tying them together and the cloud of grumpy severity I seem to have written the trilogy under.

**Counting to Oblivion**:

Backgammon Man is real. And he's more like his literary counterpart than I intended for him to be. A moment of madness where the time and the money in his wallet aligned happened for him and so when I realised I was telling a story along much the same lines it was the work of half a day to tweak the draft to include that personal touch.

Backgammon Man – or Crazy Dave, as he actually is in my phone contacts – is someone I have an enormous respect for and especially during Sixth Form I'd usually see him two or three times after school. Nothing sinister, you understand – literally just tea and backgammon! He and I had met through Oxfam volunteering and has slowly realised how alike we were, seeing reality in a certain way and rallying against the neurotypical way of thinking.

To those curious about what my A-Levels were: Religion, Ethics, and Philosophy; English Literature; Theatre Studies. I mention this not to bore you, but to put down my sonic screwdriver and hold my hands up that this entire collection is in fact one long, ridiculous philosophy essay for that unintentional reason. I loved English, and Theatre Studies, but the actual nitty gritty of Philosophy I took to in a way which surprised even me. Suddenly "Existentialism", for instance, wasn't just a term I'd occasionally come across in a book – it became something I could see. I then started thinking within that theory, or thinking of a rejoinder against it, wherever I went; it infected my brain in a rather bizarre way. Patt- erns appeared where they shouldn't, and I could no longer see patterns where once I had.

One of my offsets for this was with Crazy Dave. We'd actually talk about these things without the worry of an essay to complete at the end of the day. It was an exhaust pipe of sorts; after a day where I might have had to worm something into my brain to force it into an essay I felt no conviction for, I could instead separate the nitty gritty and the facets of the subject which I actually cared about and talk about them in what was to me a sensible way.

This story *is* me then. I'm not saying I go round killing people because of an unorganised universe – well, not that the police can prove . . . – overthinking everything into oblivion is something I suffer from. My nickname for one aspect of this is "Blank Page Syndrome": where you look at a blank page with an essay title at the top, and every time you try and figure out a plan the words start to make less and less sense, if you even understood them in the first place, to the extent that they end up just being fancy squiggles in random places on a page. Similarly, I have a sensitivity to numbers. I can't necessarily explain why I'll only allow certain numbers for the TV volume, nor why they have no pattern to them. I mean, 28 and 32 are fine and dandy, but 29, 30, and 31 make me want to tear off my flesh and smother someone with it. Then, of course, there's also the sensitivity to volume, which adds an entirely new spin on things! Trust me, it's bloody exhausting. The point is that all those coincidences, the way my Sixth Form brain (more than ever before in my life) saw patterns where none might have existed, and my need to see things in a rational construction needed to go somewhere. And so they went into 'Counting to Oblivion'.

One such point of strange reality happened with the title of this story. I don't keep a diary of when I write my stories, but my computer tells me that May 2022 is when I created the document that became 'Counting to Oblivion'; I'd have been nearing the end of my first year of Sixth Form and so I can say almost with certainty that that's when I re-read the story 'Decanting Oblivion' in the fantastic collection *Voices*, written by none other than Lawrence C. Connolly (or, as I know him, Larry). Notice a similarities in the titles? Consciously at least, the "Oblivion" of both is the only connection between them both, but Larry's story is one I'm vastly fond of and I knew immediately upon re-reading it that I wanted to use the word in a story of my own.

How coincidental then that Larry agreed to do the foreword for this collection? I wish I could say it was some divine strategy on my part; I imagine it's actually the universe telling me I asked the right man for the job.

**In the Forest of Bones and Shadows**:

COVID-19 has mostly obscured my memories of the aftermath of myself and Dad's joint collection *Uneasy Beginnings* being published in 2020, but as I touch upon in my note for 'Crucial Decisions', something I do remember was the impostor syndrome. Or, at least, this ridiculous insecurity that when we all came out of the pandemic there'd be an expectation for me to have written far more;

I'd started a ball rolling, hadn't I? I couldn't let its momentum drop!

When COVID then began settling down in 2022 (at least, in terms of its impact on me: I could return to school by then, the lockdowns were over, and ostensibly things had returned to the "new normal"), the impostor syndrome never really left. But this story is where I channelled it. That dislocated sense of self found their way into Toby (who is based after another of my A-Level thespian friends, though in name only – that Toby is a far more genial and indoors-y person than park ranger Toby), and a lot of my general frustration at the world coloured my writing of the character. Like 'A Lenity for Ghosts' and 'A Loathing for Ghosts', the story ended up digging its claws into the dynamic of its characters, but the original draft was far more impermanent, barely reaching 2000 words. Unsurprisingly, it received a volley of rejection and in hindsight I'm quite grateful for that; the story sat in a folder for a year until I finally reconsidered it. When I did, the path towards fixing the story just felt clear; originally, after Toby finds the carcass of one of the animals, it's the shadows from their innards which chase *him* from the forest and instead of suffering the underside of a car tyre, he ends up plummeting to his death in a stream where the shadows pick his bones clean.

But I knew that, to paraphrase the words of 1980–9 *Doctor Who* producer John Nathan Turner, it needed a monster! Hence why the bone creature is a part of the story – the name never makes it into the story, as my character rationalises it as "The King of the Darkness", but in my head it's called "Ossorum Rex" (Latin for "The King of Bones"). The actual *why* of its existence within the logic of the story I shall keep to myself, since my brain continues to flirt with the idea that its story hasn't fully concluded, but I imagined its plight much like some kind of gestalt worm. He's making a home for himself beneath Farrowpine Forest and mortals should fear what eventually will be housed there! The revised draft also gave me chance to cut, among other things, a myriad of tawdry dialogue and a very strange arc where one of Toby's loves of being in the forest is rooted in him looking for the best spot to embrace his inner flasher – the kind of arc Guy N. Smith might've smiled at! However, I am sadly not him and I cringe at the naivety with which I wrote that first draft.

As for the realisation of Ossorum Rex itself, I'd be doing you a disservice if I lied and said my visualisation of it I don't picture in very Junji Ito terms. I love horror films as much as I do horror literature – for every H.P. Lovecraft story I've read, there's been a watch of *From Beyond* (1986) or *Lurking Fear* (1994) to cement that – but of manga and graphic novels, I can't say I'm an especially avid reader. Nothing against the medium, it just isn't *me*.

Junji Ito's work is the exception to that. I find his stories/art supernally sublime, as haunting as they are beautiful, as sinuous as they are visceral, an anatomy textbook given form and narrative and an unworldly quality. Here is where I might owe Dad an apology too; when I had just begun high school, he lent me his copy of *Uzumaki*, Ito's 600-page epic about a town haunted by spirals, and I mocked him by asking how a spiral could possibly be frightening? I shan't reveal how, but suffice to say Ito does make them f*cking terrifying. His illustration of a boy metamorphosing into a snail was in fact the basis of my Year 8 art project and, whether Ms. France approved or not, it still got me the highest mark I ever achieved in the subject!

**The All-Embracing Nature of a Plastic Bag**:

As I've touched upon elsewhere, bouts of depression and existential angst are something I've struggled with more and more over the last few years. And I find what makes them worse isn't so much the intensity or duration of the bout, but instead the fact that the way out of them feels so close and so tangible and yet every time you step towards it, it's as if you're thrown into a dolly zoom and suddenly one step forward becomes two steps back. Should you fancy looking at other examples of this, 'I Miss You Too Much' by Sarah Langan is a remarkably brilliant short story which explores it via a mother/daughter relationship, and you can't go wrong with either Edgar Allan Poe's 'The Tell-Tale Heart' or a myriad of stories by the inimitable Shirley Jackson.

One of the few ways I have of coping though is to go for walks – it's where I do my best (and my worst) thinking, often with an audio drama of some description: this story was fully planned out on one such walk. It was after a particularly difficult weekend in my first year of uni, where all my other plans for taking my mind off my depressive episode seemed to have crashed and burned, but I finally convinced myself to walk around the Town Moor at about 3 a.m. (accompanied by the *Blake's 7* audio drama 'The Sevenfold Crown', though don't ask me how I can remember that and yet frequently forget the names of half my cousins!)

on the Monday morning. I returned home a good two hours later and wrote this in one sitting, maybe against saner judgement since there's an argument I should have instead caught a bit of sleep before my 10 a.m. lecture.

I'm pretty sure it remains the only story I've ever written in one go and – at least to me – it feels like one of my best flowing stories. I rarely write in the first person *and* in the present tense, and so my decision to use the style here stems from that, I reckon. As for what inspired the narrative itself, I'll leave that to a psychoanalyst with too much time on their hands. But perhaps stories from the perspective of a serial killer's plastic bag-cum-murder weapon sometimes just need to exist and the universe finds a way to make it so?

What I can say without a shadow of a doubt is that I really like Paul Albatross as a character; he's not a nice character, but the almost radio-sitcom-esque style of someone in most of the stories, but with no actual appearance I liked. Sometimes you don't catch the madman; or sometimes the madman catches themselves. I wanted to explore the downfall, just in a "by proxy" way.

## Paradigm of Pains:

For the majority of high school and Sixth Form, Dad and I would only see each other every other weekend and alternate Thursday nights (divorced parents, what can you do . . . ). It was during one such weekend early on in my first October of Sixth Form we were in the midst of a mini binge of the three "main" Clive Barker films – to the uninitiated, that's *Hellraiser* (1987), *Nightbreed* from 1990 and *Lord of Illusions* (1995). The first was a rewatch, but the latter two I was watching for the first time; my favourite of those three is actually still *Lord of Illusions*, though Barker is one of those authors who, at least on screen, I've never warmed to as so many other creatives. The latter might explain why, for all the flaws I can still see in the film, it took me until yet another rewatch of *Hellraiser* just after going to uni to appreciate it in full.

What does this have to do with 'Paradigm of Pains'?

Well, for a start, it began life under the tit- le 'Raising Hell', a deliberate homage to the 1987 film, before becoming 'The Sadists, The Masoch- ists, and the Innocents', and then its eventual ite- ration. On that first rewatch, the story threshed itself into being in my head almost at once, or at least planted were the seeds of a plot which would revolve around a sadist and a masochist caught in a kind of symbiotic relationship. I was intrigued, I think, by the notion that two things at two extre- mes of the sexual spectrum could somehow be two sides of the same coin.

This did, of course, make it slightly awkward when I scribbled out the rough plot of this story – with special regard to where and when the grues- omeness ought to feature – and accidentally incl- uded it in a bunch of things I'd printed out for a Theatre Studies class the following day. I like to think that my Thespian Tribe were quite accept- ing of my eccentricities, yet I shall never forget the look on Heather's face when she asked what on Earth a story outline written in madman script (and which had obviously had the misfortune of skim-reading) was doing among the printouts. I think she was worried I might have had plans to behead or maim her.

After that ill-placed outline, the story itself actually took roughly eleven months to get to a point where I was happy with it and another two years to find publication in *Criminal Pursuits 2: This is Me* (ed. Samantha Lee Howe). Its home was always going to be here though.

As the story was forming in my mind, the actual "thrust" of the collection was also finalising itself in my mind and so from then on any publication of the stories was in fact them escaping early like icebergs breaking off a glacier. It's therefore the first of the stories here where I was writing it with a fully fledged concept of Little Hodbury and its various machinations; a handful of unused ideas still exist in my notebook, one of which involves Satan writing messages to people via Starbucks coffee cups. I knew already that the collection's theme would be a town essentially being disrupted by gentrification and becoming an unspoken cul-de-sac where all that was good went to perish; the push specifically with this story was firstly that it made me realise just how many stories I'd set in this little Hellmouth, but secondly just how great the scope was for tales which interconnected as opposed to simply lived in the same universe. It's a tactic Robert Holmes, my favourite ever scriptwriter for *Doctor Who*, would utilise, polluting his stories with character arcs within character arcs, off-hand references, little asides which only the characters understand, and a world greater than what you see on the screen or in the dialogue; he also knew how to write duplicity beautifully and used dynamic character duos to get the most out of the ideas, both of which also affected how I wrote the interplay between Andrews and Tall Boy, and more importantly Aspinwall and Martindale. I don't know whether I explored the concept to the same degree as Holmes, but as the rest of the collection took shape and the final edits on the other stories occurred, it was something very much in my mind. It gave me the incentive to make one of the police officers of 'A Final Repose' also Martindale; it's why events of some stories are referenced further down the line; most importantly, it's why the "unseen" Albatross thread develops as it does.

More of this is hindsight and coincidence than I'm maybe making out – and to that I hold out my hands and admit it! But whether deliberate or not I think it's something I'm proudest of about *Into Wrack and Ruin*.

**Mother Dearest**:

As previously mentioned, a number of these stories are set either in facsimiles of places in Sedbergh, or are places I know which I've bolted onto the Sedbergh scenery. In the case of 'Mother Dearest', the house which this crazed family live in is the house Dad and my stepmum first rented after his divorce. How we survived there as long as we did, given how isolated and in various states of disrepair it was, baffles me – good job it makes for good writing fuel!

Thankfully, the events of the story are far less realistic to anything I've experienced. They owe a debt to *Doctor Who*, and more specifically one or two of the various *Doctor Who* scripts I've hammered out for my private amusement over the years. The traces of its *Who* foundation are, by the draft you're reading, barely present, yet it's why the tale's conclusion involves a mutant creature. Those original iterations of this story are too shockingly cliched and tawdry ever to see the light of day, and like so much I've written they're expelled to a folder entitled "The Work of an Idiot"; in intent, I wanted an amalgam of a number of classic novels like Emily Brontë's *Wuthering Heights* and Thomas Hardy's *Tess of the D'Urbervilles*, because if there are two things they're good at capturing it's dysfunction and beautiful description. In the case of those two specific ones, I have my teacher Ms. Gibson to thank; Hardy's novel she taught at A-Level, but Brontë's she actually gifted me a lovely clothbound edition of (thus beginning my collection of Penguin clothbound classics which I adore and which my bank account grouches over) and it was a seminal novel for me in many ways. Although anyone who says they like romance and dislike horror, like a certain (other) Y9 English teacher once tried to, can book themselves into the local asylum; eleven of the thirteen non-narrating characters die in *Wuthering Heights*, and over the course of the book people suffer attacks by dogs, death during childbirth, intense neglect, rape, domestic abuse, implied racism, profound xenophobia, bullying, and even a goddamn haunting. That's horror in my book!

With any luck, this explains the "meaningless" death in the story, simultaneously blink-and-you'll-miss it and central. You can escape from your parents, the weird alien monster thing that used to be your mother, or your alcohol addiction, but it's tripping and banging your head that'll really do you in, just as hope is rearing its head.

The other element I consciously inserted into the story was the mood of *The Monster Club* (1981), an anthology film based on the works of R. Chetwynd-Hayes. It's very possible that even horror aficionados won't have heard of *The Monster*

*Club*, since it's generally considered the devious empty wrapper at the bottom of a box of chocolates. I've always found that a rather unpalatable attitude – I much prefer to regard it as the coconut cream, disliked by many but which I take an intense pride in liking. 'The Ghouls' segment of the film involves an isolated village where the inhabitants eat corpses and you get to see a hapless film director get trapped in that world. Profoundly bleak and subtly insalubrious, there's a lot going on within that portion of *The Monster Club* that I recreated in 'Mother Dearest', most obviously seedier notions underpinning a pulpier narrative. Sadly, and I'm sure my good friend John Llewellyn Probert will lament this alongside me, I couldn't find a (rational) way for Stuart Whitman to wander into the story and encounter a Humgoo!

Incidentally, another facet of Sixth Form carried over into a lot of these stories was that at one point I asked my Theatre Studies group if any of them fancied being immortalised in print – they could even choose the manner of their death! Nico (hence Nicolas) was insistent on dying by tripping over a rock, which just so happened to mesh with this story. And so he did.

**A Final Repose**:

Like 'Paradigm of Pains', 'A Final Repose' is one of the two reprints here – it escaped early to go join the circus but instead got captured by J.E. Feldman for the anthology she was editing called *Beautiful Darkness 3*. If 'Paradigm of Pains' was the story that took the longest to write a first draft of, and 'The All-embracing Nature of a Plastic Bag' was the story I found easiest to write in a single sitting, this was the story which I had the most fun writing.

It is another one that the idea for had long been percolating in the back of my mind. It wasn't written in one sitting, but I felt no need to plan or outline – it wasn't there one minute and was the next! Most of it grew organically too, very little needing to be tweaked or edited; not out of pomposity, just out of a realisation that I was onto something and was having great fun in finding out how far I could stretch the possibilities of it. It's why I can't place where the epiphany struck me that it needed a final wrongfooting, it just seemed the right thing to do. The whole point was a story where you discover the narrator is unreliable at the conclusion of a story rather than gradually discovering it at first, as well as the contrast between someone very easily excusing and thus editing their memories of killing two children while finding a piece of roadkill on their conscience so inexcusable. Not of those British stereotypes of people who know what's happening and handily decide they want a quiet life – this is self-delusion at its finest!

Should one day I ever decide to make a short film, I imagine this shall get the treatment. You can have great scope with short stories, but there's a lot of fun in seeing how insular and almost trippy you can make them, for which I think this would be perfect. I know who I'd (ideally) cast as well – shall we just say that should a spectral version of Niall MacGinnis be reading this and in need of resurrection from the dead, the part of Ross Bainbridge (clad in dishevelled tweed and troubled by a grasp on reality) is yours! As for the roadkill – I'm sure Basil the Brush must have a disreputable cousin who doesn't mind being lathered in make-up and special effects goo.

**The Fifth Demographic**:

Since so many of these stories have been influenced by my love of horror cinema, it feels only right then that the denouement of the collection was influenced similarly. Gary Sherman, Jorge Grau, step up to the pedestal!

Sherman's *Dead and Buried* (1981) and Grau's *The Living Dead at Manchester Morgue* (1974) are two films I love intensely. I'd go so far as saying they're my favourite zombie films, although their unique complexions extend beyond the subgenre, and to various degrees I wanted to include what made them special. The overall grim tone of both films I think found its way into here – most of the horrors of this story aren't built around the stigma of what makes old people scary (I'd direct you to *Frightmare* [1976] for the answer to that question), I tried to build them around the fact that this isn't a town ready for change. It enters the fifth demographic (the "declining" stage, where birth rate is low and the death rate is low only because the population is generally at its lowest point) because the outside, gentrified world is impinging on it and because Albatross' schemes have weaponised the few remaining population.

*Dead and Buried* and *The Living Dead at Manchester Morgue* also have the allure which I adore from "possessed town" stories – no, *The Monster Club*, shh! You've already had your turn to be mentioned! – and cultivate a sense of lacking individuality in most areas of the setting, from the sordid to the heroic. Not to say townsfolk are without personality, but you find in those kind of communities most hold the same values and most live by the same traditions. And there's nothing necessarily bad about that! However, among people like me, it can seem a little taciturn being somewhere that the days blur into one another. When every day of your life you wear anything from bow ties to cravats and waistcoats to velvet jackets, amid other peacock-like displays of sartorial elegance, at best you stand out and exist on a different wavelength – and at worst people stick their nose up at you for being unalike.

That I'm autistic comes into play here – and Seb was a character I ummed and aahed over including for quite a while. Because, I admit, he is somewhat stereotyped. But the difference is he's a stereotype only if you could isolate him from his surroundings. He isn't mute because autistics are mute, he speaks less because the conditions need to be right for him to feel able to express himself – and let me tell you, despite the bow ties and waistcoats, it took me a long time to discern what those conditions were. Equally, he's not sensitive to noise and having a panic attack because that's what all autistic people are – but with autism there frequently comes a heightened set of senses. Because the world is built for neurotypicals, we're told to get on with the world, and so most of us therefore find coping strategies. In my case, I find I can usually cope with one sense going into overload as long as I expect it and can make sure the others are harmonious in preparation. When the world enacts a private vendetta against *all* your senses though? It can feel like the world is crashing down around you; and often to stay sane, "perfunctory" things like the ability to speak can go out the window because you enter the fight-or-flight world. Or, sadly, the fight-or-crumble, because fighting takes a lot of energy and most people with autism or ADHD are to some degree already working off reserves they don't have.

It's a sad reality, but please take this as representation. If you've read above something you can recognise in yourself – don't worry! You're seen. If you can't? That's okay – but be aware, you'll likely know someone who does recognise it and might benefit from you being aware of it.

**O Little Town**:

Like 'Mother Dearest', this very loosely began life as one of my *Doctor Who* script ideas – on this occasion, one where an alien culture uses Christmas as a bellicose punishment against invading humans. Again like 'Mother Dearest', almost the entirety of its *Doctor Who* iteration isn't evident in the story anymore, but it still possesses an ode to the show's Target novelisations range. There are very few Target novelisations I haven't read now, and one of my favourites is *The Dalek Invasion of Earth*, quite simply for its opening sentence: "Through the ruin of a city stalked the ruin of a man." Poor Robo-man. For all that I don't have a ruined city here, the temptation to co-opt the general structure of the line felt too strong, hence my opening sentence: "Beside the wreck of an aged cottage, of which only a chimney and fireplace remained, fought an aged man in red."

The actual writing of this story is far more bizarre than the story itself though. Since it's only quite short, and I knew that from word one of page one, I'd decided to write it on a train ride down to Manchester. I get the train regularly, but by the time I'm in the zone for the metaphorical juices to begin flowing the journey is usually over and the idea has disappeared in a puff of logic, and so I was taking full advantage of actually feeling up to writing.

I'd written the opening paragraph. I was about to start describing the snowy landscape – and then a gaggle of ABBA lookalikes appeared.

Stag parties? I can deal with those; they pollute most trains past 10 p.m., as do those celebrating football matches with drunken exultations. People dressed in ways that draw quizzical eyebrows? Can deal with them as well, I'm one of them. I dress in enough velvet and have enough bow ties to begin my own tailoring shop. But, these ABBA aficionados . . . there were about thirty of them, I think a little tipsy, and they seemed determined to play "Fizz Buzz" across the central aisle for the entire journey! And, though in the midst of them there did seem to be one person cosplaying in the guise of a coked-up John Lennon, me and a poor man trying to read his *Fortean Times* (I wish I was joking) were being harangued to and fro.

So, whilst I've no idea whether the page picked up my stress energies or a particularly disconcerted vibe, I can confirm that most of this chilly tale was written with two Agnetha Fältskogs in their 'Waterloo' outfits opposite me and an obscenely foul-mouthed Bjorn Ulvaeus to my left. Odd doesn't quite cut it, methinks.

## Acknowledgements

My family put up with an awful lot: mad tangents, the tumble of words when I haven't had a helpless audience for a while, my need to wear waistcoats no matter the weather. My life has had two very different complexions since Mum and Dad separated in the early 2010s, but I love you all.

Dad, I can blame you for an *awful* lot. Either because of some recent family curse or black magic, or perhaps even good parenting, I reckon I picked up the author gene from you. You gave me the shoe-in to the genre, gave me unfettered access to the bookshelves, and were instrumental in placing me in front of a TV and telling me we were going to watch films, a lot of which I would then come to adore. You're wrong about *Evil Dead II* (1987) though – it's terrible.

Samuel Forrest; Laurence and Adele and Tom and Jamie Clark; Ele and Seb Raw; John and Kate and Magnus Probert; Ramsey and Jenny Campbell; and Kayleigh Dobbs – with all of you I found kindred spirits and you're some of my fondest friends from across all my spheres of pandemonium. Sorry if my love of *Doctor Who* is far too intoxicating – it shan't *ever* stop, though. Although if you aren't accustomed to my madness at this point, I don't know where you've been hiding. All my love.

As touched upon in the notes, my Sixth Form years surrounded the writing of a lot of these stories. And so to those who helped me traverse the complexities of A-Level and provided me with life lessons, my utmost thanks: Mrs. Gibson, Mrs. Owens, Mrs. Livesey, Ms. Ball, Ms. Jenkinson, Mrs. Ennis.

There are many people within the writing community who have supported me and welcomed me into a family I now cannot imagine living without. You know who you are!

Especial thanks go to Anna Stephens for an utterly horrible editing tip that I'm infuriated to say works really well, as well as CC Adams, Sam Howe, Dan Howarth, and Ross Chapman, not only for their support of my various insanities, but also for providing invaluable beta-reads and advice along the way. Lawrence C. Connolly, I'm so grateful you wrote the foreword to this – you were my first choice for the job and the support you've given me means an awful lot!

**—Benjamin Kurt Unsworth,
August 16, 2025**

# About the Author

*Benjamin Kurt Unsworth*

Because his obsessive love of *Doctor Who* and horror films isn't nerdy enough, Benjamin Kurt Unsworth is currently embarking on a degree in Classics. When he isn't doing that, he enjoys confusing all and sundry, writing short stories and reviews for various outlets, drinking copious cups of tea, knitting, and buying far too many waistcoats, bow ties, and velvet jackets. His TBR pile threatens to topple over and crush him any day now. The collection he co-authored with his father Simon Kurt Unsworth, *Uneasy Beginnings*, is available from Black Shuck Books.

Printed in Dunstable, United Kingdom